The Seventh and last Pentacle of the Sun from the Key of Solomon is for freeing those unjustly imprisoned:

If any be by chance imprisoned or detained in fetters of iron, at the presence of this Pentacle, which should be engraved in gold on the day and hour of the sun, he will be immediately delivered and set at liberty.

PHOTOS BY JOE BERLINGER

The Last Pentacle of the Sun

Writings in Support of the West Memphis Three

M.W. Anderson & Brett Alexander Savory, editors

To Mike,
Thanks so much for your support and for your
friendship over the years – Both mean more to
me than you know.

Cheers, bro!

ARSENAL
PULP PRESS
Vancouver

ARSENAL PULP PRESS
103 – 1014 Homer Street
Vancouver, B.C.
Canada v6b 2w9
arsenalpulp.com

Design by Solo
Front cover photograph by Grove Pashley
Back cover photographs by Joe Berlinger

Efforts have been made to locate copyright holders of source material wherever possible.
The publisher welcomes hearing from any copyright holders of material used
in this book who have not been contacted.

Printed and bound in Canada

Library and Archives Canada
Cataloguing in Publication

The last pentacle of the sun : writings in support of the West Memphis Three /
M.W. Anderson and Brett Alexander Savory, editors.

ISBN 1-55152-162-8

1. Short stories, American. 2. American fiction – 21st century.
3. Murder – Arkansas – West Memphis. I. Anderson, M. W. (Michael W.), 1960–
II. Savory, Brett Alexander, 1973–

PR1151.L38 2004   813'.010806   C2004-903026-4

Contents

Illustration from Weaveworld, CLIVE BARKER

. . . And Justice For All

James Hetfield

Halls of justice painted green
Money talking
Power wolves beset your door
Hear them stalking
Soon you'll please their appetite
They devour
Hammer of justice crushes you
Overpower

    The ultimate in vanity
    Exploiting their supremacy
    I can't believe the things you say
    I can't believe
    I can't believe the price you pay
    Nothing can save you

        Justice is lost
        Justice is raped
        Justice is gone
            Pulling your strings
        Justice is done
            Seeking no truth
            Winning is all
            Find it so grim
                So true
                So real

Apathy their stepping stone
So unfeeling
Hidden deep animosity
So deceiving
Through your eyes their light burns
Hoping to find
Inquisition sinking you
With prying minds

    The ultimate in vanity
    Exploiting their supremacy
    I can't believe the things you say
    I can't believe
    I can't believe the price you pay
    Nothing can save you

        Justice is lost
        Justice is raped
        Justice is gone
            Pulling your strings
        Justice is done
            Seeking no truth
            Winning is all
            Find it so grim
                So true
                So real

Lady Justice has been raped
Truth assassin
Rolls of red tape seal your lips
Now you're done in
Their money tips her scales again
Make your deal
Just what is truth? I cannot tell
Cannot feel

The ultimate in vanity
Exploiting their supremacy
I can't believe the things you say
I can't believe
I can't believe the price we pay
Nothing can save us

Justice is lost
Justice is raped
Justice is gone
Pulling your strings
Justice is done
Seeking no truth
Winning is all
Find it so grim
So true
So real

Seeking no truth
Winning is all
Find it so grim
So true
So real

Introduction

Joe Berlinger & Bruce Sinofsky

It is hard to believe that eleven years have elapsed since the horrible tragedy that, indirectly, led to the creation of this book. Had they not been murdered, Stevie Branch, Christopher Byers, and Michael Moore would be older today than Damien Echols, Jason Baldwin, and Jessie Misskelley, Jr were at the time they were wrongfully convicted of the killings. We are both parents – Bruce's son Alex was the same age as the three boys at the time they were murdered – and we often wonder, particularly as we've watched Alex grow up, what kind of young men those little boys might have become, had their lives not been taken at such a young age. We also wonder how the lives of the three young men who rot in jail as we write this might have been different, were it not for the gross miscarriages of justice in that Arkansas courtroom ten years ago.

We first heard of this story in 1993, right after the arrests of Damien, Jason, and Jessie. Sheila Nevins at HBO faxed us a small article from *The New York Times* about these alleged Satanic ritual murders. As we later learned, *The New York Times* was simply reprinting an AP-wire piece from the local paper, the *Memphis Commercial Appeal*, that unfairly characterized the three as presumed guilty. We flew to Arkansas, intending to make a film about disaffected youth. Thinking we'd make a real-life *River's Edge*, we wanted to explore how three teenagers could be so cold-hearted and ruthless as to brutally sacrifice three eight year olds to the Devil.

But as we spent more time in West Memphis, with the families of the victims and the accused, as well as the police, prosecutors, judge, and attorneys, a clearer and far more logical picture than the one being printed in the newspapers began to emerge – Damien, Jason, and Jessie were not the killers. What we couldn't understand was why so few others seemed to see the facts for what they were. Rather than looking at the evidence (or lack thereof), the community and the media preferred to explain the unimaginable horrors of May 5, 1993 with rumors, innuendo, prejudice, and salacious tales of blood-drinking and devil-worshipping. It seemed to sell more newspapers to buy into the prosecutor's version of events than to really do the digging to show that these teens were innocent.

Brother's Keeper, the film we'd made just before *Paradise Lost: The Child Murders at Robin Hood Hills*, was also about a criminal case, only in that situation, we felt that justice was served. We went to West Memphis feeling that the system worked, but as we watched the events in this case unfold, our feelings changed dramatically. There were countless times that we just wanted to shake people and scream, "This is an injustice! This is not how things are supposed to work in America!" Instead of jumping up and down, we made a film.

In the summer of 1993, West Memphis, Arkansas was a wounded corner of the world, reeling from one of the most vicious crimes in the region's history. It is also a Bible Belt community where many believe that angels and Satan are as real as you or us. For some people in town, perhaps the explanations put forward by the police and prosecutors (and reinforced by the media) were easier to digest than imagining some other scenario in which the killings could have taken place. For others, it might have been a desire to see *someone* pay for the crimes, regardless of guilt or innocence. And if the people paying for the crimes were a little bit different – labeled as "social misfits" because they read Stephen King novels, listened to Metallica records, wore black clothing, and, in Damien's case, were enamored with the "strange" Wicca religion – it was easier to accept the injustice, no matter how outlandish or devoid of proof the allegations were.

Making *Paradise Lost* was an intensely emotional experience for us personally, as well. Both of our wives were pregnant at the time we were making the film, and as we spent mornings grieving with the families of the murdered children, then afternoons with the families of the accused, our own loved ones were always on our minds. Joe has often said, "The making of this film robbed me of my fatherly innocence. We edited the film as my first child was born. After long days of reviewing the horrible autopsy footage in the editing room, I would go home late at night and pick up my sleeping six-month-old daughter from her crib, and flash upon the awful images we had waded through during the day."

The pain, horror, and despair that consumed everyone involved in this case often became overwhelming. There also were many times where it was clear to us that two black-leather-clad "New York City Jew-boys" (as we so often heard), especially ones with cameras, were not wanted in West Memphis. As we became personally involved in this case in which emotions ran so high, we also found ourselves carrying guns to protect ourselves from the death threats we received, something neither of us had considered doing before. The year we spent off and on in West Memphis changed us both forever.

The experience was not entirely negative, though. We also made some good friends – people we still maintain contact with. We learned about the strength of the human spirit, and observed with admiration the dignity of people who endured things that we ourselves could never imagine living through. We also grew to admire the supporters, from all walks of life, who have tirelessly campaigned for the West Memphis Three's release.

When *Paradise Lost* came out, we had very mixed feelings – not about guilt or innocence, but about how the film was received. As artists, we were thrilled by the overwhelmingly positive response it received from audiences and movie critics, but as advocates for the West Memphis Three, we were devastated that the film never made the leap from the entertainment pages to the editorial pages. We hoped there would be an uproar, as people saw this situation for what it was: the railroading of three innocent teenagers while the real culprit(s) remain(s) free somewhere, perhaps to kill again. We hoped that the film would open the eyes of people in the media, as it demonstrated the terrible consequences of sensationalism over truth. We hoped that *Paradise Lost* would lead to new, *just* trials for Damien, Jason, and Jessie in which they would inevitably be acquitted. And we hoped that the investigation would be reopened and properly handled, culminating in the arrest and conviction of whomever is actually responsible for the deaths of those three little boys.

The failure of *Paradise Lost* to make Arkansas rethink how it handled this case caused us to make the second film, *Revelations: Paradise Lost 2*. As filmmakers, we were wary of treading the same ground from a creative standpoint. However, as first-hand witnesses to one of the most significant miscarriages of justice in American history, we felt we had an obligation to continue to shed light on this horrifying case, particularly after learning that the same judge who presided over the original trial would preside over the appeals! We also saw a growing international movement to "Free the West Memphis Three" start to coalesce, and we thought that by putting that movement on film, it would only widen the circle of outrage. It worked – due to the films, the constant work of a number of concerned citizens, and books like this one, grassroots groups have popped up around the world and across the United States (including Arkansas), to raise awareness and desperately-needed funds for the appeals.

We are starting a third film this summer, funded by HBO and slated for theatrical release in 2006. It aims to tell the definitive story, from the initial arrests until the absolute conclusion of the appeals process. We hope it will have a happy ending.

Perhaps we are idealists. In the ten years since the convictions and the eight years since the release of *Paradise Lost*, very little has changed. As we find our country mired in a war made possible by a lack of interest in facts by the public and the media, it is clear that things may be worse than they were ten years ago. Whomever committed the West Memphis murders is probably still walking the streets, and perhaps has killed again. Jason and Jessie remain in prison, while the lethal injection needle casts an ever-looming shadow over Damien as he sits on Death Row, his eyesight fading as he struggles to read in the dark of his cell.

Despite all of this, we, and many others around the world (including the contributors to this book) maintain hope that justice will eventually emerge from this long, dark saga. Numerous artists, musicians, actors, and others have stepped forward in ever-increasing numbers to show their disgust over the situation and their support for Damien, Jason, and Jessie. And now there is this book, a remarkable collection of work by a diverse group of individuals who still care, as so many of us still do, about truth and justice. If reading this book makes you angry, frustrated or sad, take solace in knowing that you are not alone.

Free the West Memphis Three!

May 13, 2004
New York City

She Saw a Young Man

Peter Straub

She saw a young man in a loose black sweater and black trousers come toward her down the street. His dark hair was blowing, and his face seemed to be illuminated by a smile. It was always nice to see someone smiling on the street, she thought – a grace note. When he was nearly abreast of her, she saw that he was grimacing, not smiling, and that his eyes were wet. This was on that day in New York when the sky is gray and the air is gray and cold and people are wearing jackets and sweaters for the first time. She turned around and watched him go past her, wondering what had happened to him. Some sort of strange illumination still clung to the young man, and the woman noticed several other people staring at him.

From top: Damien Echols, Jason Baldwin, Jessie Misskelley incarcerated, 1996.
PHOTOS BY GROVE PASHLEY

California to West Memphis in Ten Years

Burk Sauls

I think about the Robin Hood Hills murders a lot. I think of the murders themselves, so horrifying and hard to believe, and the effect that this horror had on the people who lived in West Memphis, Arkansas in 1993.

It's not hard to imagine how helpless and confused you'd feel if you had children and lived near where the bodies of Steve Branch, Chris Byers, and Michael Moore were found. It could have just as easily been your child all over the newspapers and TV, naked, mutilated, and dead.

The known facts can't be erased or argued. Three children were killed and left in a ditch. They were stripped and tied with their own shoelaces. Someone did it. Someone apparently undressed them, or found them undressed. Someone took their shoes and removed the laces from them and tied them up. Unlacing six shoes takes time, and we can only wonder what the three children were doing while this was taking place.

Were they conscious? If they were not, why were they tied up if the killer or killers planned to leave them there in the woods? The fact that they were tied up suggests that they were transported from another location. The kind of binding is one used by hunters to make deer easier to take home. It doesn't seem like something someone would waste time doing if they were simply going to roll the children into a ditch a couple of feet away from where they were attacked. This is only one of the troubling mysteries surrounding the Robin Hood Hills murders. There are many things to think about that keep this case alive in the media and on Internet discussion lists. I'm not the only person who spends a lot of time thinking about what might have happened a decade ago in those woods and elsewhere.

Robin Hood Hills is a name that suggests a housing development or a park, but in 1993, the small chunk of woods was an undeveloped lot beside a Blue Beacon truck stop. After the murders, people came forward with tales of devil worshippers performing human sacrifices in that small lot, and it appeared that the local police were convinced that the murders were just too horrible to have been committed by anything less than a supernatural force in the form of a satanic cult under orders from Satan himself. They enlisted the help of self-proclaimed experts in the occult who inflated these tales until they convinced themselves and many in the community that devil worship was the only possible motive for the murders. Due to inexperience and overzealousness, the West Memphis police destroyed what might have been valuable physical evidence. They were left to struggle with the shambles of their own investigative bungling, and were forced to resort to wild stories of satanic cults and human sacrifice.

The only thing left for them to do was to identify someone who fit the image of a devil worshipper. With satanic ritual human sacrifice as the motive, it was easy for them to identify a suspect; according to the local occult experts, a genuine devil worshipper could be identified by their appearance: black clothing, tattoos, black hair, maybe even black fingernail polish. Since people who looked like this were rare in the area, it wasn't long before the police zeroed in on a young man named Damien Echols. He became their suspect, but until they had more evidence than just his appearance against him, they had to dig further. They interviewed and photographed him at his home; they got lists of books that he'd bought or checked out from the library; they asked the public to help them find out more about Damien. Finally, they managed to intimidate a teenager named Jessie Misskelley until he agreed with their fantasies. Jessie provided them with confirmation that their suspicions about Damien were true. Jessie did what he was told to do and gave police a fragmented and inconsistent scenario in which he not only implicated Damien's friend Jason Baldwin, but himself as well. Oddly, the police didn't seem to care that Jessie's story didn't mention devil worship. They had enough tape of Jessie stating that he'd seen Damien and Jason kill the children, seemingly without motive or planning. According to Jessie, the three victims just happened to walk into the woods where Damien and Jason were, and for no reason, Damien and Jason decided to kill them. Jessie apparently hadn't been coached enough to include details of satanic ritual in his story.

Despite this, and despite the fact that no evidence of a satanic ritual was found in Robin Hood Hills or in the way the children were killed, the police promoted their stories of devil worshippers. The local media obliged. Once this fantasy was the basis of a criminal investigation, it was no longer necessary for the West Memphis police to bother with things like forensic science, crime scene reconstruction, or any of the techniques used by responsible investigators. They no longer had to think about criminal behavior or physical evidence. They had chosen their path, and it had nothing to do with reality.

I saw the film *Paradise Lost* before it was released because my friend Kathy Bakken worked for the agency that provided the film's advertising art. I watched it, expecting a documentary about three deranged teenagers who murdered some children. What I saw was even more disturbing. The film seemed vague and unfinished to me. There wasn't enough information to convince me that these murders had been solved, and in the final scenes when the teenagers were convicted and hauled off to prison, I felt like a lot of information had been left out. I decided that if I was going to understand why these teenagers had been convicted, and why the local authorities were so stubbornly convinced that they were guilty, I was going to have to find more information about what had been presented in court as evidence. What had the jury seen that made them believe that those children had been killed in such a bizarre and difficult-to-believe ritual?

Kathy, our friend Grove Pashley, and I began to talk about the case a lot, and before long we were gathering bits of information about it. The more we found, the more we wanted to know. Every door we opened revealed several new doors. I contacted people who were involved with the case and managed to speak to quite a few of them. The ones who were willing to speak with us only made us more suspicious. We flew to Arkansas to meet with people who had worked on the case, and the prisoners themselves. When we arrived, we really didn't know what we would find. Would there be something that would open our eyes to the things that the police claimed were so obvious? Would we finally be struck with the ability to see these elusive facts that would prove to us that Damien, Jason, and Jessie were guilty? But this would not be the case. When we met one of the investigators for the defense, Glori Shettles, she shook her head in frustration over how wrong things were. We tried everything we could think of to find even one thing that pointed to guilt; instead, we found more information that suggested there wasn't any *real* evidence that these three young men had killed the children. The film *Paradise Lost* had presented a shortened but accurate picture of why Damien, Jason, and Jessie had been arrested and convicted. The words that kept coming up to describe them were "weird" and "evil," and the explanations that surrounded their convictions were vague and unsatisfying. We were told by police that we simply didn't know the truth; that the truth was invisible to us because we were from California, and that Damien, Jason, and Jessie's guilt was obvious to the people who had "been

19

there" when it all happened. But we talked with many people who had "been there," and nobody seemed nearly as convinced as the police said they would be.

The prevailing attitude from the few who agreed with the verdicts was always something along the lines of "They just look guilty," "You can tell by looking at them," or "I could see it in their eyes, and by the way they were acting." Obviously, this wasn't the kind of evidence we were looking for, and we concluded that Damien, Jason, and Jessie had been railroaded by Satanic Panic. They were in prison because certain people in power had been convinced that devil worshippers had killed the children in a satanic ritual human sacrifice, the kind of thing that they had seen discussed by silhouetted "cult survivors" on hysterical talk shows hosted by the likes of Geraldo and Sally Jessy.

When we visited the prison, we were searched more thoroughly than ever before at airport security. We walked through an electronically-locked chain-link fence that was topped with dense rolls of concertina wire, past a grassy space filled with more wire, and finally another fence. The front door and lobby area of the prison reminded us of a high school, complete with a trophy case and T-shirts for purchase. From there, we were taken through metal doors that looked like they could withstand the blast of a military jet engine.

Damien is on death row, so on our visit, we were separated by what I assume was bulletproof glass, with a little strip of metal mesh under the window through which we could talk to each other. The light came from dim fluorescents overhead, and the smell was what you'd expect from a building that's full of people all the time.

I'd been talking with Damien on the phone for a while before our prison visit, so it was disconcerting to see him in these surroundings; on the phone, I almost felt that he was just across town in some noisy high school cafeteria.

He entered his side of the visiting booth through a door that had a slot at wrist level, and once he was locked in, he placed his shackled hands against the slot in the door and the guard outside unlocked his cuffs. Damien seemed embarrassed to have us see him in this situation. He was almost apologetic in the way you'd be if you had friends over and your house was a mess. Once the initial strangeness had passed, though, we found ourselves laughing and joking about everyday things. We felt like maybe we were helping him escape for a few hours by not talking about how grim and depressing things were.

I guess we were hopeful that our visit was at least a little fun or interesting for him, and I think it was. At this point it didn't seem to us that there were a whole lot of people who believed that Damien, Jason, and Jessie were innocent; they seemed like they had been completely abandoned by everyone but their close friends and family.

Visiting Jason and Jessie was similar, but a little less strict. We were allowed to sit in the same room with them, although a guard was present the whole time. We were in a conference room when Jessie walked in, nervous, and almost too polite. He sat at the end of the large table, and looked wary of us.

I remember asking all three of them if anything was being done on their behalf, if there were any efforts being made to help them get another trial, or even if anyone was advocating for them in the media in any way. They all said that aside from friends and family, there wasn't anything going on. They hadn't spoken to their attorneys in a long time, and they all seemed sadly resigned to their fate. I got the impression they found it strange that there were three people from California who cared enough about their situation to come visit them and ask questions. I think this depressed us more than anything. Kathy, Grove, and I had never been activists, and we'd never taken up a cause this important, but I think when we walked into those prisons, we stepped through a doorway that we couldn't back out of. We now felt personally connected to this story, and we commented more than once that it was like we had stepped into the film *Paradise Lost* itself.

When we got home, we gathered all the information we had and published it on a website, even though none of us had any experience creating Internet content. Soon, people from all over the world began visiting the site after seeing the film or hearing about the case on the news. We found that we weren't alone; we were heartened to discover others who were just as concerned as we were, and just as willing to make trips to Arkansas to attend hearings, dig through archives, and talk with attorneys and investigators. Our site became a hub for people who wanted to help. We created an Internet discussion list, which became important for putting people in contact with each other, generating ideas, and organizing benefit efforts. Finally, it seemed we'd started something that was too big to ignore, and the media began to take notice. Joe Berlinger and Bruce Sinofsky, the filmmakers who made *Paradise Lost*, decided to make a sequel, and asked us if they could follow us around with their cameras. At first we were reluctant, because we were afraid it might look like the attention was being diverted to us as an organized cause and away from the facts of the case. Eventually, we decided that we were almost obligated to participate. Not that we felt like we were qualified to be spokespersons, but we realized that nobody else out there was so publicly committing themselves to the idea that Damien, Jason, and Jessie were innocent.

When the second film, entitled *Revelations: Paradise Lost 2*, aired on HBO, we were flooded with emails from people who were outraged by the case. A small percentage of the emails were hostile, but we felt redeemed when we read the huge volume of heartfelt correspondence from people all over the world who agreed with us. Joe and Bruce had made another film that affected an amazing number of people, many of whom claimed that their eyes had been opened to something they never realized could ever happen in the U.S.

People started their own websites and organizations, and eventually we captured the attention of a few celebrities who got the information out there even farther. A defense fund was set up by Damien's wife, Lorri, and the money started pouring in. Now, in 2003, it looks like there might finally be some serious investigation into what really happened ten years ago in West Memphis, Arkansas. It's sad to think that money is so important to achieving justice, but that's the way things are. We realize that there are many other innocent people out there in prisons all over the country who are there because they can't afford the price of justice.

Damien, Jason, and Jessie had two documentary films made about their struggles, and because of those films and the hard work of people who value honesty and fairness, they've got more of a chance than most. One thing we hope we've achieved with our involvement in this particular case is to provide inspiration to other people out there.

If you think you can't change things, think again.

Night Story 1973

Caitlín R. Kiernan & Poppy Z. Brite

"'It rained and it rained and it rained,'" the old woman said, reading aloud from *Winnie-the-Pooh*. She held the book close to her face, squinting to see the words by the yelloworange light of the kerosene lantern. "'Piglet told himself that never in all his life and *he* was goodness knows *how* old – three, was it, or four? – never had he seen so much rain,'" and then she paused, lifting her head to stare at the front door of the two-room mountain cabin she shared with her grandson, whose name was Ghost.

"'Days and days and days,'" said Ghost with just a touch of impatience, prompting her. But then he sat up straighter in bed and stared at the door too, recognizing the alert uneasiness on his grandmother's face.

"Ghost child, if you already know this story by heart, why am I botherin' to read it to you?" But she didn't take her eyes off the door as she spoke, the door and the rainslick windows on either side of it. Those windows worried her most of all. Nothing to see out there but the stormy night, blacker than pitch in a bucket, black as a coal miner's ass, except for the brief and thunderous flashes of lightning.

"What did you see, Dee?" Her name was Deliverance, Miz Deliverance to most everybody, and Dee-for-short only to this boy. Deliverance frowned and nodded her head, nodded it very slow, and then she looked back down at the familiar pages of the book.

"I didn't see nothin' at all," she said. "I expect it was just a dog."

"Which?"

"Which what?"

The boy sighed, leaned back into his big goosedown pillow. A small vertical line appeared between his eyebrows, more than a hint of impatience now, that suspicious expression far too mature for his six-and-a-half years. "Which one *was* it?" he asked. "Was it nothin' or was it a dog? It can't be both."

"You know, boy, sometimes you sound just like your mama," and sometimes he could look like her too, but Deliverance didn't say that. Hard enough thinking it, seeing the careless bits and pieces of her only daughter in his fox-sharp face, her eyes become his eyes, irises the pale blue of a clear mountain dawn. She reached out and brushed Ghost's long hair from his face, that cornsilk hair so blond it was white, or as good as white.

"Nothin'," she said. "I didn't see nothin'. So don't you worry."

But there were no secrets between these two, and she knew he did not believe her. Instead of pretending to, he pointed at *Winnie-the-Pooh*. "'It rained and it rained and it rained. . . .'"

"Ghost, honey, why don't we read somethin' else? Somethin' where it *ain't* rainin' so much. Maybe that one about old Eeyore losin' his tail, or Kanga and Baby Roo comin' to the Hundred-Acre Wood."

Ghost looked disappointed, then frowned and glanced up at the ceiling of the little house. The storm drummed at the tin roof with a thousand fingers, the icy, late-October rain that had started a few hours before sunset and showed no signs of letting up any time soon. The wind roared and rattled the roof, trying hard to find a way in, trying to help the rain, and he was pretty sure this storm wasn't just any storm. This storm was *mean*. This storm, he thought, wouldn't mind hurting them, picking them up like Dorothy Gale and blowing them all the way to Oz or someplace not so nice.

"It's after me, ain't it, 'cause of what I done down at the creek yesterday, at the rocks?"

The old woman closed the book and laid it down next to the lantern on the small walnut burl table beside the bed.

"It's only a thunderstorm," she said sternly, trying hard to sound convincing. "Storms don't come lookin' for people. You know that, don't you?"

"I think this one is," he replied. "This one's come out lookin' for me," and then lightning so bright that it might have been the Second Coming, cold wash of noonday brilliance to drown the inside of the little house. And the old woman turned towards the window, turned fast but not nearly fast enough, too old to be racing lightning, and the windows were already black again. Nothing there but thunder and the rain streaking window glass.

"That was its eyes," Ghost said. "It has big shinin' eyes so it can see where it's goin' in the dark."

And Deliverance turned back to her strange, pale grandson snuggled into his nest of old quilts and a mint-green blanket she'd bought at Woolworth's years ago. The big flannel shirt he always slept in, a work shirt that had been his grandfather's once upon a time, to keep him warm and safe from his dreams. She took a deep breath and leaned closer to him.

"Ghost, you listen to me now and pay attention," she said, using the sober, old-womanly voice she always reserved for the things that she had to be certain he understood, copperheads and steel-jaw traps, poisonous mushrooms and the leaf-covered pits of abandoned wells.

"I'm listening, Dee," he said quietly.

"Sometimes we gotta be brave, even when we're scared. We gotta not let being scared keep us from thinkin' straight. That's all brave is, boy, when you come right down to it, not lettin' the fear get you so turned around you start doin' stupid things, instead of what you know you *ought* to do."

"I didn't know about the rocks," the boy whispered, and he looked away from her, watching the flame of the lantern instead.

"Ain't nobody blamin' you. I should'a told you about that old pile of stones a long, long time ago. But sometimes a body forgets things, even important things like them stones. All that matters *now*, Ghost, is that we do the stuff we know we gotta do and don't get so scared we forget anything else important."

"Like the salt?" he asked solemnly and she nodded her head, even though she knew the storm had surely washed away the double ring of salt she'd carefully sprinkled around the house that afternoon. There were still neat white lines of it on the thresholds and window sills.

"Yes. Like the salt," she said. "And the chamomile and St John's wort."

And then Ghost sat up again and pointed at *Winnie-the-Pooh*, where Deliverance had set the book down on the table beside the bed.

"How about we read 'In Which Pooh Goes Visitin' and Gets into a Tight Place'?" he asked. "There ain't too much rain in that one, is there?"

"Maybe you best get some sleep. It's almost midnight."

He shook his head no. "I ain't sleepy."

"I didn't ask if you were, now did I? And don't say 'ain't.'" She scowled at him, but picked the book back up off the table anyway. "It's bad grammar. I ain't havin' people thinkin' my grandbaby's no better educated than some ignorant hillbilly."

"But *you* say 'ain't' all the time, Dee. You just said it."

"When did I say it?"

"Just *now*."

"Well, I'm old," she said. "It's too late for me," and she opened the book to Chapter Two and began to read, but Deliverance listened, too, to the wind blowing wild through the trees, the rain on the roof, the thunder rolling like angel voices across the valley.

"'Well, Edward Bear, known to all his friends as Winnie-the-Pooh, or Pooh for short, was walkin' through the forest one day,'" she read, and far away, off towards the creek and the place where the sandstone bluffs got steep on their way up to the bald crest of Lazarus Mountain, there was another sound. The one she'd been waiting for all night long, the reason she'd drawn hex signs on all the doors with a piece of chalk. She didn't have to ask him to know Ghost had heard it, too, the wary flicker in his pale eyes all she needed to tell her that he had, and so she kept reading, Pooh gone to see Rabbit, and tried to remember if the shotgun on the big table across the room was loaded.

Sixty years since the first time Deliverance saw the pile of stones by Lame Rabbit Creek; 1913 and she was barely eight years old, the same year her mother married a tall, red-bearded blacksmith from Tennessee who made horseshoes and ax heads and lightning rods. Deliverance would go down to the gurgling, snakewinding creek with her mother and together they would pick watercress and dandelion greens and look for sassafras trees growing along the banks. Sometimes they would sit very still and quiet in the bright patches where the sun found its way through the sheltering oak and sycamore branches overhead, dangle their bare feet in the cold water, and wait for deer or raccoons to come down to the creek for a drink. Sometimes they saw otters or mink, and once, a bobcat that sat and stared back at them warily from a tangled hawthorn thicket.

Her mother showed her fossil sea shells embedded in the mossy rock walls of the creek, proof of Noah's flood, taught her the difference between the harmless water snakes and cottonmouth moccasins. "This here creek runs all the way down to the sea," she would say, as if maybe Deliverance had forgotten since the last time. "All the way to the Pee Dee River and the South Carolina marshes and finally out to the wide Atlantic Ocean."

But on the late September day they found the stones it wasn't sunny and her mother hadn't said much of anything, one of her silent, melancholy moods, and Deliverance kept running on ahead alone, threading her way expertly through the ferns and pricking creeper vines. The two of them strayed farther up the creek than they'd ever gone before, wandering past a wide, beaverdammed pool and then the creek bed made a sharp bend and disappeared into a dense wall of tall, dead trees. Twisted, moldrotting trunks stripped of bark, stark branches naked except for the clustered, infesting growths of mistletoe and greenbrown fungi. The trees seemed to have grown too close together, to lean towards one another, intertwining and blotting out the cloudy sky.

"Livvy, *stop!*" her mother shouted, but she'd already gone past the first of the dead trees, stood among them looking back out at her mother.

"Come on back now, baby," her mother said, whispered urgently, and she motioned to the girl. "We shouldn't be here. This is. . . ." and she hesitated, looking up at the ugly, ancient trees, the birch and hickory corpses standing guard like a column of wooden soldiers. "This is a bad place," she said, sounding frightened, and Deliverance couldn't remember her mother ever having been afraid of the woods before. Cautious, because there were things that could hurt them if they weren't careful where they put their feet or what they touched, but never frightened.

"No, I want to *see*," she said, and turned and ran deeper into the stand of dead trees.

Later, she clearly remembered the sound of her mother calling after her, the crunchy rustle of her mother's feet running through fallen leaves, but she could never recall exactly why she'd disobeyed, why she'd turned and run away laughing. Even then, some small part of her understood what her mother was saying, could feel the sick and spiteful energy rising from the trees like heat from a crackling fire. Sometimes she would think there had been a voice, another child's sweet, inviting voice, calling her to come and play. And other times, it would seem as though there might have been an unseen hand pushing or pulling at her, driving or dragging her on as the trunks of the trees closed in tight around her.

"Deliverance!" her mother cried out, sounding at least a hundred miles away.

Towards the end, hardly enough room left to squeeze between the trees, and she couldn't help but touch their raw bones, that malevolent wood slick with the things that lived off decay. Her arms and hands and face, her dress, smeared with the corrupt and stinking juices that leaked from everything she touched, and then it was over and she stood alone in a small clearing on the bank of Lame Rabbit Creek, and the pile of stones was waiting for her there. The stand of dead trees entirely surrounded the clearing, encircling it in a protective shroud and the creek wound down the middle, dividing it neatly in half.

The cairn was nearly as tall as Deliverance, each and every charcoalgray stone so smooth, so evenly shaped, round and flat as a pan of cornbread, dark as the cloudbruised sky overhead. There were glinting crystal flecks of mica and quartz in them, and no moss or lichens growing anywhere on the stones, as though someone came here every day and scrubbed them clean.

She held her hand out just a few inches above the topmost stone and saw that there was something carved there, circles held within circles, wheels within wheels like what the prophet Ezekiel saw come down to him from Heaven. And a voice that wasn't a voice murmured words she didn't hear, but felt through the tips of her outstretched fingers; the kindest, most beautiful voice she'd ever imagined and somehow it knew her name.

"No!" her mother shouted. "Don't you touch it!"

Deliverance looked back at her, but all she could see was a pale, terrified face, her mother's face framed by a gap in the trees much too narrow for her to ever squeeze through.

"Come back to me, Livvy. Come back exactly the way you got in there and don't touch *anything*."

"It won't hurt me, Mama. It already promised it won't hurt me. It's just lonesome," but her mother was shaking her head, straining desperately to reach her through the gap in the dead trees.

"Don't be afraid," Deliverance said, and turned back to the cairn again, the honey and summer sunlight voice seeping up from it, and in the last second before she touched the intricately-carved surface of the stone, she *might* have seen something rising from the rippling creek. Something vast and glistening, with a crown of eyes that blazed like the coals in her stepfather's furnace, eyes like redhot iron. And then her hand hurt and there was only the sound of her mother screaming before there was nothing at all.

Somewhere in the short space between Pooh getting wedged in Rabbit's front door and Christopher Robin reading the bear a Sustaining Book, Ghost drifted away, sleep not nearly as far off as he'd thought, the rhythm of the rain and his grandmother's voice to lull him reluctantly down. But he only fought a little, blinked himself awake once or twice to the storybook rise and fall of Deliverance's words that sent him right back to the soft, indefinite places dividing wakefulness from dreams. Not far to fall, to settle slow, like a yellowgold leaf to the sandy, pebblelittered bottom of a stream.

"No, the Indians," she said, in answer to a question he didn't remember asking his grandmother, but in this dream her hair wasn't gray and the splotches on the backs of her hands were gone; her skin as smooth as his mother's was before she got sick and died, the mother he remembers mostly when he's asleep, and sometimes he thinks she's *only* a dream, the kind that was never true and never would be, and his real mother is Deliverance after all.

"The Cherokee people who lived here before us," his grandmother said. "They put the stones there."

Ghost was sitting on a chair in a small room that smelled too much like dying, the brittle winter scent like peppermint tea and stinging red centipedes, *that* smell, and men and women sat or stood around a bed. Only candlelight, and he thought the child lying on the bed might be where the death smell was coming from, the girl with raven hair and wildflowers strewn about on her pillow. One of the women leaned down and wiped the sweat from her forehead with a damp cloth and one of the men began praying quietly to himself. Log cabin walls, one small window with a pane of cloudythick glass, and outside the night so full of stars that Ghost thought the sky must have exploded.

"She's so *hot*," one of the women said, the one who wiped the little girl's forehead. "I swear, I think she's gonna burn up alive."

Another woman was sitting on the edge of the bed holding a small cobalt-blue jar, an ointment or salve that she was rubbing into the skin of the little girl's right hand. The hand was swollen and purple and looked snakebit. He'd seen a beagle that was snakebit once and that was the way its paw looked.

"But there were other things here before the Indians," his grandmother said, the young woman standing beside him, and she pointed to the dying girl on the bed. "I opened my eyes that night and there was this white-haired boy child watchin' me from that very chair you're sitting in. I thought he was an angel. I thought he was the Angel of Death come to take me away with him."

"I didn't know," he whispered, afraid the girl would open her eyes and look at him and see an angel instead of a boy named Ghost. "I didn't know what was under the rocks."

"Nobody's blamin' you," his grandmother said. "This ain't your fault. This ain't nobody's fault."

And then Ghost looked at the window again and saw what was looking in, watching them, and he started to scream, opened his mouth wide so the sound rushing up from his belly wouldn't tear him apart trying to find its way out. But the sickroom had already dissolved, like sugar in scalding coffee, melting so only the taste remains, and he was wet and sailing through the stormlashed night on the back of a great black bird.

"Don't you fall," the bird cawed, a crow or an eagle or maybe even an owl, all of those or nothing he'd ever seen before, and Ghost dug his fingers deeply into its feathered shoulders. Its wings rose and fell, rose and fell, and Ghost looked down at the world so small and wet below them.

"You be careful back there," the bird said. "I should think poor old Rabbit is about flooded out by this time."

Lightning and thunder and below them Lazarus Mountain and Big Henry Mountain and all the others flinched and cringed at the terrible commotion from above. Ghost knew they would hide from the violent sky, if there was anywhere for them to go, any sanctuary for a mountain, and then he saw the things marching single file up the narrow dirt road that led to his grandmother's house. Dancing things with torches and some of them had long sharp sticks that they jabbed at the sky and each other.

Deliverance put her thin arms around his waist, and he wanted to ask her how she got way up here on the bird with him when she wasn't there just a second ago, why she had to get old again, wanted to ask a lot of questions, but "Hold on, Ghost child," she said. "Hold on tight as you can," so that was what he did. And the great bird folded its wings and swept lower so that Ghost could see the faces of the loping, trotting, prancing things, their dogsnarls and vicious, blazing eyes.

"The rocks didn't hurt me," he said to his grandmother. "They didn't burn me when I touched them."

"You got magic about you," she said. "A fierce magic and sometimes it keeps you safe."

One of the dancing things stopped dancing, stood in the mud and the muddy water rushing about its splayed hind feet, and it pointed a crooked finger up at the bird and Ghost and the old woman flying above it through the rain.

"You gotta go back now, Ghost," his grandmother said. "You gotta wake up," but he didn't want to. Thought if he could dream all this maybe he could also dream himself back into the clearing, back to the day before when he went walking in the woods alone, splashed up Lame Rabbit Creek and found those strange, dead trees and the pile of stones in the clearing. Back to the moment before he lifted the top stone off and heard the whistling deep beneath his feet, the whispering, eager voices that wanted into his head but couldn't find their way. And then he wouldn't have to do or see any of this, and the storm wouldn't come looking for them, or the long-legged dancing things, and he'd never even have this dream.

"Sorry, but it don't work that way," his grandmother said, sounding like she wished it did, sounding tired and afraid and old, and then the wind turned her into dust and fallen leaves and she blew away.

"Wake up, Ghost," the bird screeched, spreading its dark wings almost as wide as the stormy Appalachian night. "Wake up right this minute or you'll *fall* and that's what they've wanted all along," and then the thing crouched in the muddy road below them hurled its sharpened stick, a bewitched and tainted spear to shatter the sky itself and Ghost tumbled through the mad cacophony of thunder and gunpowder, time and breaking glass.

Deliverance sat in the dark in her rocking chair a few feet from the front door of the little house. The oak rocker that was her mother's before her, and the big shotgun that was her husband's across her lap. The Winchester 12-gauge he used for hunting squirrels and possums, fat tom turkeys and coons, but she figured it'd work just fine on whatever had been scratching at the door for the last hour or so. Outside, the wind was a bold and fleshless demon, battering the world with cold, invisible fists. Perdition come crawling out from under a rock, spilled from the prison that had held it since the continent seethed with buffalo and white men were only a distant nightmare for shamans to keep to themselves.

"Don't you think I don't know you," she said, talking to the other side of the door, talking to keep herself alert, just to keep herself company. But the storm made it hard to hear herself, so Deliverance raised her voice. "I *know* you! I know what you are!" she shouted. "I know who you are and what you come here after!"

And she couldn't be sure if what she heard next was laughter, mocking laughter for a presumptuous old woman who thought she could slay dragons with birdshot, or just a fancy new trick of the wind. One or the other and it really didn't matter which; something to make *her* blink first, to get the best of her and then it would all be over in a heartbeat. She concentrated on the words and symbols drawn on the door instead, Bible verses and darker phrases, chalk and the paste she'd made from arrowroot and angelica and chicken blood.

"Oh, I know you. Yes sir. I *remember* you. I got this scar right here on my hand so I won't never forget."

She held up her right hand, held it palm out and never mind the thick, pine door or the charms scrawled there, she knew that the thing on the other side wouldn't have any trouble at all seeing the crooked pinkwhite scar cutting her life line in half, dividing soul line and heart line. That scar she'd carried with her sixty long years and it still looked so fresh, so raw, she might have gotten it a few months ago; might only have grabbed the handle of a hot skillet or burned herself trying to light the water heater.

The taunting, snickering sound again, then, but much louder than before. *It is* laughing, she thought. *You ain't fooling nobody but yourself, old woman.* Deliverance put her hand back down and swallowed, a rasping, sore-throat swallow because the spit in her mouth had dried up; she took a deep breath and slipped her index finger around the trigger of the shotgun.

You ain't fooling nobody at all.

There was a flash of lightning, the stormy, mountain night stripped straight down to broad daylight and for the stingiest part of a second she could see it standing out there in the wind, glaring in at her through one of the windows. Brief glimpse of shaggy, stooped shoulders and spindle arms, a horsey-long face and black wolflips curled into a sneer or a hateful grin, snaggled teeth, and then Deliverance shut her eyes. Squeezed them shut tight and counted, one, two, three, four, waiting for the thunder and when she opened them again the night had washed mercifully back over the hollow and there was nothing out there but the rain pelting hard against the windowpanes.

You didn't see anything out there but what you were afraid you'd see. You didn't see anything at all.

But the immediate and scraping sound of claws on the door to contradict her, and the knob began to turn, teasing, slow game of clockwise and counterclockwise motion, and she raised the shotgun, set the brass butt plate against her shoulder, and aimed the barrel at the door.

"Come on ahead then, you old bastard. But you ain't gettin' him, not this night or the next," she said, trying hard not to sound afraid, trying to sound like she believed a single word of it herself. Just a little more pressure on the trigger and the Winchester would tear the night to smoky shreds.

"No, Dee," Ghost said, "That's not the way it ends," speaking very softly, calm and velvetedged words from his lips held close to her left ear. A warm pool of light from the oil lantern he carried and she hadn't even heard him get out of bed, the storm raging too loud, all her attention focused on the door.

"I *saw* it out there, grinnin' in at me, *darin'* me," she said. "You stay behind me, boy." But Ghost took a step closer to the door instead, put one hand on the barrel of the shotgun and gently pushed it aside and down towards the floor.

"I called it out," Ghost said, turned towards his grandmother and his pale eyes glinted like the thumbprints of God, two shining points of certainty in the fickle, faithless night. "I didn't mean to, but that's what I did. Now I gotta send it back."

And she watched, helpless, too exhausted or afraid to argue, as he stepped past her and stood in front of the door, her crude charms visible in the flickering, pale wash of orange light. Ghost touched one of the chalk signs she'd made and he whispered something, but nothing she could hear, nothing meant for her anyway, and then he sat down on the floor. He put the oil lamp down nearby and leaned forward, pressing himself tight against the door, and then Ghost began to trace words or shapes on the wood with one finger.

"There are *still* worse things in the world than you," he said. "Still things to watch the ways in and out of darkness," speaking louder than before, and his finger moved faster, faster, smearing the chalk and powdered herbs and dried blood, tattooing the door with his own secret ciphers. Lines of power woven from innocence and mystery and the clammy night air, and after a moment Deliverance realized that the doorknob had stopped turning.

"Go home," Ghost said, and the lightning flashed again, the thunder right behind it this time. "Go on home before they come lookin' for you."

And then the old woman heard the sudden, feather-rough flutter of a hundred small wings, a great flock of blackbirds all taking to the air at the same instant, or the defeated sound of running feet, or nothing but the wind, shrieking cheated through the trees. Ghost glanced back at her, bright beads of sweat standing out on his sharp, ashen face, and the finger he'd been using slid slowly down the wood until his hand lay limp on the floor at his side.

"Is it gone?" he asked, and shut his eyes before she could reply.

Deliverance looked at the windows, at the night that was no different from any other stormweary North Carolina night, the storm that was only rain and lightning, wind and thunder.

"Yes," she said. "It's over, Ghost. I think it's all over now," but she didn't get up, stayed there in her grandmother's rocking chair, the practical, reassuring weight of the shotgun in her lap, until the rain had finally stopped and the sky turned the first purplegray shades of dawn.

La Bête, CLIVE BARKER

Weird Tales:
The Story of a Delusion

Philip Jenkins

Teaching in a university can be a humbling experience, a reminder of how short-lived public concerns can be. You are, after all, dealing with young people with very short time-horizons, who often can remember no president before Bill Clinton. Today, then, virtually nobody knows about the satanic scare that roiled the United States as recently as ten years ago, and few are prepared to believe that such a thing existed. Witches' sabbats and black masses? Human sacrifices? Ritual murders? You mean in Massachusetts three hundred years ago, right? The 1690s, not the *1990s*? What do you mean, people are still in jail for such things? That's just silly. Probably, the fact that the Satanic Panic has dropped so entirely off the map is a good thing, though it doesn't inspire confidence about people's ability to resist a new panic, should the media ever feel inclined to launch another one. Remember that phrase about those who do not remember the past being doomed to repeat it?

Some very fine books have been written about the Satanic scare, and all the associated nonsense of ritual abuse. The best are probably *Satan's Silence* by Debbie Nathan and Michael Snedeker (1995) and Dorothy Rabinowitz's aptly titled *No Crueler Tyrannies: Accusation, False Witness, and Other Terrors of Our Times* (2003). Nothing I say could improve on those accounts of the rise and triumph of a national lie. We now know how the Panic started in the early 1980s among fundamentalist religious groups and anti-cult theorists, among "cult cops" looking for a niche in life and among anti-child abuse activists, all of it broadcast by a prostituted mass media in quest of higher ratings.

Yet perhaps in one way I could make the story a little more harrowing than it already is, because I believe I know where it started. A hundred years ago, nobody believed that real witchcraft still existed, except among marginal rural communities, a far cry from stories of sabbats and great organized underground religions. And the Black Mass? Well, that was a fantasy, though maybe one that some European brothels would provide for a lot of money. But real, honest-to-Beelzebub satanists did not exist. In the 1920s and 1930s, though, tales of secret satanism became a genre

35

of popular fiction through the writings of Herbert Gorman, H.P. Lovecraft, and the contributors to *Weird Tales* magazine. What they were doing was trying to sell stories to a public that was fascinated by some bizarre theories in contemporary anthropology.

And this would just be a curious note in the history of pulp fiction if at some point, people had not started taking it seriously. That's right: the Satanic Panic that blighted lives, destroyed entire communities, and sent hundreds of innocent people to prison has its origins in fantasy fiction, in weird tales. I am hard-pressed to find a modern example as outrageous: it's almost like creating a national panic over the threat that the *X-Men* pose on society. But when anyone talking about satanism argues that there's "no smoke without fire," they need to be told forthrightly: this one is *all* smoke – and mirrors.

How did this all happen? We have to go back to the 1920s, when we find the first tales of clandestine alternate religions operating in the American heartland. This was a time of rapid change in the American countryside. The 1920 census was the first to show a majority of Americans living in cities rather than in rural areas, while the popularity of the private automobile vastly increased the opportunities for city-dwellers to explore those country landscapes that now seemed so quaint. As tourism boomed, entrepreneurs made all they could of the exoticism of the countryside, selling as commodities the authentic folk-traditions of regions like New Mexico, the Ozarks, or the Louisiana bayou.

The extent of popular interest in the "pagan countryside" became obvious in 1928–29 when an incident in Pennsylvania's York County attracted worldwide attention. In November 1928, three young men murdered a reputed witch, whom they accused of hexing them. A media frenzy followed. The York story was reported across the globe, as rural Pennsylvania was portrayed as a medieval community living under the constant shadow of spells and superstition. In this area, said the *Literary Digest*, "Witchcraft rears its head and flourishes as it did in the Medieval Ages, and does now along the Kongo." Based on such stories, witchcraft continued to be a hot topic in the American media in the 1920s and 1930s.

In these same years, a diverse group of anthropologists and sensational writers reinterpreted witchcraft to construct a mythology of a powerful organized movement. The ultimate influence was Sir James Frazer, whose book *The Golden Bough* first appeared in 1890. Frazer claimed that fertility cults represented a universal primal religion, which practiced regular human sacrifices. In turn, Frazer's theories influenced Margaret Murray, whose 1921 book *The Witch Cult in Western Europe* formulated the concept of widespread secret religions. (This book is, incidentally, the grandmother of all modern theories of Wicca and neo-paganism.)

Murray argued that the witch hunters of the sixteenth and seventeenth centuries had exposed an authentic underground religion, which was a survival of ancient European paganism dating back to the Stone Age. In her view, the so-called witches of early modern France or England had been adherents of this goddess-worshipping Old Religion, organized into cells (covens), each comprising thirteen members. Each coven was headed by a disguised leader who bore some title such as The Devil or The Black Man, and the groups met periodically at sabbats.

Now, no reputable scholar believes Murray's work today – and her work grew much crazier as the years went on. But her prominent use of the word "cult" popularized it as a description of covert occult or satanic groups, in North America as well as Europe. She argued that the Salem trials genuinely had exposed at least one pagan coven, with Puritan minister George Burroughs as Black Man, the literal Devil of Salem, and that other covens could be found in the history of seventeenth-century New England. This view ran contrary to the accepted notions of the early twentieth century, in which Salem had become a symbol for Puritan intolerance, greed, and wild superstition.

The speculations of Murray and Frazer would have remained an academic curiosity if they had not been taken up so avidly by a new generation of sensational writers, for whom they offered wonderful new material. During the 1920s, the world of popular fiction was revolutionized by mass marketing, and by the pulp magazines. By 1934, about 150 pulps were being published in New York alone, and a few famous names redefined entire genres. The key title in the horror genre was *Weird Tales*, the legendary magazine that published all the major American horror authors from 1923 until its demise in 1954. As exemplified by writers like H.P. Lovecraft, the *Weird Tales* horror story often used the American backwoods as a setting for depictions of cults, witches, and sacrificial religions. While *Weird Tales* did not reach a mass national audience, it was representative of a growing interest within popular culture, and similar themes now pervaded not just the pulps but the cheap novels, as well as radio serials and films.

The notion of an American witch-cult proved attractive for Lovecraft and the *Weird Tales* generation. Fantasy writers began treating Salem as if the witchcraft genuinely represented a serious occult movement, and that the village had been the scene of actual evil rituals. The pioneering fictional work was Herbert S. Gorman's novel *The Place Called Dagon* (1927), which portrays a secret cult in a western Massachusetts town populated by descendants of refugees from Salem, and still practicing what Lovecraft describes as "the morbid and degenerate horrors of the Black Sabbat."

Because it would be so critically important for later developments, I want to focus on Gorman, who is certainly not a well-remembered writer today. He is best known as an early biographer of James Joyce, whose genius he recognized by the early 1920s. However, his career had two other main aspects. First, he was thoroughly familiar with nineteenth-century France, and drew on French speculations concerning the Black Mass. This parody of the Catholic ritual was celebrated by a defrocked priest, who used a naked woman for his altar, and who sacrificed living creatures, including children. The Black Mass achieved a literary revival in the decadent literature of late nineteenth-century France, and an extensive account appeared in J.-K. Huysmans' novel *Là-bas* (*Down There*). Gorman knew this literature very well.

Second, he extensively researched nineteenth-century American writers like Longfellow and Hawthorne, and it was in 1927 – the same year as *The Place Called Dagon* – that Gorman also published his biography, *Hawthorne: A Study In Solitude*. The Hawthorne link is critical, since that writer was deeply interested in New England witch persecutions. His "Young Goodman Brown" can be read as describing a genuine witch-cult, though the standard reading is that the story involves a fantasy or delusion. What Gorman did was to bring that idea into the twentieth century, and to take the unprecedented step of situating an occult or Satanic theme in contemporary America.

Reading *The Place Called Dagon* today, we are struck by how commonplace it is, since so many countless fictional treatments have depicted secret witch-cults and sacrificial rings in American villages and country towns, but in his day, Gorman's work was radically innovative. Gorman argues that the Salem witches "belonged to a secret and blasphemous order that met all over the world, that they were divided into covens or parishes, that they each had their leader in the shape of a Black Man who represented the devil, and that they attempted to practice magic. . . . The trappings and the ceremonies and the results might appear supernatural, but that was because the people in those days did not know about such things as thought-transference, auto-suggestion and the impulsion of the will." Some of the group fled to "Dagon" where they raised the great altar of the Devil Stone. "By day they were taciturn people, carrying on the quiet masquerade of pioneers, building up homes in the clearing, pushing the forest farther and farther back; but when the moon rose, the madness that was in their blood swept them out of themselves and they became other creatures employing pagan symbols and ancient phallic ceremonials. They existed in a domain out of place and time then, in a land of hallucinations and dreams and primitive urges." In modern times, a charismatic leader "reinstituted witch meetings, formed a coven here, and made himself the ruling Black Man. . . . These people lead two lives, and one of them is the surface life that we see going on about us. The other is the secret life that centers about the place called Dagon."

At the climax, we see the secret rituals at Dagon, at which Asmodeus is invoked in a kind of Black Mass. The affair culminates in the attempted sacrifice of a woman, which is interrupted by the forceful intervention of the hero, who attacks and kills the group's leader, the Reverend George Burroughs (this was of course the name of the actual minister at Salem). Virtually every allegation about real-life American satanism, particularly during the Scare of the 1980s and 1990s, can be located in this one novel.

The name Dagon evoked some bitter controversies of Puritan New England, which suggested that this Puritan society really had had its covert pagan side. The case in question was the notorious incident in 1627 in which dissidents erected a maypole similar to that from the English countryside, and held a festive gathering under the auspices of the Lord and Lady of the May. The story is recounted in Hawthorne's "Maypole of Merry Mount," and echoed faithfully by Gorman throughout *The Place Called Dagon*. Aware of its pagan connotations, outraged Puritan leaders denounced the maypole as a Dagon, after an idol mentioned in the Bible.

Both Gorman and Lovecraft appropriated the name "Dagon," implying that the maypole gathering had been part of an American chapter of the witch-cult. The theme appeared in Lovecraft's "The Shadow Over Innsmouth" (1931), one of his best-known stories. This portrays a forbidding New England town dominated by an evil race whose secret rituals are carried out under the cover of The Esoteric Order of Dagon, "a debased, quasi-pagan thing imported from the east," "a degraded cult" linked to devil-worship.

Lovecraft often used this idea of subterranean colonial cults. In *The Case of Charles Dexter Ward* (1927), Lovecraft depicts Salem's Rev Burroughs as the leader of a group of evil sorcerers, some of whom escape to carry on the cult into the present day. In "The Dreams in the Witch-House" (1933), reincarnated Salem witches in a modern city wait to celebrate Walpurgis Night, when "there would be bad doings, and a child or two would probably be missing." In "The Haunter of the Dark" (published in *Weird Tales* in 1936), Lovecraft cites the work of both Murray and Frazer, in addition to creating his own battery of spurious occult texts that sound so convincing that many readers then and since have thought them genuine. (You can still buy alleged copies of the bogus *Necronomicon* at many bookstores.)

Reading *Weird Tales* and its ilk, one would naturally believe that America not only had real witches surviving into the twentieth century – the York case proved that – but that they might be part of an ancient historical tradition, a deeply-rooted homicidal cult. None of which would have mattered for practical purposes, if the media of the 1930s did not buy into these stories wholesale, partly due to the ferocious newspaper circulation wars of the Depression era. From about 1932, the media had itself a bad case of satanic theory, and headlines about "cult killings" and "human sacrifices" appeared in amazing number – in stories about Black Muslims, Voodoo devotees, even Pentecostal "Holy Rollers." The relatively sober *New York Times* also offered stories about "Three 'Devil Murderers' Held In Baby Death." Also, for the first time, police were taking these theories seriously as possible explanations of multiple murders. A series of grotesque mutilation murders in Cleveland in the 1930s led police to explore "a wide range of unorthodox sects – blacks practicing Haitian Voodoo, covens of self-proclaimed witches and warlocks, and even a Hispanic group observing some obscure, ancient Aztec religion." Though none of these leads proved relevant to the case, the national public was further sensitized to the idea of authentic human sacrifice.

By about 1940, America was in the grip of a proto-satanism scare, an anti-cult movement, which looked very much like the horrors of the 1980s and 1990s. Though this eventually faded away, it left a body of memories that remained at the back of the public consciousness, ready to be revived when fringe religions and counter-cultures came to public attention once more.

What we are describing, then, is the prehistory of the modern cult scare. And it clearly originated not in actual events, but in bogus anthropology, media sensationalism, and in the fantastic imaginings of pulp writers – in short, of weird tales.

That is all there ever was to it then, and all there is today.

Homecoming

John Pelan

It had been nearly twenty years since Callie died; even though I was married now and had two little ones, I couldn't help but think of her every so often. Maybe it was looking down the barrel of the big Four Oh that made me grab a six-pack of beer and head out on the highway through the hills, back up toward Twin Oaks.

Twin Oaks was a tiny, dying flyspeck of a town, but that's where I told people I was from. At least Twin Oaks was on *most* maps, not like Creech Hollow, which lay farther up in the hills, 'bout twenty miles by dirt road from Twin Oaks. That's where I was from; I'd grown up there, and likely would've taken over the family feed store and spent my whole life there if it hadn't been for Callie dying and all that came with it.

Yeah, I could've stayed and run the feed store when my aunt and uncle decided to turn it over to me, but I'd always wanted to leave and they were as much a part of what happened as anyone else in town. I didn't know if they were alive or dead now, though I suspected the latter; they'd be in their eighties if they were still around. I figured that they were probably in the little cemetery beside my parents.

Callie Kilby and me had grown up together; I was a couple of years older and my earliest recollection of her was when she was maybe five or six years old and I saw her sittin' in her pa's truck when they came into town for supplies. Maybe I'd never seen anyone with such milky-white skin or with freckles before, but if I had, I sure didn't recollect it. Callie caught my imagination then and held it for years. We got sent off to Sparta to school together and probably would have got hitched sooner or later. That is, if she hadn't died all those years ago. . . .

I shook my head, as I'd nearly missed the turn-off to Twin Oaks. I slowed the Ford down and took a swig of beer. The country hadn't changed much at all; the road cut through the mountains is a gray twisty ribbon that seemed like it could get swallowed up in no time by the rhododendrons and scrub pine that grew almost to edges of the highway. There's a sense you get if you're from the mountains that's sort of like what the Cherokee believe – we're just visitors here; there's older ones than us humans up in the mountains and if we don't cause too much of a fuss and take care of the land, then everything's okay; but the land ain't ours, never will be, and we'd do well to remember that. . . . Hard to think that way back in the city when all you see is cement and smokestacks and the textile mills, but out here I felt very small and alone. . . . Knowing that if your car broke down, you could walk for most of a day and maybe not see another soul – sort of puts things in perspective.

They'd found Callie dead of a broken neck at the bottom of the gorge that runs under Creech Hollow. You take the path from behind Tucker's General Store and follow it along the cliffs . . . it's a beautiful place to walk among the beeches and silverbells with just the songs of the veeries and nuthatches for company. A peaceful sort of place, not a place where you'd go walking expecting to find someone dead. You go along the trail a bit farther and you come to Nahum's Bald. The old farmhouse still sits up on the plateau, but there's nary a growing thing to be seen for about three hundred yards in any direction from the house. A few rocks sticking out like the spurs on a gamecock and some scrubby bushes scattered here and there. Not a place where many folks would want to live, not with all the rest of the mountain country to choose from, but that's where Jory Tanner lived, and him being that close to the gorge was damning evidence to the folk of Creech Hollow.

But I'm getting ahead of myself here. See, Jory was reckoned to be a witch-man; after all, it was in the blood. His ma had been a conjure-woman and people came from all over to get charms from her, healing potions, luck charms, and (it was rumored) even more powerful spells if the price was met. She was the great-granddaughter of Nahum Tanner. Nahum Tanner had come to settle here after the War of Northern Aggression. The history of the Tanner clan is pretty sketchy before that. Some said he'd come west from Kansas and had ridden with Quantrill and Bloody Bill Anderson, but nobody really knew for sure. What is known is that he married a Cherokee woman and together they built the farmhouse that still stands up there today.

Maybe it was good farmland when they got there, or maybe not; over the years things just up and died near the Tanner house. Their land stretched a good few acres past the desolation, and most folk would have just given up and built a new house on the good land, but not the Tanners. No sir, they stayed right there in the center of the dead earth and went on as though it was the most natural thing in the world. Folks always said that either Nahum or his wife had conjured up an Anisgina, and that's what had blighted their land. . . . In any event, generations of the Tanners lived there, supposedly handing down their witch-lore from parent to child over the years.

I didn't know Jory real well; he was a few years older than me and we weren't really friends or anything, but when there's only a handful of people approximating your age anywhere nearby, you tend to get to know each other somewhat. Jory kept to himself for the most part. He was tall and spindly as a daddy-longlegs and had one eye with a silver cast to it. Of course, folk considered that silver eye his witch-mark and it did make you right uncomfortable when he looked straight at you and you couldn't be sure if that eye was really blind or not. . . . Jory gave a lot of folk the shudders, but Callie and I both thought of him as sort of a friend.

Jory was four or five years older than we were, so it's not like we spent a lot of time together; when you're young, four or five years is a gulf of age that seems unfathomable. Still, there weren't too many people around that were our age and only a few that were closer to Jory's age, so we did hang around together somewhat on the rare occasions that he got away from the house to come into town. We'd sit and drink sodas and talk, mainly talk about what we were going to do when we finished school and whether we'd move away or not. Callie talked about going and seeing the places that we read about in school, Richmond, and Raleigh, and maybe even going up north to see New York City. I thought it might be fine to travel somewhat, but I surely wouldn't want to live anywhere else. Jory would just sigh and say that with the special chores he had, he didn't see as how he could ever leave, even for a little while.

I remember Callie sort of staring at him all quizzical-like and asking, "What kind of chores you mean, that you couldn't ever leave even for a little while?"

He just smiled sadly and replied, "Sometimes you jest sort of get bound to a place, if you know what I mean. There's been Tanners up here on Nahum's Bald since the War of Northern Aggression, and there's always got to be a Tanner there. That's jest the way it is. I figure there's always going to be a Tanner up at the bald, leastways long as there's a town here."

I didn't think anything of it at the time or connect it to the stories I'd heard about Guardians. There were lots of stories that got handed down, ghost stories mixed up with Indian legends and the kind of wild imaginings that one naturally gets when you're way up in the mountains and hear the owls screeching in the dark and things moving about through the pine trees. We just sat there enjoying the afternoon without any idea that this would be one of the last few times we'd be together. That was the day that Jory handed us each a little crystal stone on a leather cord. The rock was sort of quartz-like with a pinkish hue and a splotch of dark red running through it; with the hole bored into it, it caught the light in a colorful way.

"Keep this with you, it's powerful; this here's a piece of the Ulunsuti. When it was whole it had a life of its own and was very powerful. It got broken years ago but the pieces are still protection against most things. . . ."

I had to show my ignorance and ask, "What's an Ulunsuti?"

"The Ulunsuti was a Cherokee demon; it stayed in the form of a stone unless it was hungry – when hungry it would take another shape. Story is that years and years ago the Ulunsuti was broken into pieces by a great medicine man who gave my great-great-grandfather some of the pieces. Maybe it's just some kind of quartz, but I've always worn one and so did my ma and pa. These here are a couple of extras. I've still got three, that should be plenty. . . ."

I couldn't tell if Jory really believed this Ulunsuti stuff himself or not. With him you never could tell when he was being serious about the witch stuff. Sometimes he'd get mad if you joked about it, other times it seemed like it was all just a big joke to him and nothing to take seriously. Still, the stone was unusual and it would have been bad manners to refuse a gift like that, so I looped it over my head and tucked it under my shirt.

I pulled in to Twin Oaks just as the afternoon sun was starting to peak. The old gas-station/general store/post office had apparently been torn down years before. There was big sign saying "Beer/Gas & Propane" in front of one of those little stores that you see all over the south. That accounted for the general store and the gas station, but no telling where the post office had been moved to. Across the street was a small shop with a neon sign proclaiming "Wine & Spirits." That sounded pretty good to me; I parked the Ford and went in. Wasn't much to it. Apparently folk round here were still pretty content with their own 'shine and homebrew and didn't have much use for store-bought booze. The selection was pretty much limited to a dozen different bourbons and two each of the other major types. I looked in vain for Wild Turkey or something equally good and finally settled on a pint of Jim Beam. Ol' Jim's nothing special, but he sure is consistent – for a sipping whisky to drink in memory of old friends, he'd do just fine.

I handed the old man behind the counter a ten and tried to place his face as he made change. He had to be someone I was at least acquainted with. . . . People may move out to the areas that the big companies are developing with golf courses and strip malls and condos, but nobody moves out to Twin Oaks or Creech Hollow. Those are places you move away from, not to. . . . Finally, to break the ice, I said, "Anything new up in Creech Hollow?"

"Ain't no Creech Hollow round here. . . ." His tone was sharp as though I'd annoyed him by speaking. "You must not be from around here —"

I cut him off. "I was born here, and Creech Hollow's 'bout twenty miles up the road just over that way." I gestured across the street to where the dirt road snaked up through the hills.

"No sir, ain't nothing up that way, hasn't been for years. I should know, I've lived here my whole life; my pa built nearly this whole street."

It dawned on me then who this old man was; he had to be one of the Mulkey brothers. The family had been here near as long as mine. I figured he didn't believe me when I'd said I was a local and was just trying to run me off. . . . Fine, I didn't much care to stick around here in any event. The memories of twenty years past were coming back fast and furious.

They'd hung him. You don't think of a lynching as taking place in this day and age, but that's just what it was. Someone spotted Jory standing up in the hills looking down at the cemetery as Callie was being laid to rest and that's all it took for a grieving town to convict him of murder in their minds. After all, he was the witch-man and she was found near the trail leading up to his home. Didn't no way matter that half the people in town counted on Jory and his Ma before him for everything from potions to ease a cow in labor to charms to keep the crops safe to talismans to warn when danger was near. That was all forgot now in their grieving and all they thought about was that he was different, he was the witch-man and that meant he had to be the one that done killed Callie. I tried to stop it as best I could, but I was just one kid arguing with a whole town of angry, grief-mad people.

I didn't see the actual hanging, but I saw them leading Jory to the big oak in the cemetery and the noose already cinched into place on a branch. I'd been packed and ready to leave for a week before Callie died. I got into my beat-up old Chevy and started driving, worked my way here and there all the way to Wheeling and never did look back. Until now, that is. . . .

I took a slug of JB and headed the Ford up the dirt road; maybe Mulkey was right about there being no town of Creech Hollow. The road was pretty overgrown in spots with nothing to indicate that anyone had driven or even hiked up this way recently. I didn't know what I was expecting to see, maybe the old feed store boarded up, maybe a couple of the houses gone to ruin. I parked in what had served as the center of town and headed over to the bench where the three of us used to sit and talk. As I neared the two wooden steps leading up to the skirt porch that extended all along the storefront, it was obvious that the store was closed. Well, not *closed*, exactly, maybe abandoned would be a better word. It looked for all the world like Rafe and Janey Tucker had just up and left without a care in the world about what might happen to their store.

I walked in, the door was wide open. There was no one is sight – the register stood unattended and empty; the rotten vegetation stink from long-since-spoilt produce made it impossible to stay inside more than a minute. I walked back outside and looked down the street, saw a few scattered houses, weather-beaten and with paint peeling and dry-rot settling in. Mulkey was right; nobody had been living here in quite a spell. Maybe they all had moved away after the hanging. . . . Still, if this was the last time I'd be home, I should probably make it a point to see everything. Everything, that is, but my old house. I had no desire to go there. I figured I'd save the visit to the little cemetery for the way back. Maybe finish off the bottle in a toast to old friends. Whatever answers there might be about what happened weren't going to be found here in the town. Maybe there weren't really any answers. . . .

I wondered, was it possible that the whole town was so afeared of the repercussions of the lynching that they all fled Creech Hollow? I supposed that was possible, though it didn't seem likely – after all, the closest real law was over in Sparta, and how would any outsiders ever know? I couldn't imagine that they would have thought that I'd go to the Sheriff's office, they'd have known better than that.

I walked over to the trail that ran up to Nahum's Bald. I wasn't sure that I really wanted to see Jory's place, but something inside said I needed to go up that way. I took a pull of the bottle of Jim Beam and started up the trail.

Oddly enough, the trail to Nahum's Bald was in much better shape than the road to Creech Hollow. No weeds or vines intruded onto the dirt path. I glanced around. Something was different about the trail, but I couldn't quite place it. . . . I walked slowly, looking around and trying to figure out what was different. It finally hit me and made the hair on my neck rise – it was quiet, deadly quiet. There were no birds, no cracking of twigs, no rustling in the leaves, nothing. I hadn't seen or heard any living thing since I'd left town. I almost turned back, but I was so close to Nahum's Bald that I just had to go the rest of the way and see what, if anything, was left of Jory's place.

The little farmhouse stood in the middle of the desolation, just as it always had. I walked slowly across the bare earth, glancing around to see if there was any sign of life anywhere. Of course, there wasn't; if the woods were deserted, there surely wouldn't be anything living up here on Nahum's Bald. The door was open, as I'd known it would be – up here folks didn't bother with locking doors, (nothing to steal and no one that would steal, anyways). The house was in pretty good shape for being well over a hundred years old; it was small, a main room connected to the kitchen and a short hall leading to two small bedrooms. The only thing that made it stand out from a hundred other little farmhouses in the mountains was the odd stick lattices and chalk markings scattered here and there as wards. That was the sure sign of a witch-man's house, but it didn't look like much else of interest. There was a small shelf with some old, old books. I picked one up and examined the title *Long Lost Friend*. . . . I glanced at a few pages, didn't make a whole lot of sense to me, seemed like long passages of poetry and recipes and the like. I placed it back on the shelf and turned to go.

I don't know what I thought I'd find. Jory had been by himself up here for three years before he was killed and far as I knew there weren't any other Tanners 'round here likely to want to take possession of the place. I guess Jory been wrong about there always being a Tanner up on Nahum's Bald. . . .

I stepped back out into the sunshine and noticed something; the wooden cover to the root cellar was ajar. I walked over and peered down into the darkness. Didn't make much sense that anyone would have come up here and gone poking around in the root cellar; wasn't like Jory was likely to have anything squirreled away down there. I bent down and slid the cover to the side for a better look.

There was an awful smell that hit me all of a sudden, a smell of rotten meat and death. Somehow the dark of the cellar seemed to be *shifting*. At the same time I felt a sharp burning on my chest and clasped my hand to the pain. Jory's stone was hot to the touch, hot enough to burn. Something told me to run, and run fast. I looked down into the cellar and something was definitely moving down there, moving and making a buzzing sound. . . .

I covered the distance to the edge of Nahum's Bald and the start of the footpath in seconds, then glanced behind me. There was a figure standing by the root cellar; it wasn't human, though it was man-shaped. . . . It had to be at least ten feet tall and black as night and was moving slowly but steadily towards me. It was close enough that I could see why it sort of shifted and melted and reformed as it moved; a huge black cloud of every kind of fly that you could imagine – horseflies, bluebottles – all the biting, stinging flies you ever heard of. I could almost make out their distinct shapes as they swarmed together to make this gigantic form. I ran, heading down the trail with a horrid buzzing just behind me, Jory's talisman burning on my neck.

I rushed down the trail as fast as I could. The thing wasn't gaining on me, but it wasn't slowing down neither. I kept to the edges of the trail trying to remember where some of the shortcuts we took as kids were. Even if I made it back to the town, what then? Barricade myself in one of the houses and hope this thing went away?

Whatever it was, it wasn't just flies – flies don't twist and turn and follow a trail with the kind of awful purpose that this thing had. Where was the shortcut? I remembered a steep cut-off that you had to practically slide down, but it could put some distance between me and the black cloud that followed. If the thing could go any faster, it would have already caught me. . . .

There! I recognized the old pine with the twisted trunk; I shot over to the right and hit the ground like Pete Rose sliding into first – the slide was a lot steeper than I'd remembered and the ground a hell of a lot harder – still, a broken neck would be better than being caught by that thing.

I felt a sharp pain as I slid face first over a root and a sudden jerk as the root snagged the cord around my neck. It was strong leather lace, but my momentum was such that it snapped like kite-string and I continued my slide, finally hitting some bushes well over two hundred feet from where I'd started. I was alive, knees and stomach raw and bleeding, but alive. I rolled over and looked up. The thing was coming down the hill, slowly, relentlessly. I had to get up, had to start running again. The buzzing was getting closer. . . .

Just as suddenly it stopped. The cloud dissolved and a million flies darted off in separate directions. Near as I could figure it was right at the spot where I'd lost Jory's stone. For a second I thought about climbing up after it, and then I reconsidered and limped over to where I'd parked the Ford.

I didn't stop to say anything to anyone in Twin Oaks, just kept going straight to Sparta, where I went to the hospital to get patched up. I told the nurse I'd slipped while hiking and got a lecture about hiking up in the hills by yourself and a couple of aspirin and that was about it. Waiting in the hospital gave me some time to think, time to draw some conclusions; I guess the stories about old Nahum conjuring up something were true, and that Jory was dead serious when he said that there always had to be a Tanner up on Nahum's Bald. Jory saved my life, twenty years after he'd been lynched. No doubt in my mind that it was his talisman what stopped that thing. Of course, it probably reformed itself by now – I figure a thing like that can't be got rid of so easily.

I guess I finally got the answers that I'd gone home to find, though now I sort of wish I'd never asked the questions. Near as I can figure, the generations of Tanners that lived up there kept that thing in the root cellar where it couldn't do no harm. Maybe they fed it somehow, to keep it quiet. As to what happened to the people of Creech Hollow, I don't rightly like to think about it. They made a real bad choice and killed the man that was protecting 'em all that time. I don't reckon that it makes much sense, and like I said, I really don't like thinking about it. Nor do I want to think about what might happen when that thing up on Nahum's Bald gets hungry enough to come down off the mountain.

Horizon, CLIVE BARKER

How to Spot a Serial Killer

Michael Oliveri

This could have been me.

The more I read about these three unfortunate kids and the hell they have been through due to the ignorance and ineptitude of others, the more I realize this could easily have happened to me had I been in the wrong place at the wrong time. And that just scares the shit out of me.

I wore black all the time in high school. It felt good, and I thought it looked cool. As a matter of fact, I still wear black all the time, though for entirely different reasons (I haven't been kind to my gut). I wear it so much, people who know me are shocked when they see me in another color. People who don't know me tend to give me these funny, sidelong looks.

As I got into high school and could afford to buy my own tapes (CDs still came in those goofy, oversized boxes and cost quite a bit more), I bought my first metal album: Mötley Crüe's *Doctor Feelgood*. I soon picked up Megadeth, Metallica, Judas Priest, Iron Maiden, Black Sabbath, Pantera, Slayer, and more. You know, all those "evil" bands that only devil worshippers listen to.

I dug the concert tees the bands sold. Unfortunately, twenty-five bucks a pop was too much for a kid putting in just enough hours making minimum wage at a toy store to fund his music and comic book habit. So, I found the next best thing: "death" shirts (as my friends referred to them). My family did some target shooting as a hobby, and we went to gun shows. One vendor there carried these black T-shirts with various gruesome pictures and slogans featuring military and/or death themes, most for a ten spot, though you could snag three for twenty-five. Over time, I stocked up.

The shirts said all kinds of things. "Born to kill" was one. Then I had "bred to Kill, not to Care," "Mercenaries Never Die, They just go to Hell to Regroup," and the ever-popular "Kill 'em All, let God Sort 'em Out." Odd thing to see on a chunky, nerdy freshman who routinely got his ass handed to him at wrestling meets. It permanently labeled me as part of the stoner crowd, though I never did drugs, and even friends teased me that I'd be the next Jeffrey Dahmer. I would just kind of smile to myself at the time, and not bother to deny it; it usually made most people leave me alone.

If I only got three strikes, I guess that would have been it for me. Yet there are a few more things that could be held against me if one follows Crittenden County Juvenile Officer Jerry Driver's "How to Spot a Killer" manual.

Next up, I played role-playing games. I played *Advanced Dungeons & Dragons* for starters, and had loads of books and modules for the game. Then I read H.P. Lovecraft and played *Call of Cthulhu*, and wondered if the fabled *Necronomicon* really existed (it doesn't) and how I could get my hands on it. Surely that must mean I worship the devil.

Which brings me to the next bit: I had a strong occult interest. Werewolves, zombies, and ghosts, oh my. If it was big and mean and evil, I wanted to read about it. If it had something to do with the supernatural and people dying, bring it on. And it was all non-fiction. Or at least as close as one could come to it, anyway. When I read fiction, I entertained other dreams.

Then, finally, we have the *coup de grâce*: I tried to get a look at *The Satanic Bible*. (Cue ominous horn music.)

The Helen M. Plum Memorial Library in Lombard, Illinois was a cool place. It was huge, and they carried *everything*. They even carried both first and second edition AD&D books when the older kids actually bothered to return them. So I decided to look for *The Satanic Bible*. I didn't have any real interest beyond idle curiosity, but by the above, I imagine most folks would have assumed otherwise.

Lo and behold, they *did* carry it. A Styrofoam board with brown duct tape disguised as a book binding marked its place in the Dewey Decimal System on a shelf in the reference section. An index card taped to the front indicated it was not eligible for checkout, and I would have to bring the board to the reference desk to see the book.

So I did. The librarian first asked if I was "old enough." She didn't give a specific age, so I shrugged and told her yes, I was. She looked over her glasses at me, looked me up and down. Then she went in back for a moment. When she came out, she stashed the faux-Bible under the counter and informed me someone must have taken it, as it's not in the back.

Did I believe her? Not really. I thanked her and left. Maybe she thought she did her good deed for the day by saving me from a life of evil. Or maybe it really was gone. Doesn't matter. Still, every time I see the scenes dealing with the library books in the movie *Seven*, I smile to myself and wonder if there's a tick mark next to my name somewhere.

That makes what, six things to throw at me in a courtroom, depending on how you count 'em up? Maybe you can call it seven things if someone knew I collected *Killer Cards*, which were trading cards with gory death scenes on one side and survival tips on the other. Almost bought a pack of serial killer trading cards once, too, but they were too expensive.

I guess it's a good thing I don't live in West Memphis, Arkansas.

I may not have had a juvenile court officer to point a finger at me, but I had a suitable replacement. One kid who only knew me from one class often referred to me as MOD – Messenger of Death. He once told me I was a "loose cannon" and was dangerous, and that I'd get into trouble some day. Never quite figured that one out myself, but there you have it. All he would have had to do is drop my name to the para-pro security guard or the part-time liaison officer from the Lombard Police Department, and I would probably have been hauled off for questioning.

Surely my friends would have come to my defense, right? Thinking back, I'm not so sure about a couple of them. As I mentioned, I already drew the Dahmer comparisons. Then came the threat.

A friend of mine encouraged my younger brother to steal a few CDs for another friend's birthday. He claimed he was joking, of course, but I figured he was full of shit. In the middle of a crowded hallway, in front of several other friends, I pushed him against a locker and told him if he ever asked my brother to do something like that again, I'd slit his throat from ear to ear. I pointed at the base of each ear for emphasis, and walked away.

Much as I would deny it then out of sheer bravado, I would never really go through with it. I never *could* really go through with it. But a short time later, I found out each and every witness, including the other close friends and a girl who later (ironically) became my girlfriend, were one-hundred-percent convinced that Dan would be a dead man by the end of the week.

Wow. I say again, it's a *damn* good thing I don't live in West Memphis, Arkansas. Combine the above with an inept and short-sighted law enforcement team and I'm sure I would be sitting in jail alongside Jessie Misskelley, Damien Echols, and Jason Baldwin, if not in their place. For as you probably know, the evidence used to convict these three poor guys has been little more than perception and assumption.

It's the kind of thing that's not supposed to happen in America. It's the kind of thing we hear about going on in Nazi Germany, the former Soviet Union, and modern dictatorships. Unfortunately, even our supposedly superior legal system is run by people, and reason doesn't get handed out with a gun and a badge. When the cops in this case destroyed all the real evidence and the emotions resulting from the brutal murder of three young boys ran hot, what little rational thought they had went out the window.

So what's the solution? Giving these guys a fair shake is a good start. With a little hope, you've helped do just that by purchasing this book. As we all know, legal matters and evidence testing are far from cheap. Similarly, I hope once these young men are exonerated, the authorities will do their damn jobs and attempt to track down the real killer(s); Christopher Byers, Steven Branch, Michael Moore, and their families deserve justice, too.

The Afterlives of SweetDeath

Adam Roberts

There was something uncommon about this customer as soon as he came into the shop. Allow me to stress the point. I may add that I have dealt with all manner of customer in my time in the company: I have seen men and women happy, sad, apprehensive, enthusiastic, cynical, ingenuous. But this one was something *quite other*. Of course, I did not realize quite how disastrous a series of events he was to inaugurate.

He came into our sales chamber late on Gateday. It may still be Gateday, as I write. Perhaps it is Flyday. But it was summer outside the emporium. It is still summer outside, which is a comforting thought. Light shimmered through the city-shield above the rooftops, yellow as custard, bright like strip-lighting, as hot as bathwater. High summer. My favorite season. The city environment was fine-tuned for heat, brightness, and joy.

I wore my company white Lanret, pressed smooth, which hung neatly from my shoulders. I was happy. I am no longer wearing those clothes and I am no longer happy.

When the customer entered, I said: "Good day to you, prospective-customer, my name is Vanice and I will be your sales-guide to the afterlives of SweetDeath – material immortality at affordable prices. With our trade-protected nano-insertion-vR compounds, we promise you perceptions of infinity *more* vivid, *more* real, and *more* lasting than any of our competitors – where they use vR-helmets and similar outdated hardware, we are the *cutting edge*." I smiled my best salesman smile. That same smile had won the SweetDeath Employee customer-interface personal skills competition on three separate occasions.

But in return I received no politeness, no gracious chitchat, none of those normal human niceties. "I wish to purchase a death," he said, baldly.

"For yourself, sir?" I asked. "Or for a relative? You'll understand the reason for my question, I'm sure – you seem yourself both young and in good health, although, naturally, outward appearances can deceive –"

"My own death," he interrupted.

"I understand, sir," I said.

He was a young male with a plump face, on either side of which projected two bunches of curly black hair. His eyes were white-blue, porcelain-like, and in constant movement, as if he mistrusted where he stood. He wore a mauve droho with a white seaque, and expensive-looking meadhres. In that respect he appeared to be a promising customer, an individual worthy of my time – clearly an individual of wealth, and of some taste as well. It is true that he was younger than most of the customers who come to visit SweetDeath, being, I gauged, no more than thirty-five. (Our typical customer is in his thirteenth or fourteenth decade.) But his age was not, in itself, an impossible thing. On occasion we do, of course, get young customers. Diseases of the body and mind can afflict the young, even in our advanced society.

So, the usual sales procedure is for me to sit the customer in the Moar Chair, and take up a position somewhere behind him. All walls project a soothingly attuned blueness downloaded from actual sky (by actual sky, I mean, of course, from well above the city shield). Clouds float white-laced in the cyan. The air is warm with sunshine the color of lemonade, fretted by birdsong captured from twenty-second century databases. Most customers find it relaxing. But no sooner had I settled this customer in the Moar Chair than he barked out:

"None of that! I require neither that noise, nor those images!"

The walls faded to an inoffensive flux of pale colors.

"I apologize, sir," I murmured. "Most of our customers find the environment an aid to the process of their choosing."

"Choosing?" he snapped at me, as if not understanding the word.

"Choosing," I said, "which of the many popular Deaths we retail that most suits the customer."

"Is it true that your customers are able, if they wish it, to design their own deaths?" he demanded.

"Quite true," I said. I had summoned the preview device from its alcove with the crook of my hand: it snaked silently through the air and positioned itself behind the customer's head. "Customers base their design upon a popular pre-designed Death, so as to be able to take full advantage of the capacities of the machinery. But any Death can be customized."

I then activated the preview device. It broadcast to the customer and I simultaneously.

*You are in a large and comfortable bed, propped up on
goosedown pillows. You are surrounded by a dozen or more*

family members and loved ones, all of whom are quietly
distressed about your condition, but you are calm – contented
– happy. You see the sunlight through the open window, you
smell the clean air, you hear the birdsong. And with words of
reassurance to your family, and a smile on your face, you pass
from this earthly veil on a waft of softness, and are carried up
into a light that floods down, and yet does not sting the eyes.
[phased pulsed electrical stimulation of the medulla oblongata
and certain circuits in the cerebrum set up a reinforced cerebral
feedback giving the hallucinatory experience a deep sense of
solidity, and chemical supplementation in the hindbrain produces
a deep-felt sense of well being]

You drift up through infinite light and infinite love to a
towering gate of pearl and mahogany swathed in strings of
bluebells. Through these gates you walk on pavements of felt
past buildings of marble and gold, and you meet the spirits
of your departed loved ones, as well as the spirits of famous
people. You ascend to a sunlit meadow beside a blue-purple
lake, beneath a beautiful range of mountains. Here you spend
many days: all your questions are answered, all your wishes
are met. You may explore an extensive city of rose-colored
stone constructed beside the lake. You may fly with angel's
wings. Your every minute of afterlife is suffused with bliss.
[please note: if your Death requires that more than twenty-four
attendant spirits be programmed, additional fees may be charged]

The next stage takes place when your spirit is ready: you rise
again, traveling through the cosmos, stars surrounding you
like glittering white spangles. You visit a thousand worlds
and see strange life and strange civilizations. Yet you are
drawn, happily, towards the great central Om, the truth of the
Godhead, and to this you move ever closer, your sense of bliss,
harmony, and meaning increasing. You approach ultimate
meaning and ultimate contentment. . . .

It was then I noticed the customer had risen from the chair, broken the
connection, and was standing by the door. "Stop! Stop!" he called. "I did
not give you permission – to pour all that – syrup into my head –"

"Sir, I assure you," I said, "this is a perfectly normal sales strategy.
Most of our customers –"

"I do not like it," he cried. Petulant, like a child. Imagine that!

"It is our most popular product," I replied, with, of course, a certain professional pride. "If you had waited until the conclusion of the simulation, you would have seen –"

Again he interrupted me. Such ill-breeding! "It was ghastly. Although," he said, more to himself than to me I think, "not as bad as some." He scratched at his chin with his thumb, and settled in the chair again. "*You* must tell *me*," he snapped, "precisely how long all this lasts – how long? *Precisely* how long?"

"Your question is an acute one, sir," I replied. "To understand the difference between perceived time and actual time –"

He nodded, which I took as a prompt to continue.

"The feedback stimulation-loop repeats," I explained, smiling again, "every fifty-two seconds. In effect, folding over itself every minute. Which is to say, the first minute of the simulation is perceived as lasting a minute, the second is perceived as lasting two minutes, the third as lasting four minutes, the fourth eight." I smiled. "I'm sure you can see how quickly the time in the simulation appears, to the subjective observer, to stretch. The fortieth minute of the simulation lasts 550 *billion* minutes – over a *million years* of subjective time."

He scoffed. "Long, yes. But hardly eternity."

"Oh sir," I chided gently, "a longer stretch of time than any human has a right to expect. More than forty iterations and the perceptual time degrades beyond acceptable parameters. Besides, the Court of Mercantile Ethics ruled ten years ago that, for advertising purposes, it is legitimate to advertise 'one point oh six million years' under the rubric 'eternity.'"

He snorted. Then he said, "The Death itself actually takes forty minutes?"

"A little over forty minutes, yes," I replied, "indeed." And, prompted by my salesperson's instinct, I activated the device a second time –

> *You are in a battlefield of the historical period of your choice, from Ancient Greece to the present day. You are fighting with a group of heart-close comrades, or alternately are fighting by yourself against incredible odds. You perform staggering feats of heroism against a bestial foe and* [decision to be made on payment] *either receive a swordstroke through the heart while saving the lives of your comrades* [swordstroke programmed to register in terms of exhilaration and triumph rather than pain]

or *rescue a group of innocent civilians from certain death at the cost of your own life.* [phased pulsed electrical stimulation of the medulla oblongata and the pineal set up a reinforced cerebral feedback giving the hallucinatory experience a deep sense of excitement, victory, and well being]

You pass through the smoke of battle to a Valhalla hall of feasting and drinking, meeting the spirits of celebrated warriors of all ages. From there you ascend to a sunlit meadow beside a blue-purple lake, standing beneath a beautiful range of mountains where all your questions are answered, all your wishes are met. You may explore an extensive city of rose-colored stone constructed beside the lake. You may fly with angel's wings. Your every minute of afterlife is suffused with bliss. [please note: if your Death requires that more than twenty-four celebrated warriors be programmed, additional fees may be charged]. . .

"No!" cried the customer, leaping from the chair and stomping around the shop in agitation. "*None* of that! I have already made it plain that I do not desire to experience such advertising!"

"I am most sorry, sir," I returned smoothly. "I must have depressed the control button by mistake." But of course this action had been no accident; I had hoped that this more exciting variant would sweep him past his peculiar reticence. Perhaps I had intuited that this particular customer was of the more martial sort. Something about his manner, his belligerence, his lack of *manners.* But the strategy had not worked. His brow was now compressed with exasperation, and he took an even harder tone with me.

"Mistake? I do not believe it," he said. "But it hardly matters. I have *very specific* instructions for my death. I wish you to program a *particular* death for me."

"I see," I said coolly. Occasionally a customer will come into the shop asking for a bespoke death. Almost always their aspirations are grossly sexual. I composed my features to be sternly off putting. "I might suggest the Erotothanatos organization, if your –"

"No, no," interrupted the customer again. "You misunderstand. Mine has no sexual component. That is not my purpose at all. I require," and he pulled a page-floppy from inside his jacket, "I require this. Please peruse, and tell me if such a thing is possible."

"Possible, sir?" I said, with a hint of snideness, as if to imply that nothing was beyond our possibilities. "Of course, sir."

I read the document. This is what it said:

> *You are in a small room. There is one exit, and it is sealed. You*
> *spend a night there, alone. You are wearing a single item of*
> *clothing that covers legs, torso, and arms. Your hair has been*
> *cut short. The air temperature is cold and the only heating is a*
> *warm-water pipe that runs along one wall close to the floor.*

This was such an odd scenario that I stopped reading. "Sir," I hazarded, looking up at him, "I do not quite understand. May I ask: why are you in the room?"

"Why," he retorted, "in your last product advertisement, was the warrior on the battlefield? What was the war in that case? Why was *he* there?"

"I really have no idea," I replied. "None of our clientele have ever found it necessary to – I mean to say, that nobody has ever – required elucidation on that point."

He stared at me for many seconds. "They accept the situation they find themselves in," he said.

"I suppose they do."

"It is the way of people," he said, nodding ponderously.

This, it seemed, was the only answer I was to receive. I continued reading.

> *In the morning, the door opens. There are six men beyond it,*
> *two of whom step into your room. They shackle you and lead*
> *you out. All are silent except for one walking behind you who*
> *recites certain religious catchphrases and slogans in a small*
> *voice. You pass through concrete corridors and into another*
> *room where you are strapped into a large chair. The straps go*
> *over your arms, around your ankles, and belt you in at the*
> *waist. The chair is spot-lit, and beyond the brightness you*
> *can make out, though only hazily, an audience of angry faces*
> *watching you. A helmet is attached to your head. A powerful*
> *electrical current is passed through your body. This stops your*
> *heart, squeezes all your muscles into spasm, heats your bodily*
> *fluids to boiling, and cooks your bones. The shock blinds*
> *you, turning the transparent gel in your eyeballs white, and*
> *holds you in one place, where every component of your body*

> *becomes palpable and vivid to your consciousness as pain and*
> *stress.*

Again, I stopped. I did not know what to make of this. In our dozen most popular simulations – and this really goes without saying – the "pain" of death is either blurred away entirely, or else transmuted into triumph and exhilaration. But I could not see how to program this form of excessive pain in those terms. How could the subject feel exhilarated by such a dismal circumstance?

"This is based," I hazarded, "upon an historical circumstance?"

"It is," he confirmed.

"I confess, sir," I said, "that I do not – understand –"

"Is my description unclear?" he said.

"No," I replied. "But – but why would anybody *want* such a death?"

"Who would want such a death?" he repeated, with such an uninflected, blank tone that he seemed not to be querying my own question, so much as merely echoing it.

I read the remainder of the document:

> *It is dark, and then you experience a tumbling sensation of*
> *falling. You are aware of a red glow all around you, of visible*
> *darkness, and the sensation of heat. You fall through a vast*
> *chamber, and after many days' drop you land in an intensely*
> *alkaline lake. The shore of this lake is constantly on fire. Your*
> *only choices are to wallow in the lake, or crawl on the land.*

That was all.

"I have never before," I said, slowly, "read of a SweetDeath in any way akin to this."

He nodded.

"Is it," I prompted, "your own imaginative construction?"

"By no means. It is the result of careful research in obscure historical archives. It is based in every detail upon practices documented from the Century of War."

"Ah! I see. Of course, many," I said, half-laughing, "consider that century a barbarous time."

"Indeed," he said. I expected further comment, but he said nothing.

"Can human society ever *really* have held beliefs so bizarre and sadistic? The subject here suffers a painful and degrading death *followed by* an eternity of torture?"

"Indeed they did believe so," said the customer, blithely, "at that time."

"But, given that the subject will endure an eternity of torture, why is it necessary to make his death so painful and demeaning?"

"It is hard to say," said the customer.

"Surely," I pressed, "a peaceful death would be more appropriate? A subject destined for one of the archaic religious heavens might be expected to endure a painful demise, to earn the right of bliss; but an individual in such a situation as you have delineated. . . ."

"I agree it is puzzling," said the customer. "I am by no means an expert on this period. My guess," he said, "is that this was a rudely superstitious time, and a culture that believed in sympathetic magic: that like cured like, that affinities existed between material and spiritual realms. It may have been the case that the painful and degrading death was believed to be necessary *in order* to usher the subject into their hell . . . that the manner of death was believed to dictate the afterlife. So a man dying peacefully would pass into a peaceful eternity, a man dying sickly would endure a sickly afterlife, and a man dying in pain and fear would," and he glanced around himself with a studied carefulness, "exist eternally in the manner indicated in my document."

"Sir," I said nervously, perusing the document again. It was dawning on me that this customer genuinely wished to realize this horrific death and painful material immortality. I could hardly believe it, but his manner was one of absolute sincerity. "Sir," I said again.

He was looking at me with exaggerated concentration. How to handle this grotesque situation?

I summoned my salesman's courage and prepared to contradict the customer. Such contradiction does not come easily to a true salesman. "I'm afraid that this is most irregular. It vitiates the whole purpose of SweetDeath to emphasize these – ah – *concepts* of pain and misery to this degree. To accede to your – strange – request would be to damage the reputation of the company for which I work. The purpose of Material Immortality, after all, is to bring hope and scope to human life. . . ."

He interrupted. "I have looked into the matter," he said. "Nearly ninety percent of deaths are nowadays handled via Material Immortality."

"Indeed," I confirmed. When he had first entered the emporium he had acted as if he were ignorant of the process (as is the case with many young people; for why should a youngster think about death at all?). But now it appeared he knew a great deal more than he had revealed. My suspicions hardened.

"The fifty or so companies that handle such deceases earned eleven trillion *totales* last year. Considerable wealth."

"Who can put a price on immortality? Most virtual reality programs trade in momentary elations; but ours are eternal –"

Again he interrupted me. "To walk into one of your chambers," he said, "and not leave it again for nearly *two million years* –" He stopped. "Does not this seem to figure the chamber as a prison house?"

"Prison?" I repeated, uncomprehending.

"A punitive arrangement?"

"Punitive? Most certainly not. Our virtual evocations are the most vivid on the market. Where our competitors use VR helmets, of limited potency, we inject a nanobitic compound called CTX-nervous, that travels directly to the relevant centers of the brain in order to –"

"This," he said, "does not address my concern."

"Sir!" I exclaimed, barely able to control my outrage. "I must observe that you *frequently* interrupt my speech, without the least regard to the niceties of society, when –"

"Immortality," he said loudly, and I stopped. "It is a myth, of course. Look around," he said urgently. "Science preserves and extends our lives, it is true, but everybody must die. We try to circumvent the truth of this, but the people who step into your SweetDeath chambers – in an hour they *are* dead, they have gone. Is this immortality?"

"The Court of Mercantile Ethics ruled, as I explained, that it is legitimate to advertise 'one point oh six million years' under the rubric 'eternity.'"

"You misunderstand," said the man. "You misunderstand. It is not the *shortfall* to which I object. What worries me is how much *longer* than a human lifespan these millions of years are."

"It is," I replied, uncertain as to his objection, "a long time. But if the alternative is extinction? We may choose to think, as most do, that science has given us a greatly increased –"

And once again he interrupted me. I had never before met so rude an individual. "After the first death there *should* be none other," he said. "A million years? How many possible deaths are there in that?"

"I do not understand your question," I said.

He sighed briefly, like a punctuation mark. "And if our culture is indeed obsessed with death? Yet it lacks the honesty to concede its obsession. We *dwell* on death, only because of the chambers of material immortality such as yours. We elongate the experience of dying to grotesque proportions. A woman's life may be a hundred years living and a million dying – how can that *be*, except that it overbalances her existence wholly?"

"A woman's life?" I repeated. But I was alarmed now by his aggressive tone. It appeared he was a troublemaker. Perhaps, from his views, he was a crank, a religious-person, a fundamentalist of some kind. Occasionally such anachrones would picket our emporium, declaring that material immortality violated God's will, or postponed the soul's entry into spiritual heaven, or somesuch. "I do not understand."

"I hold it as truth, as self-evidently true, that it is a short death which restores meaning to life."

"Meaning?" I smiled. "But how may there be meaning in nullity? Meaning presupposes existence. And what alternative is there to material immortality but extermination?"

"I could name," he said, somberly, "dozens of acquaintances of mine – people in their sixties – who have never gone to the trouble of gaining an education, who do nothing with their lives but slack, and play, because each of them believe that their consciousness has two million years stretching before it." He shook his head sadly.

I thought, then, that I saw the basis of his objection to the Material Immortality program. "Ah!" I said, holding up my forefinger. "So you object to the *effect* on society. But this is merely repeating the objections of the Schofield group from five years ago! You remember, of course, their proposal to keep younger generations in ignorance of the possibility of Material Immortality, revealing it only to people over one hundred, or those terminally ill. A ridiculous notion! Can you genuinely be advocating such world-wide hypocrisy? Secrecy? That would not be *polite*." I meant my last word in the deepest sense. I am, perhaps I should explain, a member of the Westron Courtesy affiliation: and I believe, as do millions, that politeness and truth are the same thing, and the very heartsblood of civilization.

"I advocate no such thing. I suggest, instead, the replacement of the treacle mock-deaths sold by emporia such as yours with the death I have researched from the Century of War, and of which you have seen the outline."

"Nobody would desire such a death!" I cried.

He nodded ponderously.

I decided then that he was less than wholly sane.

"Sir," I said, standing straighter. "I should warn you that a flick of my finger will sound an alarm, bringing security immediately into this emporium to deal with any malefactor or agitator."

"No," he said.

It was then that I knew something was truly wrong. I activated the alarm at once, of course, but there was no response. The system had been disabled.

My mind raced. Only somebody with a detailed and professional understanding could have disconnected the necessary virtual pathways of the alarm system. It was possible to do it by hacking our network, but that could only have been accomplished from within another Sweet-Death parlor.

"Perhaps," I said, my voice wobbling a little. "Perhaps there is more merit in your suggestion than my first reaction implied. I would be prepared to consider the force of your argument." I tried another smile, although it did not come out as effectively as my previous ones. Fear dented the spontaneity of the curve of my lips.

"You speak," he said, "not from conviction, but from fear. But fear has its place in life as well. Pain, and death, and fear. A life without them would be merely a fog, howsoever sweet-smelling."

He reached into the main pocket of his meadhres and drew out a weapon. My heart bobbed like a buoy in the suddenly turbulent medium of my breast.

"That," I said, "is a weapon."

"It is," he agreed.

We both looked at the weapon – he mournfully from above, I staring with my lips apart.

I tried again to sound the alarm, or to activate some other portion of the control panel that might alert the outside world to my predicament, but without result.

"Step forward," said the man.

There being no alternative, I obeyed his command.

The weapon was a black, weighty-looking thing, shaped like a miniature gallows with a bulb-shaped protrusion at the joint of it. It was presumably hand-made, modeled on some archaic instrument of barbarity that this man had uncovered in his researches. Some antique from the Century of War. But I had no doubt that it could cause injury. Possibly death.

"The weapon," he said, as if reading the thoughts on my face, "is Pretanican. The army police there use it to subdue extreme criminals, and in the small wars of that region. It is loaded with rapid projectiles that pierce the flesh and enter the main corpus of the human body, often with fatal results. But the projectiles are primed with CTX-nervous."

"You have worked for SweetDeath," I said, "or for some affiliated organization, to talk in this way."

"I have," he said. "You know it, because of my familiarity with our nanobitic solution, since none of our competitors use CTX-nervous."

"You gave the impression of complete ignorance of the Material Immortality process when you entered."

In reply to this, he said, "I have programmed the death myself. I configured it and loaded the seedbits into CTX solution, priming the projectiles of this weapon with the resulting compound."

"You asked *me* to program that death for *you*," I pointed out. "You requested it for *yourself*."

"Oh," he said, distractedly, "eventually. Eventually, I am sure, this is the death that will await me. But I have significant work to do before that conclusion. Our city-screened, our tech-assisted and idle lives. . . ." He seemed to have more to say, but stopped himself, looked sharply from left to right, and then fixed me again with his eye.

"I worked for SweetDeath in Pavannia," he said. "I personally supervised the death of my mother. She elected for a warrior death, and I personally supervised it." He stopped for a moment. "I checked the activity. It should, as you know, have been thirty seconds of brainwave agitation, followed by forty minutes of slowly flattening calm sines and regular patterns. But it was forty minutes of agitation, the peaks clustering closer and closer together."

"I see," I said, trying with some difficulty for a neutral tone of voice. "If you are, as you say, an officiated employee, you will know that the CTX cannot guarantee exactly the same uptake in every single brain. The brainwave trace of which you speak affects perhaps one percent of our customers. . . ."

He said, almost mildly, "My mother."

I was silent.

"A million years of pain," he added, in a low voice, "administered by myself."

"I see," I said. I dared not move, but could not control the trembling in my limbs and throat. "That was unfortunate. Of course it was. But there is no proof that a million years of agony ensued. There's no evidence that the brainwave pattern you mention is experienced *on the inside*, as it were, in that fashion. No empirical research has been done, of course. But common sense suggests that the sensorium would be worn smooth by such prolongation of unvariegated –"

"Research," he said, dolefully. "VR technicians fine-tuning swordstrokes through the chest so that they register in terms of elation and triumph rather than pain? And what is an appropriate punishment for inflicting such pain on one's mother?"

He raised the weapon. It occurred to me – it seems almost ridiculous to say so, but the thought had not properly occurred to me before that moment – that he truly intended to shoot me.

"Stop," I cried, as much in pique as terror. "Do you intend to shoot me? I had nothing to do with your mother's situation! It was not I who programmed the warrior scenario, and not I but you who administered it!"

"You talk, in other words," he said, without lowering the weapon, "of guilt. But guilt is general in this case. To create a paradise for the ninety-nine and a hell for the one, when millions pass through our chambers, is to replace the old theologies with an arbitrariness of destiny appalling to contemplate. Who is guilty for that? We all are. To transform the old religions of a God of judgment into a God of statistical chance, howsoever weighted? No, no, we must reinstate judgment. *Judgment* is key. The Century of War understood that. Judgment was a fetish for them."

"But there is no evidence," I insisted, speaking rapidly, "that the brainwave pattern you describe is experienced by any brain as *continual* suffering. . . ."

"You are not the first I have shot today," he said, "and you will not be the last. Guilt?" He shook his head.

I opened my mouth to say something, but instead the air was overwritten with a flash and a clattering noise, as of metal breaking. At once I was breathless, for something had punched me hard in the chest. Or rather, it felt as if I had run at full pelt and collided with a spar or pole jutting at chest height. I stumbled backwards, bumped against the wall, and collapsed. I could not breathe. The pain in my chest was significant, but not overwhelming. Worse was the impossibility of breathing. I gulped. My ears sang. The room, or my tumbled and right-angled view of a floor, a blue wall, of my assassin's form standing at ninety degrees appeared milky, indistinct. I tried to inhale, tried to form words, but the pain in my chest swelled suddenly, and –

Everything went blue.

Just that color, nothing else.

The pain went away. I cannot say where it went; draining into some subterranean reservoir or sump of pain, perhaps. I felt blithe, heady.

It felt like an immersion, oil creeping slowly through my veins and arteries, the CTX nanodevices hurrying their way to the brain centers, until –

– here I am. I am here.

I am in the small room of the assassin's program. There is one exit, and it is indeed sealed: a weighty, metallic door pimpled all over with bolt heads and painted blue. I am alone. I am wearing a single shift-like item of clothing that covers my legs, torso, and arms. My hair is short as suede. The air-temperature is cold and the only heating is a warm-water pipe that runs along one wall close to the floor. One detail that was not mentioned in the document I read is in the furniture: a low tube-metal-framed bed, a wooden table, and a single chair. On the table I have found paper and a stylus, and using them I have written what you have read.

A single window, no broader than my hand and blocked with three bars, is located near the ceiling on one wall. I have stood on the table and looked out of the window, but saw only merely of blackness.

It occurs to me (and the thought is a hopeful one) that my actual body will die in less than the forty minutes the program is designed to run, which would in turn truncate the full force of the punishment meted out to me. Naturally, I desire this death. I have been trying to calculate, drawing on such physiological knowledge as I possess, how long a human corpus may live after a projectile has impacted with its chest, but my calculations cannot be precise. And yet, I cannot believe that my future holds such a dire set of sensory inputs.

It has been many hours since my consciousness awoke here, and the quality of light outside is changing.

There is hope. I have thought long, and I have come to this conclusion: the human mind is incapable of the cruelty this customer proposed; therefore his cruelty was a sham, employed to make a point about material immortality. Ask yourself: what person could – genuinely, comfortably – enjoy the thought of another creature dying in pain and degradation in order to propel them into an eternity of suffering? No person. Hence this program, the one in which I am trapped, will lead to no such conclusion. For how could it? I could not condemn another human to such a course of events. *You* could not. The customer cannot have done so either. Of this I am increasingly sure. Genuinely: how could it be otherwise?

I do not know what will follow in this simulation, but it will – surely, surely – not be cruelty on that scale. If a human being knew he was sending another human being to eternal pain, that human would of course endeavor to make the death as painless as possible. Conversely, a painful death such as the one written into this program must only be because the culture that sanctioned it believed, as we do today, that material death is a complete extinction. And such extinction is, for my circumstance, preferable to the alternative.

There is a noise at the door –

Acetylene, CLIVE BARKER

All Sliding to One Side

Paul G. Tremblay

It was not heartbroken rage against injustice that froze me.
I had taught myself that a human being might as well look
for diamond tiaras in the gutter as for punishments
and rewards that were fair.
– KURT VONNEGUT, *Mother Night*

The car windows are open, and wind swirls old ATM stubs and gum wrappers, but you don't mind. It's too nice out for the air-conditioner. On your passenger seat a pizza box is wedged between cans of soda and empty CD cases. The smell is so good, you can't imagine anything tasting better than *that* pizza. You think about eating a slice now, but there's no sense in eating something this messy in the car when you're so close to home.

Besides, your wife and daughter are hungry and waiting for you. And you are waiting to see them. You are always waiting, and you hate the job that's taken your whole life to achieve, because for five days a week, the only time with your daughter, your precious little Mia, consists of a hurried dinner and a quick bedtime story. Because five days a week you and your wife rush through chores that only seem to accumulate, or maybe you wordlessly watch some TV together, and then you both barely have the energy or desire for a goodnight kiss. So every commute home becomes a race to steal a little back from all the time you've lost already.

You *need* to be home.

You drive down back roads to avoid the center of town and its traffic congestion. Another successful shortcut. There's a stop sign ahead and you slow down and look left, hoping you can Texas Roll out onto the street without coming to a full stop. You see a blue station wagon coming, its right directional blinking. But there's a large pick-up truck right behind it so you do stop, sending the soda cans crashing. You swear, hoping the stop wasn't so abrupt that all the cheese slid to one side of the pizza. You lift the box cover. . . .

A blaring horn, and you twitch in your seat. Hands jump back onto the steering wheel. You watch that blue station wagon turn onto your street. It's carrying a heavy-set woman, skin the color of cottage cheese, and in the back a small child who might be the same age as your Mia. And you see the souped-up truck riding right on the wagon's rear bumper. Two teens lean out the passenger window. One is a Snow-White-looking girl, with an innocent I've-never-been-touched-by-a-boy smile, and an upturned middle finger. And there's the sneering driver: buzz cut, squinty eyes, football jersey, and a sinewy arm that shoots all the way across the bench seat and out the window, displaying a middle finger like a peacock's plume.

Then you see four faces at once.

The mother's face screws and folds over itself into a what-did-I-do-to-deserve-this look, a victim's look. She throws up a hand without giving her middle finger, but it flutters, as weak and unconfident as her face, a surrender, and it makes you look away, like you've seen something you shouldn't have. Some horrible secret that should never be shared.

You don't let yourself see what's on the little girl's face.

The pick-up revs, white smoke billowing out of the duel-exhaust, and powers past your corner.

You pull out, right behind the truck.

You're shaking your head like the disapproving adult you are. Yeah, you remember what it was like to be a kid, and you remember all those chances you once took behind the wheel. But you know better now. Right? You know the road is full of danger. *This* is the thought you have every time you strap Mia into her car seat, and you then think about how this could be the last time you touch her cheek or hear her laugh or see her last-all-day smile. . . .

You are sitting in your sensible sedan and you give the truck in front of you an equally sensible birth. You watch it speed up and jam on its breaks, spotless black metal shaking on the oversized tires. A leashed but vicious animal.

This kid is a jerk. You are certain of it. You have seen enough to know this kid does not volunteer at nursing homes, nor does he befriend orphan children. You know he talks back to his parents and teachers, and you know he brawls and bullies and steals and drinks and fucks.

You tell yourself you are thinking rationally. You are deducing. You are being pragmatic. This isn't being judgmental. You are convinced *this* is different than shipping someone off to jail because of tattoos and piercings, *this* is different than a black man being pulled over for driving in an affluent neighborhood, *this* is different than rednecks beating the life out of someone because that someone looked gay. You tell yourself you're still that not-so-long-ago college student who loudly protested injustices in the name of ignorance and bigotry.

And you believe everything you tell yourself.

Mostly.

So, you know he is just some rich brat tooling around in an over-sized toy worth at least half of your annual salary, and driving it like he owns the road. Driving it like a weapon.

Traffic, even on this sleepy stretch of road, slows you both down. You creep closer to the truck's rear. And you watch. You see the kid in his side-view mirror. He's smoking. No, he's inhaling. You're not too old or so far gone from that age to know what he's doing. The kid spits dirty smoke out his window, and it's no longer the pizza you smell.

You say, "Christ, the kid is smoking dope, too."

You sound like the disapproving adult that you are, that you have been for longer than you realized, and you don't care. You don't cry for your lost youth.

Because now you *hate*. And it doesn't matter if Daddy beats him or Mommy gives him no love. You don't care if he was made. You still hate. You don't have any qualms admitting it.

You look around. Does anyone else notice or care about this menace on the road? Where's a cop when you need him? You think about pulling out your cell and calling the police. Seeing that punk pulled over just might erase that mother's victim-look from your head. But it won't get you home any sooner. And if you call the cops that would mean you'd have to testify, which would mean having to spend the rest of your life looking over your shoulder for him or his equally-punk buddies to jump you. Risking your family's well-being for a small fine and whatever toothless punishment they dole out isn't worth it.

And you hate him even more. Because this small-time punk from your small-time town is proof society is broken. He's proof there is no justice.

So you hate and hate and hate, and you want to hurt him somehow. You think about what it would take for you to do harm. It's not a fantasy. You're trying to be honest with yourself. Do you have it in you to rev your tiny, four-cylinder engine and smash into the truck or run him off the road? Would you do it if you had the money to pay for the damages? Would you do it if there would be no arrest, no outside punishment? And then you think about forcing the punk to the side of the road and beating him with your fists. Yeah, the kid's probably stronger than you. But so what? You hate and you hate and you hate . . . and your eyes flicker to the glove compartment. You remember what's inside, though you haven't given it a thought since you put it there.

A utility knife.

Part of you knows you don't want to be thinking like this. But it's all here. Everything.

You turn your eyes back to the road and try to regain the person you were before seeing the truck. You tell yourself that you'd never be so far gone as to use the utility knife over something so trivial.

Then there are two more questions:

Why did you even put the utility knife in your glove compartment?

You remember putting the knife, a cheap gift from somebody – who, you can't remember – in the car. But you didn't even think about *why*, did you?

What's so utility about a knife?

And then you understand. You know the big secret. You think of Mia and your wife, and you know that if you had nothing to live for and if there were no consequences, no *justice* that directly affected you, you could.

And you would.

Your street is just ahead, on the left. Still watching the truck chew and spit out blacktop, you turn on the directional and take the turn. The turn to home. You slink into the driveway like a wayward dog, park, then enter your tool-and-junk-filled garage. The place is a mess. Nothing is where it should be. You even have to move Mia's tricycle out of the kitchen doorway.

The pizza box is now cool in your hands.

You push open the usually dead-bolted door and you're in. You are home. Mia screams, "Daddy!" and she *is* bouncing-brown pigtails and a little pink dress and all smile. She wraps around your legs and giggles while you stumble into the kitchen. Your wife wears a chiding, took-long-enough smirk, pecks your cheek like a bird snatching a bread-crumb, and takes the pizza.

You pick up Mia and try to return her smile. It is one that thinks it'll never have reason to leave her face.

But you know better.

Your wife says, "Oh, all the cheese slid to one side."

You excuse yourself to wash up in the bathroom.

Standing in front of the sink, you splash cold water on your face.

You hear your daughter laughing and singing songs about Daddy and pizza. You think about the ride home and you are disgusted with yourself, and you vow to take the knife out of the car. But you also think about how there's nothing you can do to protect your family from *him* and all the other *hims* you read about and see on TV. You are powerless. And you are always afraid.

There, in the mirror. You look at your face. Really look at it. Mia is still singing your name and you try to hide *it* under a sliding smile. But you can't.

You can't hide that what-did-I-do-to-deserve-this look, that victim look.

And there will be a day when your daughter won't be able to, either.

Changeling

Michael Marano

I felt myself blacken as if charred, felt my skin suckle fireless smoke as I was stained with the echo of solidity. I remembered and re-lived another moment, one of freezing cold in the midst of bright warm summer, a moment of my taking the fair color of frost amid green meadows and barrows as I was made pale as lime-bleached skin scant days before I first heard the sound of a man's eyes turning to wood.

And with that long-ago press of smooth wood against the soft cups of his sight, I had been freed.

I am not now free, any more than is the boy whose shade I reflect through his demonization, through the reverse-exorcism canticles that tend the seed of spite within him. The seed sprouts. I feel it. It earth-breathes despair the boy cannot grasp, but that the boy knows with the same intimacy that he knows his dreams. The boy does not feel the germ twitch to life . . . to *my* life . . . and the lives of my distant, more bodiless kin who sleep in his imagining.

I now know no meadows, no earthwork mounds heaped over chambers of rusting swords; this is a place and a time in which eyes are not turned to wood, but are turned to things like shining dark stones. There is no sound to accompany this changing of eyes to stone, for unlike the crack of rowan bursting thin socket-walls of skull, *this* change of eyes involves no alchemy of pain; it is merely the reflection of moving light that is pulled out of the air and forced to dance in a box with a face of curved glass. The glass face of the box gives the eyes of those who stare into it the same dead sheen I have seen in the eyes of blind grandmothers who crossed themselves feeling my nearness.

Invisible, I looked into stone-smooth eyes. I breathed without lungs a darkness like deep winter midnight behind the box that flickered the blue light of moving images no less alive than am I. Invisible, I swallowed the black of dead spectra while fear of persons and things dark-skinned worm-twitched in the minds of the boy's parents and envenomed the boy's mind and his image of himself. I felt myself stamped with fears I did not welcome, fears that would further color me and force upon me un-touchable shape. I am clay molded by hands without nails, skin, or nerves;

I could be beautiful. I have been beautiful before, heralded by the crash of a snow-colored stag from out of the brush and by the songs of birch to oak. But here, now, there is no desire nor need for me to be beautiful.

I felt kinship with the image moving within the glass face of the box. The image was flax-pulled from the ether by wire and metal that flowed with tamed and thunderless lightning . . . just as I had been pulled from the air and given unfinished shape by this house of stifled, silenced anger. I am changed by this house, as a blown horn changes the air within it.

Later, as I was soured by the dreams of the child who slept above me, I wept a deaf nothingness from empty sockets of dust, knowing what I'd be made to feel and become.

The boy sweats poison, resting above me in a nest of blankets he twists about himself. His parents would welcome the hatchling of a cuckoo; they would embrace a twisted, stunted changeling, such as I had once been, running from the scalding of a font atop the backs of pews splintered by my hoofs. They desire a monster in lieu of their son, for such a monster would free them from knowing the child they have.

Longing for a monster, they craft one – and I am echo-crafted as well. Just as a smith would beat impurities from iron he shapes, so do they remove things they do not wish the boy to have, such qualities as they doubt exist in themselves, that they snuff to convince themselves of their worthlessness.

With morning comes a new crafting.

"What is this?" asks the mother. Like the air above a bellows, the room shimmers in my eyeless sight as she speaks. She kicks with a soft-slippered foot a portrait of dust-grey strokes and red glowing eyes. It's a scrawl. A collision of bracken-angry lines. A portrait of me. The paper glides upon a floor so smooth and clean as to seem rubbed with beeswax; it skids past where the boy lay on his belly next to a wall and comes to rest in my hovel that is the underneath of his bed.

The boy says nothing. I hear in his mind the belief that he speaks the word, "*Nothing.*" The belief churns the haze of the room. He draws a dragon on another piece of paper with a nub of green wax. There is no dust, here in my hovel. The picture of me, of the impressions of me that he has caught in moonlight, flutters from a slight draft that rides the smooth floor.

The boy's mother leaves. I hear her say what she does not speak. Her wish to truly say it makes the bellows-haze of the room flurry like wasps.

You're shit.

The boy presses harder with his stick of wax as his mother's thought grips the back of his neck.

There is pressure as I take the red eyes the boy has drawn, as I become a glamor just a bit more visible than I had been.

The boy feeds me poison in the night.

But only what poison he spits up.

The father sits before the box that sorcel-traps moving images. The boy is nervous as he sits beside the father, and wishes to be welcome, to not be afraid. While fear murks with desire, I am summoned to stand behind the boy, pulled as if by a rope crafted of the twitching legs of wasps. The boy is aware of me, as some are aware of the coming of summer storms in their bones. I know this limbo. It is a home to me. It is the color of the boundary suspended between the earth and sky, where Beltane offerings killed by rope or fire are most treasured – where flesh burns best and where seed that would give me a woman's form of root-matter falls best. Time shifts, as if by a farewell, or by the start of a cloaked exile. The boy conjures, out of the need to be acknowledged, and by the fear that he will be acknowledged. The motes of my being respond to the boy's silent chant before this glowing altar.

Words of power and invocation filth the air, but they are not spoken by any who have breath or throat. The words are dream-syllables that accommodate the father's dread and desire. Though I know not what the words mean, they have the bile-flavor of *weregild*, of deep shadow forests forbidden to travelers and the desperate springtime lifting of flesh with a stone knife to ensure a bounty of crops. The words are pulled from the ether. The father takes the trance of their power, as if they are spoken by a hierophant before a bloody stone table. The bodiless voice carried from the box with the face of glass has the feel of greasy metal cooling.

youths . . . disturbances . . . wildings . . .

The words of power seize the mind of the father and wave-daub the mind of the boy. The un-present priest speaking the words is made of shifting light trapped within the box; he is a spell that itself casts a spell. He is less real than is the shifting light of heat and marsh-breath that births will-o'-the-wisps, though he is much more powerful in its capacity to bewitch and lead astray.

shooting . . . unrest . . . drug-related . . .

The phrases connecting the thrawn-words are nothing. They are like the chants that bridge the uttered names of gods that are at once loved and dreaded; the bridging words serve only to pace out the invocations. The gorge of fear nourishes both father and son. The gorge of fear shores the walls, and makes this home a fortress of the imagination. It masques the walls in the guise of a haven safe from fell beings – beings who, in the minds of those who live here, carry only the shape of humanity. I had been once such a fell being of human shape in this very spot, which had been a wood-rimmed clearing scant years before the sundering of trees and the fever-swift building of houses. I had once been made a giant of a man, glimpsed. I had been the gleam of a hook where there had been a hand. I had been both the snapping of a twig and the imagined boot that snapped the twig. Fear and desire had danced in this spot before the coming of houses, though in a way much different from how they do now.

violence ... urban ... projects ...

I am made more visible to the boy's storm-seeking nerves. I drizzle the blood in his spine cold. Were he to stand, his knees would be limp for reasons he could not guess. The father is made more uncomfortable by the boy's discomfort. He looks to his child, freshly in awe of the god-words of fear he has unknowingly worshipped. He hates the boy's lack of deformity. Hates the lack of wickedness that would exonerate him from the apostasy of despising his own issue. The father looks to the box's glass face, to the will-o'-the-wisp priest whose image gives way to images of shadow-people running on city streets. The father's own face would be reflected on the glass if he strained to see it, in the same way he would see the lack of monstrosity in his child if he chose to see it.

Not my kid, he thinks for the pleasure of thinking it and the pleasure of controlling his reality by fiat; his discomfort abates, as if pressed under a poultice. And with that thought of the father's, the muscles of the boy's back clench as if a blade were drawn at his hind. It is the same tension I was aware of in a girl who long ago turned and searched for me beneath a great outcrop of rock without knowing why, but who knew that she would find me there swaddled in tresses of my own hair. The boy knows he is thought of by his father, and is in an ecstasy of hope for a kind word and of fear of punishment for an unknowable offense.

The father lets his hand drop to the back of the pillowed bench upon which they sit, and does not know that the boy expects at once a pat upon the head or a pulling of his hair; both have been bestowed to the boy with equal suddenness. The father does not know why, but is pleased by the confusion he senses in the boy; hope and dread flavor the air in a way that allows me to taste my own ether-misted physicality.

The father himself becomes a hierophant, using words of power like those that have touched his mind. He gestures to the box, to the image of a city goblin led in shackles.

"You ever become a little white nigger like that, I'll kill you."

The father pats the boy's head, and the boy waits to feel fingers close and pull.

I darken. My red eyes take sclera of white.

In his ecstasy of acceptance and fear, the boy would see my shape if he turned his head.

The pictures tell a story in bright colors of warriors and chieftains; the boy fixes upon one image that fascinates and terrifies him. He presses the image upon the paper with his gaze, and I am pinned beneath the boy in my hovel under his bed; his attentions and fears hold me fast, as would a needle driven through the back of a beetle. The boy has endured more this day. Conscripted by his mother to help make food, she reviled him for dropping eggs like those I would once have spoiled with an infusion of my essence to announce my coming with the retch-smell of sulfur. Still stinging from her reproach, he now in the night stares at the image of a monster, a beast-man, abominating it to feel superior to it while at the same time feeling kinship with it for being abominated.

The boy enters a new trance staring at the image, a new state of half-vision brought upon by half-wakefulness.

But later in darkness, the boy lies fully awake above me while he tries to sleep.

In darkness, in the deep night, he has made me densely formed enough with his trance for me to draw raspy breath that he barely hears; the branch-twig fingers of the claws he has given me can lightly click upon the floor.

I am the living *wyrd* he needs to despise. His eyes dry in the darkness; he is too afraid to blink. He fears to whistle up the flame-less light he thinks may dispel me, believing I will seize his arm in the dry bark of my grasp as he reaches for the lamp. But I cannot seize him, so immobile am I made by his fear.

The boy's eyes are dry, and I speak to them.

I change the darkness; while I am so dense, it is my food. I fill the darkness with forms as I pluck shades from pitch and depths from moon-whispered grays. I force shapes and beasts and apparitions upon the smooth stones of his sight. Immobile, I feed on shadows. I must while so physical. And I exhaust him with fear. His racing mind finally sleeps, and I am free to wander the house that has snared me.

This home is orderly. Where there had been thicket and rim of moss-draped trees before, while I had been a hook-handed monster, there is now nothing for me to straighten in the night and so incur the thanks that would free me from this place. The tables and cutting boards are wiped with oil so fine, the wood beneath cannot ever breathe or rot. There is no winter fuel to stack. No wool to spin. No residue of the eggs broken at dusk lingers to give me a homunculus-like form that would drop to shapelessness upon the crowing of the cock.

I stand above the mother as she sleeps, for she demands that I do. I become the intruder she fears. The Man with the Knife she welcomes to dread, so that she as a victim will be free of the sick burden of self-determination that she so resents. The father feels the house in his sleep more tangibly than he does the blankets he rests beneath. He feels himself shackled to his property; *it* owns *him*. His worries infuse the timbers. They vibrate and are strengthened with his sweat-slicked fear.

The boy had liked the screaming, and so I choke on remorse. Remorse is alien to me; thus I am more familiar with its cruelties than are those who are born with it. I have never welcomed it, any more than the boy would welcome the hand of another grafted to his wrist. I try to fathom remorse, to know it as would one for whom it is natural as skin. Thus am I hurt by it more.

The boy had liked the screaming; it walks his mind. And thus he presses regret out of himself. It flavors the poison that has flavored me these past six winters. The boy had liked the screaming, and the fur-warm twitching in his hands that became still.

I have lurked near boys like him, for whom the drowning of kittens had been a chore, and the screams a bother to be tolerated, like cuts inflicted by the baling of hay. I have stood behind such boys, who were infused with the smell of compost and rotting chaff. I have dried the milk in the udders of animals in their charge and made them fear for their blood in the night.

Remorse veins the air. I hate it. And in hating it, I feel remorse all the more strongly.

The boy has seen me, in the same way the farmer of long ago had seen me for an instant in glory upon the barrow I warded, in the second his eyes re-fleshed to smooth-grained rowan. The instant of the boy's blinding reveals me. The thunder of his skull shattering from scores of small stones thrown by a blast of charcoal and sulfur had been uglier than the sounds of wooden orbs pulled by the tongs of a blacksmith. The boy's eyes that had been made stone had been burst by stone.

The house, with the sundering of the boy's mind, has fully accepted the maledictions spoken to the boy over the passing years; they now invisibly right the walls. They are the hated legacy of a hated place that holds the curse of a youth dying by violence within it.

The house is like the barrow. It is like the great stone I slept under by the roadside. Yet those places had been free to the air and sky. These invested walls hold me; they have been taught to grip fast the anxious worry that first snared me. They hold the boy who had found no release for his stifled remorse other than through thunder, fire, and stones thrown through smooth and oiled pipes of metal. His remorse chokes me and thicket-traps me fast.

I am the conscripted midwife to the haunting of this place. The boy is that which haunts. He had seen me in the instant of his death. He is lonely and afraid of what I might be in the un-fleshed spaces of the place that had been home to him, and that shall be his home past death. His fear of me perpetuates the poison he had been fed; it no longer needs to be spoken. Yet despite his fear I cannot reach him. He is visible, yet untouchable as the grain of wood beneath beeswax.

We shall haunt this place separately until it falls.

Mesmer, CLIVE BARKER

An It Harm None, Do What Ye Will

Peg Aloi

I remember reading something very shocking a few years ago on one of the online discussion groups for supporters of the West Memphis Three. Perhaps not shocking in the way you might think, given the incompetence, prejudice, and ignorance that has characterized the investigation and trials from the get go. No, what I read was this: Damien Echols saw the stars. After being on Death Row for years, and not being let outside to see the night sky in all that time, he was allowed one night to stand beneath the stars in the open air, and the moment was a thrilling one for him.

Imagine . . . seeing the stars for a few moments, the jumble of animals and mythic hunters and chariot drivers, and savoring that sight as one stores up crumbs of food or memorizes lines of verse, wondering how long it might be until the next time, if there was to be one. Imagine now, the other things in the natural world Damien loves that are kept from him, the freedoms he and Jason Baldwin and Jessie Miskelley, enjoyed before their incarceration: walking among trees, playing with pets, listening to music, or just plain sitting in the sun. Most of us have never had to learn so early in life not to take such simple pleasures for granted.

Damien, who is now a practicing Buddhist, once considered himself a neo-pagan, and a practitioner of Wicca. Wicca is a term commonly used to refer to what modern witches believe and practice – it refers to a branch of modern witchcraft founded by Gerald Gardner, an Englishman who worked with a witch's coven in the New Forest area in the 1930s. Neo-paganism has its roots in animistic belief: the idea that all living things are connected and that divinity is immanent in nature. In England during World War II, the scatterings of the newly-defunct class system had an opportunity to merge in this unusual spiritual movement. The peasant classes' native love for the landscape and the gentry's penchant for joining secret societies met in the modern occult revival. In many cases, the former still observed (in the guise of observing quaint local custom) ancient fertility rites and harvest festivals, and the latter had already dabbled in Freemasonry or the Hermetic Order of the Golden Dawn.

Gardner was a colorful figure: a former civil servant who collected antique swords, an avowed naturist (that's nudist to me and you), and, some say, a man with a taste for spankings. Whatever his proclivities, he has been credited with inventing a complex and engaging structure for ritual worship which has endured to this day and has been the model for thousands of Gardnerian groups in the United States and the United Kingdom. Some of his writings were plagiarized from the likes of Aleister Crowley (the English poet, ceremonial magician, psychotropics aficionado, and publicity hound who was the Dennis Rodman/Ozzy Osbourne/Robert Downey Jr of his day), Robert Graves (another English poet), Margaret Murray (an anthropologist), and Charles Godfrey Leland (a folklorist), and some were cobbled from old Kabbalistic texts. It was the words of Crowley that inspired the so-called "Wiccan Rede" which states "An It Harm None, Do What You Will," as paraphrased from Crowley's oft-paraphrased dictum: "Do what thou wilt shall be the whole of the law; love is the law, love under will." (Even the '80s dance band the Thompson Twins immortalized it.) The Rede is the closest thing Wicca has to dogma. It is closely allied to another tenet, the Law of Three, also upheld by modern witches. The Law of Three supposes that whatever idea, wish, or action someone puts out into the universe returns to them threefold. This applies to magic, prayer, love, and generosity, as well as hateful thoughts, lies, greed, theft, or other sins. In other words, the Golden Rule most cultures live by, Do Unto Others as You Would Have Them Do Unto You, is at the root of modern day witchcraft belief. What you give out comes back to you.

What goes around comes around.

This principle as it applies to modern witchcraft was mentioned during a discussion amongst witches and pagans in the documentary *Revelations: Paradise Lost 2*, which explored the new developments in the West Memphis Three case as of 1999. Although it is common sense to suppose that, if Damien were a real witch, he'd be someone who would adhere to this basic tenet of his chosen belief system, the citizens of his community equated his occult interests with a likely involvement in devil worship, and all that that implied. In a conservative Christian community, to worship any god or gods other than Jehovah and Christ means you worship the devil; and if you worship the devil, you serve evil. When it was suggested by law enforcement officials that the murders of the three eight-year-olds were examples of a "cult killing," Damien's involvement in Wicca, his propensity for wearing black, his interest in heavy metal music, his reading choices (which included Stephen King, Cotton Mather, and Shakespeare), and his disdain for much of mainstream culture made him a suspect. He has said he did not understand how serious his situation was, and never could have imagined how far things would go, that he'd end up in prison, convicted of murder.

Although highly intelligent, Damien's innate sensitivity and idealism led him to believe that right would prevail.

No doubt the accused of Salem Village in 1692 thought the same thing; they, devout Puritans, most of them, also believed they had God on their side. Owing to the same sort of ignorance, misunderstanding, corruption, ineptitude, and superstition of the grossest sort that characterized the Salem witch trials, the investigation of the Robin Hood Hills murders ultimately ended in serving Lady Justice in a most perverse way. In *Devil's Knot*, author Mara Leveritt has said the main questions that led to her writing the book had to do with the 1994 trials in West Memphis and their uncanny similarity to the Matter of Salem in 1692. While doubt still lingers, the families and classmates of the murdered children cannot feel assured that justice has prevailed. If a child-killer still lives among them, the members of this community cannot sleep undisturbed. And if, as the villagers of Salem found so long ago, they realize they have helped contribute to the unjust imprisonment of three innocent young men, they will not be able to find peace in their religion until they have made things right.

How did these trials become witch trials? The specific details of the investigation and the trials dealing with these matters are too many to go into here, and so I enthusiastically recommend Ms Leveritt's detailed and meticulously researched book. But I can discuss some of the misconceptions held by some of the law enforcement and citizens of West Memphis, and offer my theories as to why Damien came to be seen as the so-called "ring leader" in a "cult killing" which showed absolutely none of the generally accepted signature characteristics of such a crime, as agreed upon by criminal experts.

I grew up in a small city in western New York State which is markedly similar to West Memphis: mostly working-class, church-going (although more Catholic than Southern Baptist), surrounded by farms, and full of teenagers looking for things to do. We had our share of racial prejudice, crime, unemployment, drug and alcohol abuse, and poverty too. I have lived in Boston since 1990 and have always found it to be a very religiously tolerant city. Perhaps because Boston Brahmins carry the stigma of Salem's history in their blood, they have a very open-minded attitude towards their teenagers' interest in Wicca, goth music and modes of dress, and other alternative interests. I have said before that a teenager like Damien living in Cambridge, Massachusetts in 1993, hanging out in the Pit in Harvard Square dressed in black, would have blended in like pigeon turds. In West Memphis, he was an outsider. Even though there was not an active pagan community where he was living, it seemed natural, given his interests, that he would seek it out and try to become involved in any local events or groups, such as they were. They did appear to have been a secretive lot, and not terribly sophisticated. It is possible they called themselves "Wiccan" without necessarily knowing what it meant (the same could be said of a number of practitioners today).

Interestingly, at least one prominent "Wiccan" author, Kerr Cuhulain, has determined that Damien was not a "real" witch at all, whatever that means. In an article debunking a so-called "occult expert" – David Brown – who is convinced witches are out to take over America, if not the world, Cuhulain (who was called on to consult with the defense attorneys) claims Damien practiced a pastiche of various ceremonial traditions, but not "Wicca." His exact words: "I can say with some authority that Echols was practicing a form of Satanic magick pasted together from various sources, and not Wicca. Echols described what he was doing to investigators as "Witchcraft" as he thought that this is what Satanic magick was called." Of course, in this same article, Cuhulain refers to Jason as "Charles Baldwin" and spells Jessie's name "Jessi," so I am not convinced he is an authority in this matter. I offer this as an example that not even the opinion of a respected occult author can be the last word on this subject, and on a subject as multi-faceted and oscillating as modern witchcraft, a range of opinions ought to be consulted. If only that West Memphis jury had been so discriminating. But the "expert" with the mail-order degree prattling on about "personally" observing black T-shirts and fingernails somehow had them all eating out of his hand.

It's difficult to explain to laypeople what witches do, because every witch does something different. Some of us work with groups; some of us work alone. Some of us do spells; some of us meditate. Some worship gods and goddesses; others prefer a "non-deist" approach which views deities as archetypes. Some of us read tarot cards; some of us make herbal incense. Some practice polyamorous lifestyles; some are nudists (or naturists). Some like to wear black. Some are cat people, some are dog people, and a good many of us are bird, snake and/or ferret people. Some call themselves witches; others prefer to call themselves "Wiccans." Some are vegetarians; some are carnivores. Some read books voraciously; some get all their information off the Internet. Some are environmental activists; others are tawdry consumers. You say tomato, I say "member of the nightshade family."

But some generalizations may be made. Most pagans and witches recognize that there is a divine essence in the natural world (although not all of them choose to interact with it in the same way). Most of us believe our path is a life-affirming one. And the great majority of us believe in karma: that the collective lessons and deeds of our lives will carry over into another incarnation, and, quite possibly, these lessons and deeds will be rewarded or punished in our current incarnation. We do not believe death is the end, nor do we believe this earthly life should be seen as a time to prepare for the afterlife. We tend to be hedonistic. So, incidentally, are those who call themselves "satanists." These folks actually follow a very proscribed set of ideals; much stricter in its ways than Wicca. They have an incorporated non-profit church (whose founder, modern-day Aleister Crowley *doppelgänger* Anton LaVey, a flamboyant but harmless eccentric, was mentioned more than once in the Echols-Baldwin trial).

The trouble is that there has always been some degree of overlap between these two divergent modern spiritual paths; because devils and witches were so closely linked in centuries past, the modern imagination keeps this association alive. It seems clear that Damien was at least partly interested in these overlapping qualities. The media also played its part. I thought it was painfully obvious that the so-called "occult experts" in this case (Dale Griffis, he of the mail-order PhD, and to a lesser extent, youth probation officer Jerry Driver) used as the basis of their "knowledge" the various films that have proven popular for their titillating portrayals of the occult: *Rosemary's Baby, The Omen* (people assumed Damien had named himself after the devil-spawn child in this film), *The Exorcist*, etc. It has also been revealed that the docket number first assigned to the case, ending in 666, actually ended in 555, and had been changed by one of the detectives, to further charge the atmosphere of the investigation into what was widely-perceived as a "satanic murder."

Just as the law enforcement officers and jury members and, to some extent, the lawyers, misunderstood the often Byzantine distinctions to be made between so-called "white witchcraft" and "black magic," the very practitioners themselves in West Memphis did not appear to have very authentic experiences that went much beyond Hollywood-style play-acting. The descriptions of "esbats" allegedly attended by self-appointed "investigator" Vicki Hutcheson, whose contradiction-riddled statements fingered Damien as being involved in the murders, are actually very naïve and fatuous. She describes people with black paint on their faces and arms, who sit in circles chanting, and then touching each other. I have not attended esbats with every single witch in the United States, but Vicki's description does sound like the sensationalized descriptions of witches' orgies one often read about in popular culture magazines in the late 1970s. Her son Aaron later identified a pewter skull earring (I had one of those in high school, too!) that Vicki said belonged to Damien, as being like the ones he saw worn by the men he observed "chanting in the woods." He must have been mighty close to them to see what sort of earrings these men were wearing.

This is but one example of the sort of statements made to police that fueled the atmosphere in the community and led people to believe the killings somehow involved satanic worship. It would be laughable if it were not so fucking tragic.

It has been said that during Damien Echols's trial, the local pagan community turned against him, believing that associating with someone accused of child murder (and worse) would reflect badly upon the pagan community. Pagan communities, like other spiritual communities, are microcosms: we have our upright citizens and our criminals, too. We support, and betray, each other. We want to do what is right, but sometimes we go about it the wrong way. No doubt the pagans of the West Memphis area thought they were doing the right thing in refusing to publicly support Damien during his trial. If Damien were to be found guilty, so too would they become *persona non grata*. But in 1996, after *Paradise Lost* was released, many audience members understood that a grave injustice had taken place. Pagans in the audience understood that a primary reason for such injustice was centered on a southern community's beliefs about witchcraft and the occult. In other parts of the country, pagans and witches don't have to skulk around in the woods when performing their rites, because they don't fear being ostracized. Pagans in the United States rallied to defend the defamation and misinterpretation of their religious practice, and spoke out on Damien's behalf, and many became involved in efforts to publicize the plight of the West Memphis Three. Many, like me, are still involved.

What happened in West Memphis in the early 1990s occurred at a time when paganism was experiencing widespread growth and slowly burgeoning acceptance across America. A pity that the level of awareness about witchcraft and paganism that now exists in schools and churches, in popular media and books, was not yet present in West Memphis, Arkansas. It was a city still mired in the 1980s miasma of "satanic panic," that unfortunate late twentieth-century hysteria that suspected a vast conspiracy of covens that enslaved people, forced women to give birth, and murdered their progeny in unholy rituals. Virtually hundreds of accusations were made; dozens of people "confessed" to having been victims or participants in "satanic ritual abuse." Eventually, the psychological techniques used to exact these startling admissions were deemed spurious and overly suggestive and discounted by the medical community. To this day, not a single actual corpse of a child has ever been found, despite years worth of investigation by the federal authorities, and despite the burial locations having been "disclosed" by the former "members" of these groups.

It is now widely believed that the whole satanic panic scare arose as a result of spurious rumors spread by the Religious Right to counter the growth of various counter-culture movements in the United States, most of them falling under the relatively innocuous umbrella of "new age beliefs."

It is a substantial leap in logic to compare meditating on the healing power of crystals to aborting children in the service of Beelzebub, but such dark times were the 1980s. It is unusual that a good-sized city like West Memphis was, as late as 1993, still trapped in the superstitious aspic of this 1980s obsession, but neo-paganism has always met its worst opposition in areas where Pentecostal, Southern Baptist, or other extreme sects of Christianity hold sway. Now that Wicca is mainstreamed to a ludicrous degree, a cynical person could look at the events that transpired in West Memphis as a pocket of ignorant ineptitude, characteristic of a time when ideas and attitudes were ready to shift. But to understand this as some "big picture" cultural trend, we must acknowledge those who got lost on the way to enlightenment.

If all this had happened ten years later, things might have turned out very differently. Damien and his friends might still have dabbled in the occult, but they would have had thousands of teenage counterparts on the Internet to communicate with, which they could easily access at school or the local library. Concerned parents or teachers would have had a plethora of sources with which to educate themselves about such activities. Federal rulings would have already been passed which recognized Wicca as a legitimate religion.

But it happened when and where it happened. Ten years ago, in West Memphis, being a teenager interested in the occult made you a devil worshipper. Ten years later, these young men are still in prison.

A recent article in the *Atlantic Monthly* suggests that the fastest-growing fanatical "cult" in America may well be Christianity. Meanwhile, we witches have become media darlings, campus club presidents, bloggers, celebrity shop owners, moms, dads, lawyers, teachers.

Ten years from now, where will evil reside?

Not By Its Cover

A SEMI-BIOGRAPHICAL
MEMORY-BAT FLAPPING THROUGH THE BRAIN

David Niall Wilson & Adam Greene

High school is a different world from the one you inhabit as an adult. It is worlds away from the years that come before as well. You walk through those doors for the first time scared shitless and filled with misplaced hopes that in this new place, and this new life, things will be different. Classmates will see you for who you are. You will be popular, because you are interesting, intense, and worth knowing. You will meet girls, even though, for the most part, those available will be the same fifty or so who ignored you when they weren't spitting at you for the last eight or nine years of your life. The things you have been made fun of for in the past are there – in the past. Removed from the new you by a teenage rite of passing.

And it's all bullshit. You know that, as well. That's why, when you slip through those doors, you don't raise your hands in the air, fingers pointing to the rafters, and scream "Yes!" at the top of your lungs. You slink along the walls, stare nervously at the frosted glass windows of the principal's office, and march down the aisles of lockers, standing like sentinels who will trumpet your arrival to all the wrong people, hoping against hope for a space in a corner, or beneath a stairway. You want anonymity, to be there, but not seen, and that, of course, never happens.

Face it: high school sucks in much the same way as any other school. Those who have watched you with glee, aware that they are in a position to use putting you down as a means of lifting themselves up, avoiding ridicule by sloughing it off onto your shoulders, have graduated the same as you. They are older, but in most cases this only serves to make them meaner, stupider, and more worthy of active avoidance than ever. It's the pattern of the world, littered with grease-spots and potholes. The trick is to wind your way through it all without getting pushed into too many potholes or smeared with too much grease.

I read the truth of it all pretty quickly as the summer dreams of a new life faded, and the hallway walls closed in like a giant vise, pressing me from disappointment to disappointment. I got my locker assignment – dead center in the main corridor. No way to avoid anyone. I made a mental note to learn the hours of the school, so that I could be in and out of that hallway quickly and quietly, books in hand, and not return until it had cleared in the afternoon. Some people plan their school schedule around their classes. I planned mine around avoidance. It was a pattern that had served me well in junior high, and I saw no reason to deviate. Though I'd dropped a good fifty pounds and no longer fit the nicknames I'd sported since grade school, I saw no reason to make that an occasion to campaign for new ones.

Still, though the dark pit of a world that surrounded me had not changed other than to spread its walls wider and present more traps and dangers, I had changed. The inner world I inhabited had fleshed out, been hung with band posters and with music in the background. Books lined the shelves in my room, and their words had spread their influence and stained the walls of my mind. If I had little to look forward to in school – that was fine, as long as I could drop back into my own world regularly.

After a few weeks of avoidance therapy, I noticed that the very act of keeping to myself was a sort of defense. I dressed the part of the lone wolf: dark jeans, black t-shirts. I hit my locker early and returned to it late, when the halls were all but deserted. When people noticed me at all, it was to notice that I was a shadow on the wall, that I always had a book, and my Walkman with me, and that the lack of their presence did not seem to be depriving me of any sleep. It didn't make me popular, but it piqued their interest just enough that they didn't break the spell. They whispered behind my back, I'm sure, wondering what I was writing in my spiral notebook during lunchtime, sitting alone by a tree out past the parking lot. I wouldn't have known, and couldn't have cared less. No one would tell me they were whispering, because there was no one to tell me. I was too busy being apart to care.

Of course, it didn't last. Time has a way of shifting planes of existence so that one day you are one thing, and the next you find you have become something else. I still remember the first day Micky Williams walked over to where I was sitting during lunch, listening to Skinny Puppy on my Walkman and reading. He came over and just stood there – I don't know for how long – before he said a word. I noticed him, but figured the safest route was the silent one. I didn't know him. We didn't attend the same junior high school, and though a Nine Inch Nails button on his backpack encouraged me, I didn't want to make a mistake.

Micky was staring down at the cassette covers littering the grass beside me, and finally he leaned down and snatched one up. Knowing it had gone beyond the point where I could ignore him, no matter his intention, I snapped my finger down on the stop button of the Walkman and slid the earphones down around my neck.

Micky looked up then, and he smiled. "I love this one," he said. It was a tape by Filter, one I'd played until it was stretched and worn out.

I nodded in return.

"What were you listening to?" he asked.

I flipped him the cover to the Skinny Puppy tape. He snapped it out of the air easily, turned it over a couple of times, then flipped it back.

"I've got that."

I was already gathering my books and tapes and stuffing them into my backpack. I stood quickly, not knowing where to go with the conversation. Micky figured it out for me.

"I've got most of their stuff," he continued. "You like Nine Inch Nails?"

We were walking back to the school before I knew it, and deep in Reznorland. I was sort of half-conscious that others had taken notice, two loners walking as one, heads bent and deep in conversation. Black T-shirts against the blacker asphalt, long hair hiding the intensity in my own eyes, and the enthusiasm in Micky's. Nine Inch Nails and Trent Reznor, when viewed in comparison to high school, other kids, football pep rallies, and Intro to College Algebra, was on an entirely higher plane of existence, and we were there. Fuck the rest of them if they didn't understand.

That was how it started, but that isn't the story. The story is how it ended, and it sucked. Listen.

Micky and I were tight pretty much from that moment in the parking lot on. There weren't many kids in the school who shared my taste in anything, and to find someone else who listened to the music that kept me sane was tantamount to stepping through a portal into a better world. And to top it all off, Micky was more popular than me; always had been. His acceptance of me opened doors, and it wasn't long before the two of us attracted our own crowd filled with questions about the music, and the T-shirts we wore, and the way we wore our hair.

We talked a few times about forming our own band. I had a guitar and a small amplifier. I'd had them for years, toying with the chords and rhythms late at night with the volume down low. Nothing ever came of it, but it was there, in the background, the great "what if" and "wouldn't it be cool" world of creative release. I kept writing in my notebooks, and Micky bought a car. High school, in short, sucked somewhat less.

Don't get me wrong. I was still the weird kid with the long black hair who wore mostly black, was never seen without the Doc Martens boots and the Walkman. I was not voted most likely to succeed and I was not Valedictorian of my class. I dated no cheerleaders and I was never going to be the poster child for the National Honor Society. Still, I had a friend, and that grew into several friends.

That is why it was bad. Listen.

I had another friend. He'd been a friend for so long that he was more like a brother, or a cousin, than another kid in school. Shane's mom and my mom were tight, and we'd been playing together since we were crawling like little spit-up robots across each other's kitchen floors. I didn't mention Shane before because he was so much a part of my life it didn't seem relevant. He walked different circles in school. We ate lunch together sometimes, and we talked in the hall, but Shane was the school newspaper type. He was everyone's friend, and no one's close friend – except mine. People talked to him, and hung out with him, but it wasn't because he was cool, only because he was there. He sort of walked a tightrope of loser-wire, wanting to be on both sides at once. I knew his score, and I didn't grudge him his mid-list placement on the school food chain, just like he didn't give me any shit about my music, my clothes, or Micky. It wasn't something we thought about, it was just the way we were. Tight.

Then along came Jane. Jane Brennan-Downey. Jane of the blue blue eyes and long tanned legs. Jane of the cheerleader squad and boyfriend on steroids. Jane who liked to see that boyfriend's eyes shift all shades of green – liked to be fought over and craved like a bad drug. Along came Jane, and Shane was a sitting duck.

But that is getting ahead of the story, and it's better I tell it the way it happened.

I came to school on the eighteenth of January just as I did any other day. I walked to my locker, scanned the halls for anyone I knew, anyone I hated, anyone I lusted after, and Micky. Not always in that order, but mostly. It was a ritual, but this day was different. I sensed it before I'd even stepped into the hall, but when I saw the lockers, more than half of them with white papers dangling through the vents at the top of each door, I stopped cold. The school didn't distribute papers directly to our lockers. The school paper was picked up in the library, or at study hall. Short of an invitation to an unscheduled pep rally, I couldn't wrap my brain around any good reason those papers would be there, flapping in the air from the vents as if waving to me.

I walked to my locker feeling the air pressing in on me like the water at the deep end of the pool. Everything echoed and my ears rang with the buzz of the overhead fluorescent lights. I slung my pack to the floor in front of my locker and snatched the paper out of the vent, unfolding it so that the bold-faced computer-generated title glared up at me. *The Underground.*

I stared at the paper, started to scan it, and then thought better of it. I grabbed my backpack, stuffed the paper in my pocket, and headed back out the door and across the parking lot to my usual spot beneath the tree. I could read it there without anyone noticing, and something told me I didn't want to share. I could hardly breathe.

Once I was settled I drew the single, two-column sheet out and began to read. My heart was pounding like some out of control drum and bass beat. The first paragraph was fluff, nonsense about how *The Underground* was the student's voice, their chance to express their truth in the face of fascist, dictatorial educators and conniving administrators. The usual stuff you heard in the parking lot, smoking behind the dumpster and hoping the vice-principal didn't catch you and call your parents.

Then it got worse. The next section, titled simply POSEURS, was a list of names. On that list were cheerleaders, jocks, honor students, and one or two hoods. All of the names were high-profile students in one area or another. All of their names had neat little notes appended.

> *Bobby "Stop it or I'll tell my dad" Blanchard*
> *Mindy "You can't touch this" Tyner*
> *Micky "Nobody understands me" Williams*
> *Jane "I'm all that and then some" Brennan-Downey*

I grew angry at that last, and I stopped for a second, the letters and words on the page blurring. Then I concentrated, and read on. There were more than a dozen names, all with comments – that any number of students might have made – attached to them. There were some articles on other things about school, a couple of insulting poems obviously aimed at certain faculty members, but my gaze kept sweeping back up the page to that fucking list. I didn't know who printed this thing, but they had a serious attitude, and one thing was sure. If Todd "bucktooth-badass" Martin got hold of them, they were going to wish they'd never seen a computer, let alone printed this damn thing out.

I glanced up. It was nearly time for class, and while I'd been reading, a lot of others had arrived. I saw there were small knots of students gathered by the parking lot, outside the doors, and near the track. In every crowd the white papers flapped. When the bell rang, it found a good half of the student body unprepared and tardy. I slipped through the masses, the paper folded and folded and folded again into a tiny square in my hip pocket. It burned through the cloth and imprinted itself on my skin.

All that day I kept to myself. I saw Micky a couple of times, but there wasn't any time to talk. He looked a little pale, but otherwise normal. I saw Shane twice, but each time he ducked around a corner and out of sight before I could call out and stop him. I let it ride. No one in the school was happy, with the possible exception of a few of those not mentioned in *The Underground*, who found gossip a good second choice to a life. Everyone was talking or thinking about who might have done it, and why. Everyone stared at everyone else, and only the closest of friends were spending much time together. That was how it ended the first day. Everything was a little off, but behind that sensation, everything had the appearance of slipping back toward normal.

Never trust appearances.

Despite what educators and parents would have you believe, high school is not about learning. High school is about who's dating whom, and what to wear on Saturday night, and whether or not Mary-Jane so-and-so saw you catch the game-winning pass in the game last week, and how the fuck do I get rid of this pimple without leaving a crater the size of Vesuvius on the side of my face. It's about backbiting and gossip, cruel jokes and anything that can be done to boost fragile, insecure adolescent egos beyond the miasma of pre-adult angst. There is a backdrop of education, but half of that is gloss, and the other half is in place only for the few with sense enough to take it seriously.

That noted – the next day was my first in hell. The minute I hit the main hall, I felt it. For one thing, I wasn't the only one there, and that in itself was enough to throw my day off. There were pockets of students, still gathered with their much-folded, sweated-over copies of *The Underground* clutched tightly. As I passed each group, the silence deepened. I caught furtive glances in my direction that on a normal day would never have happened. Sweat broke out on my neck, and my skin felt clammy, but I managed to saunter in what I hoped was my normal, casual slouch to my locker. No papers flapped from the vents, and that was good. When I opened the locker, nothing dead was sitting in the bottom. I dropped off half my books, grabbed the other half, and slammed the locker, retreating through the doors and across the parking lot to my normal spot.

The grounds were filling up more quickly than normal. Students I didn't know walked toward me, around me, and past me – glared at me, and moved on, but no one spoke. It was like having a seat in the middle of a *Dawn of the Dead* mob scene, hundreds of angry, hungry zombies circling, but unwilling to attack. I buried my nose in a book, pulled my earphones on, and cranked the Walkman, knowing the batteries wouldn't last long if I kept it up.

Then I saw Micky's car pulling into the parking lot, and I relaxed a little. At least, whatever the hell was going on, I wouldn't be facing it on my own. I turned off the Walkman, grabbed my stuff, and headed over to where Micky was locking his car door. He turned before I was quite there, and walked right past me. I know he saw me. Just for a second, I caught his eye, and then he was gone, moving quickly across the parking lot toward the school.

I read a lot in his expression, though I caught it for just a second. There were questions, accusations, and pain. There was a wall that had never been there before. There was no hesitation, no explanation, but all of it was there to be read.

It hit me so hard I nearly blacked out. I saw another small knot of students hovering over that stupid fucking piece of paper, and I knew. He thought I did it. They all thought I did it. I wanted to scream at them, right there in the parking lot, but the image of myself doing just that popped into my head, and a wave of nausea flushed through me as I considered the spectacle. If I wanted them to believe that I *did* do it, the best way to that end was to scream at them like a lunatic in the parking lot.

So I did nothing. I went to class. I slipped back into my old routine, coming in even earlier, leaving even later, and moved my tree-shaded seat to a spot on the far side of the parking lot from the school, out of site of the dumpster smoking section and the track. I stocked up on batteries, cranked up the music, and watched them all.

The school administration performed their own investigation. There were enough insults to members of the staff in that paper to incur their wrath, inept as it was. I was questioned, as were a few dozen other students, but nothing ever came of it. I kept my head down, my mouth closed as much as possible, mumbled in response to all questions, and escaped as soon as I could. When I came out of my "interrogation," other students were waiting to see what had happened. They wanted me to be "caught," of course. They wanted the school to do something about my attitude. They wanted me to be punished so they could sit back, smug in the knowledge that my "kind" could be kept quiet and down and shoved off in a corner somewhere so they could continue their own empty, fluff-filled lives. All they saw was my back as I exited the building and headed for my customary reading space.

"No hanging today," I muttered in passing.

When the yearbook came out, there was an entry in the "Stuff That Happened" section. "A Nine Inch Nails T-shirt-wearing, introverted geek is still wanted for the publication of the first and only issue of *The Underground*." That was the nail in the coffin of my innocence in more ways than one.

Micky never spoke to me again, not then, not after high school. Every person whose name appeared on that list remembers me as guilty. Most of the world never saw, read, imagined, or gave a fuck about the thing, but then, they weren't me. They didn't spend their hours with only music to relieve the boredom. They lost no friends and they gained a common enemy. Me. So it went. Years passed, and I'd nearly excised the thing from memory. I got a job, got roommates, and went to college. A lot changed, though the NIN CDs had only grown in number, and the attitude and persona I'd been developing through high school intensified. Shane eventually moved in with a group of us when he finished college. Shane was the one person who hadn't completely cut me out. We'd been friends forever, and *The Underground* hadn't changed that, though I understood when he quit sitting near me at lunch in high school.

One night, it came out. Irish whiskey, late night, loud music reminiscences were flapping about the room like the ghosts of days passed, and out of the blue, Shane told me. He printed *The Underground*. It was that fucking cheerleader, blue-eyed Jane, who put him up to it. She'd even been certain to put herself on the list to divert blame, not that such a tactic had been necessary.

I sat there, half-drunk, half blind with – I don't know. I wasn't really angry, just incredulous. Just fucking *floored*. He was sorry, of course. I heard it in the tone of his voice; his ignorance floated about the room and chased the bat-memories. He knew it had been bad, he said. He didn't have a clue. He doesn't have a clue. And all of those people, students, teachers, cheerleaders, jocks – and Micky, who I still haven't talked to since – all of those people were taken in so easily.

I glanced down at the black Skinny Puppy shirt I was wearing when Shane confessed, threw my head back, and stared at the ceiling; then I started to laugh. As I contemplated the ceiling, tears streaming from my eyes, I wondered if I could choke Shane with the folded and folded and folded again copy of *The Underground* I still kept in my desk, but in the end, I knew it wouldn't matter. The headline would read "Nine Inch Nail T-shirt-wearing, introverted psycho chokes roommate with paper."

Maybe high school isn't a completely different world from the one you inhabit as an adult. Some things never change. Whatever they tell you about judging books, albums, or people – they will *always* judge by the cover.

Self-Portrait, CLIVE BARKER

In Their Satanic Majesty's Service

Brian Hodge

Evil is a word rife with baroque connotations, and often these are will-ingly, even eagerly, exploited by those most prone to flinging the word around. Whether it comes from a pulpit or the Oval Office, the word implies battles waged on a cosmic scale, on which the whole of civili-zation depends . . . even when the circumstances of its utterances are, underneath, little more than playground sneering. See George W. Bush package his three-headed hydra as the "Axis Of Evil." See one of those heads denounce the United States as the "Great Satan." See clergy on both sides stand and nod with righteous fury.

It's an appealing perspective, not in the least because it allows you to stake out an intractable position within a timeless drama – and automati-cally you become part of history, part of the Great War between Good and Evil. Your life is invested with meaning, your motivations directed by a higher power. Yes, a few folks can be counted on to align themselves with the side of Evil, but since this is usually more of a fashion statement than a serious call to arms – and fodder for even more cautionary rhetoric pounded out by the champions of Good – let's leave that pathology over in the sideshow tent. In the grand scheme, the evildoers are *always* the other guys.

There's a part of me that loves the aesthetics of the baroque – I grew up on Hammer Studios Films, so I can't help it. It's comforting, in its way. Baroque evil may be monolithic, but it always goes down in the end. Oddly enough, though, even as I've turned a buck or two fictively exploring various faces of evil, it's been a long time since I've been able to bring myself to resort to the reassurances of traditional baroque out-comes . . . probably because they feel so fundamentally dishonest.

If there is such a palpable force as Evil, its triumphs come not in the guise of the faces that leer from stained glass and the landscapes of Bosch, but from beneath bland everyday anonymity and from bureau-cracies that can paralyze otherwise good people by urging them, in the words of Edmund Burke, to do nothing.

In the mid-1980s, in the Illinois town where I was born and raised and at the time still lived, there came a period of sixteen or so months during which the local murder rate shot upward in a dramatic spike. For a time, my hometown (along with the outlying county) was alleged to have had the dubious honor of the highest per capita homicide rate in the state of Illinois.

They weren't all your typical garden-variety killings, either, if indeed there is such a thing. Certainly these factored in: impulsive murders of jealousy or rage and too much to drink. Always those. As for the rest, it was – to put it in baroque terms – as though an ill wind had blown through and left behind some terrible malignancy.

There was, unsolved for more than a decade, the rape and murder of a young nursing student in her home.

A few blocks away, a fellow named Tommy Odle, not long out of high school, got up one morning and throughout the day killed the rest of his family: his parents after breakfast, and that afternoon, his young brother and sister as each came home from school. According to his testimony, Odle escorted his final victim into a room where he'd stacked the previous bodies like a cord of wood, saying, "Look what I did today."

These occurred within the same school district where I had attended kindergarten through sixth grade, but the killings of that era hit close to home in ways beyond mere geography. A very good friend – my best friend's older brother, whom I'd known since age five – was kidnapped by two guys who saw him drive past where they were parked downtown one night, just after he got off work. One decided he wanted the new car that my friend Stan had bought a few weeks earlier. They followed him, waited until he stopped at a convenience store for gas; one guy commandeered his car while the other followed. They drove Stan miles out of town before stopping along a desolate stretch of interstate. They ordered him onto the ground and fired five bullets into his head and neck. Then drove on. They got to enjoy Stan's car for about three days. Those of us who loved him got word of their arrest while we were at the funeral home visitation.

As horrific as these murders were, and all the others left unmentioned, they were not the worst.

In November of 1987, in the tiny rural community of Ina, about a dozen miles away, a family – Dardeen, their name – was wiped out. They were killed with such unrestrained savagery I'm sure it made even devout believers question if not the existence of God, at least his sense of hearing. The unanimous consensus among the county sheriff's department and the detectives of the State Police was that this was, by far, the worst thing they'd ever seen. Some were veterans of Vietnam, and said even there they'd never witnessed anything as bad.

As I write this exactly sixteen years later, the only thing left to hope for is that none of them have since had the occasion to revise their judgment.

To describe what happened in the Dardeens' trailer and beyond, even in general terms, feels uncomfortably close to pornography. It feels intrusive, a bit like exhuming a grave for no better reason than to gawk at the bones. And yet not to would feel as though it was understating the depths that were descended to on this little plot of land.

Around five-thirty in the evening, both Ruby Elaine Dardeen and her three-year-old son Peter were bound, gagged with tape, and beaten to death with a baseball bat. At the time, I heard – second- or third-hand from the supposed source, so I can't swear to its accuracy – that the coroner found that Ruby had been struck with such force her skull had been knocked loose of her spine and driven down over the upper vertebrae. She'd been seven-and-a-half to eight months pregnant, and went into labor. Her newborn daughter was also beaten . . . so reduced beyond recognition that the first investigators on the scene didn't initially realize they had a third murder victim.

For several hours, husband and father Russell Keith Dardeen was the sole suspect. He was nowhere to be found and his car was gone, although I can imagine that he was considered a suspect only in the most reluctant terms, that everyone involved feared the worst for him as well. His car later turned up five miles away, in a parking lot in a nearby town named Benton, notable only for having been the hometown of actor John Malkovich. The next day, Russell Dardeen went from suspect to final victim, after hunters discovered his body in a wheat field. He too had been beaten, then shot three times in the head. His penis had been excised and placed in his mouth.

More than a thousand leads and tips.

All of them dead ends.

For more than twelve years.

Unsolved murders leave behind huge holes torn in the fabric of the lives left behind. I cannot fathom what it would be like to go a decade, or a lifetime, not knowing what had really happened to someone I cared about deeply. For three days I had a tiny taste of it, as Stan's family and I and others with devastated hearts wondered who had crossed his path and left him in the weeds. Three days were plenty.

When unsolved murders are sensational enough, the lack of certainty creates a void, a Petri dish that can breed its own mythology. Few today would likely know of Jack the Ripper if he'd been caught after Mary Kelly.

As for the Dardeens and why they were killed, theories abounded. The silliest of them held that Russell had been in the Federal Witness Protection Program, and he and his family had been murdered in retaliation for his testimony in some organized crime case – this theory's proponents ignorant of the fact that, in the WPP, you don't get to keep your birth name and live in the same town as your parents.

In preparation for writing this, to refresh my memory on certain details, I looked up archived news articles online and came across an unsolved crimes website that still posts its profile of the Dardeens' killer. With his identity known for nearly four years now, the profile is more wrong than right:

He did not go to the residence of the Dardeen family to kill them but to try to talk them out of something.

He will be a deeply religious person, perhaps even active in the church.

He is very familiar with the trailer. . . .

This person has never killed before. . . .

[H]e is still living close by, living his secret life.

All wrong.

For years I was haunted by the Dardeen family's killing, in that distant way you can be haunted by the fates of people you've never known. I'm sure this was, in part, because their fate was the bloodiest in an aberrantly bloody time; more powerful yet was the uncertainty at the core of it all. Since there was no face to the killer, I was free to imagine one; given the horrid strength and the extreme inhumanity of his acts, it was easy to envision that face as something more or less than human. Although no one could actually seriously *believe* it, there was something perversely comforting in flirting with the notion that Hell had coughed up a devil that evening who did his work, left a family dead and the surrounding communities terrified, and then returned to . . . wherever.

It was certainly more appealing than admitting that, more than likely, there would be no appreciable outward difference between him and the person seen in the mirror every day. It balanced the scales better than speculating that maybe their deaths were the payback for nothing more than an act of human kindness.

On the night the rest of the country was wondering how all the computers were going to weather the rollover from 1999 to 2000, in the border city of Del Rio, Texas, two friends were having a sleepover: Kaylene Harris, age thirteen, and Krystal Surles, ten. That night a man broke into their room at the Harris family's mobile home, sexually assaulted Kaylene, slit the throats of both girls, and left them for dead.

Incredibly, Krystal not only survived, but was cogent enough to provide a description of her attacker that was so accurate he was caught within two days, on January 2. His name was Tommy Lynn Sells. A perpetual drifter and a carnival roustabout, he was thirty-five years old at the time. He had committed his first murder around the age of sixteen, and had been wandering and killing ever since, a meandering two-decade (interrupted by periodic jail terms for assault and auto theft) trail of carnage with no pattern, no consistent methodology, and of course no rationale. Using whatever weapon was at his disposal – in lieu of anything else, his bare hands – Sells was the most elusive kind of serial killer: an opportunist who can get away with it for years, decades, because he wanders from state to state and leaves behind no dots to connect.

He hadn't been in jail for long before the confessions began. Tommy Lynn Sells estimated that he had killed dozens of times; accounts vary, the figure ranging between fifty and seventy. I don't know how many have been corroborated by investigators by now . . . but the first thirteen came pretty quickly. Sells claims to feel remorse and that he's found religion. It's said that he finds the murder of an Illinois family particularly difficult to talk about. He heralds Krystal Surles as a hero "for bringing a stop to the madness" even as he admits that if he hadn't been caught, he would still be out there killing; that his only mistake was leaving someone alive.

The instincts for self-preservation that he must have had humming on an animal level beneath conscious awareness are terrifying to contemplate.

"I've woken up before in places where I don't know how I got there and I got blood on myself," he is quoted as saying by the sheriff's investigator who arrested him.

Meaning that he did his work, left behind the dead and the bereaved and the terrified, and then returned to . . . wherever. Hell may not have literally coughed up a devil, but on paper, at least, Sells' credentials are impeccable.

A year or two, give or take, after Sells was arrested for the final time, I got a call from my mom telling me that the Dardeen family's killer was going to be on one of the prime time news shows, CBS's *48 Hrs.* Much of the story focused on the trial in Del Rio, Texas, and the courage and composure shown by Krystal Surles as she had to face in court the man who'd left the scar plainly visible on her throat.

But this was interspersed with footage of Sells himself, in jailhouse interviews and out in the field, wearing shackles and an orange jumpsuit, walking investigators through the scenes of old crimes. He also spoke of the Dardeen murders. It seems clear enough, after the fact, that their paths crossed at a nearby truck stop, where Russell struck up a conversation with Sells, then in his early twenties, and decided to invite him home for a meal. Whether true or not – the truth will probably never be known with any certainty – Sells claimed his rampage began because Russell made a pass at him.

It was my first look at the man . . . but after thirteen or fourteen years of deeply personal mythology, it's hard to imagine a more anticlimactic revelation. I'd foreseen a hulking brute. Nothing else would do; nothing less could have inflicted the damage he had. Instead, while I don't know his height, he looked like a runty fellow. And while I'm sure that he can wear another face, one far more terrible, to look at him in the light of a calm day, you would never need a second glance. At the time I thought that, with his stupid mullet haircut, Tommy Lynn Sells looked as though he should be playing bass in some '80s-fixated Holiday Inn lounge band.

How dare he.

I'd known better all along, of course; known that he would have to be something like this, that a bland and anonymous appearance would be one of his greatest assets, his camouflage in a world in which he had forfeited his right to belong.

Yet we have such a fervent need for our bogeymen to look the way we think they should.

And along with our bogeymen, our scapegoats.

The Dardeen murders were still years away from being solved when I first learned of the killings of three young boys in West Memphis, Arkansas, and what appeared to be a gross miscarriage of justice that followed in their wake; learned the same way that many others have, by viewing the first *Paradise Lost* documentary on HBO.

Ever since, it has haunted me as well, in ways that are both similar to and very different from those killings that rocked a small town just a dozen miles from my door.

The slaughter of innocents, or the slow, grinding, sanctioned theft of lives based not on irrefutable evidence, but on an obdurate need not to be proven wrong ... I've yet to decide which act is more evil.

But even if the scales of injustice were to tip one way or another, I don't suppose it matters.

Either way, the devil is well-served.

From the Books of Alice Redfearn: a didactic parable

Gary A. Braunbeck

*There are no moral phenomena, only a moral
interpretation of phenomena. . . .*
– Nietzsche

They came for her shortly before midnight.

She sat in her dark cell and listened as they broke through the heavy wooden door and overpowered the jailer. She waited as they moved into the corridor. She heard the keys jingling in someone's hand. The flickering light from their pitch and kerosene torches cast dancing shadows on the wall opposite her cell. She stood close to the bars so she could see their faces when they arrived. The stench of their fear, hatred, and frenzy reached her before they did.

The corridor seemed aflame.

The shifting shadows merged into a dark stain.

The stain resolved into a crowd of human beings.

As one, they moved toward her cell.

Bouget, the Witchfinder, led the pack. It was his hand that held the keys.

He stepped forward from the rest, a Bible clasped in one hand, a bodkin in the other. "Alice Redfearn, be ye ready to receive punishment for thy loathsome deeds?"

"Would it matter if I were not?"

Bouget smiled. In the torchlight, his lips looked like two wriggling worms. "'Tis true, then; a whore of Satan can only answer a Christian's questioning with questions of her own. A pity. Ye might have spared your body much pain."

She opened her ragged robe, exposing the festering wounds and seeping blisters. "Your torturer was very skillful, Bouget."

"Enough!" spat the Witchfinder. The key clanked in the lock, the door swung open, and six men chosen by lots rushed in, stripping her naked and forcing her to her knees. One of them slipped a noose around her wrists and pulled it tight. Another kicked her legs from under her so that she fell face down upon the rough stone floor. A third man removed a blacksmith's hammer from the pouch he carried and shattered her ankles.

She did not scream.

They dragged her from the cell, down the corridor, past the unconscious jailer, and into the street. Villagers lined both sides of the path and none missed their chance to kick her, or spit upon her, or empty buckets of filth over her head.

Finally, they reached the center of the village square where the stake and pyre had been erected. The six men carried her to the top and bound her tightly to the stake. One of them placed two large stones on the sides of each of her ruined ankles to help support her weight. Then each of them inflicted a small degradation upon her body before leaving.

A ladder was placed against the stake and Bouget climbed to the top. His face was less than a foot away from hers. He held his Bible high and said, "In such a dark time as this, when a good Christian carrying out the will of God might shudder at the terrible form of His wrath, comfort can be found in these words from Deuteronomy: 'If any entice thee secretly saying, "Let us go and serve other Gods," thou shalt not consent to them, neither shall thine eye pity them, neither shalt thou spare, nor shalt thou conceal them, but thou shalt surely kill them. For if it be true that such abomination is wrought in the midst of thee, none amongst thee shall be safe until the abomination hath been smote.

"'So sayeth the Lord.' Amen."

He closed the Bible, then removed a sheet of parchment paper from his pocket, unfolded it, and read: "'It is deemed and judged this day that Alice Redfearn, having been found guilty of the unholy crime of witchcraft, has been condemned to be burnt alive, that she be bound to a stake expressly erected for this purpose at the appointed place for such executions, so that at least she will feel the flames keenly before being suffocated. Her worldly goods shall be declared forfeit and confiscate to whomever shall have them, reasonable expenses for the trial first being deducted.'" He folded the decree and placed it between the covers of his Bible, then leaned forward.

"Alice Redfearn, there be no place in God's Kingdom for the likes of thee. In Hell, thou wouldst be rewarded by thy master, Satan. We of this village agree there is no more just punishment than to imprison thy soul upon the Earth in such a manner that thou wilt see life continuing around thee and hear the laughter and music of which thy shall never be part of again.

"To whit: upon thy death a pit will be dug in this spot, and the ashes of thy body will be poured into that pit, then covered with rich soil and fresh dung. A tree shall be planted in this soil and thy condemned soul shalt forevermore reside within this tree." Bouget removed his bodkin, touching its tip against his finger to test its sharpness. A bead of blood rolled from the wound. He reached forward and drew a bloody cross on her forehead. "I mark thee with this Godly symbol, to ensure thine soul's imprisonment." He pulled his finger away. "Hast thou any final words? 'Tis not too late to renounce Satan and save thy soul."

She stared into his eyes and knew it was useless. She had tried to tell them about alchemic philosophy, about the miracles God gave to mankind through the medicinal remedies created by Philippus Aureolus Paracelsus; she had begged them to consider the vast wonders of the universe uncovered by Galileo Galilei; she had tried to explain the differences between the Black Arts and the White Magic she chose to practice, but they would not hear. Her words had been scrutinized, shredded, mocked, then filtered through Bouget's fanaticism to emerge with their meanings tainted and twisted.

She looked down and saw that they had torn her books apart and scattered their pages at the base of the stake. A tear formed in one of her eyes. All her wonderful books, all that knowledge. Agrippa's *De Occulta Philosophia*, the ancient notes of Anaxagoras of Clazomenae detailing his conclusions that the Earth was spherical, *The Gospel of Sri Ramakrishna*, the Hindu *Ris Veda*, the poems of Ovid, the plays of Aeschylus, Lucan's *De Bello Civilia*, the *Popol Vuh* . . . all ripped to pieces as if by wild animals, their wisdoms and insights soon to be lost to the village forever.

She lifted her head and blinked back her tears. "Tell me, Bouget, if you dare: Why is it that I am the only woman in this village who knows how to read?"

The Witchfinder slapped her face. "Foul concubine of Satan! Thou shalt not enchant me with thy confusing words of bewitchment!" And with that, he plunged the tip of his bodkin into her right eye, then her left. He quickly descended the ladder, which was then tossed upon the pyre. Bouget was handed a fiery torch and threw it high. It landed at Alice Redfearn's feet. The blood from her fractured ankles sizzled as the flames tongued her flesh. Within seconds, the other villagers had added their torches to the fire, then stood back and watched the conflagration.

The faces of the villagers shone and glimmered from the light. Many of those faces wore expressions of satisfaction and righteousness, none more visibly than Bouget's own, as they watched Alice Redfearn's agonizing death.

But had an outsider been present and chosen to look closely at the faces in the crowd, they would have noticed that some of the women standing behind their fathers or husbands seemed . . . distracted, even contemplative, as if they were thinking of something they had never pondered before.

Alice Redfearn did not scream, even though the pain of her dying was great.

The fire burned well into the night; a few flames could still be seen licking upward from the embers at noon the next day, when the men of the village set about the final stage of their holy task.

The pit was dug, the ashes poured in, soil and dung spread atop the smoldering remains, and the following morning, a sapling was planted in the spot.

Alice Redfearn's soul was absorbed into the young roots, then slowly into the rest of the tree.

The Earth spun. The moon waxed and waned. Vegetation grew around the tree, snaking up through the ashes. The scarred spot where Alice Redfearn had met her death gave way to a blanket of green. The tree grew straight and tall, its branches reaching toward the sunlight.

A season passed. Then a year. Then ten more.

Many of the villagers came to the tree to admire its beauty and to enjoy its shade. Many a young man proposed to his true love there. Weddings were performed beneath it. Children were christened there.

A decade passed. Then another. Then forty more. The stars shifted their courses. Constellations appeared, then vanished. The sky changed.

As did the village. Bouget was dead, as were his few ancestors. The villagers who had watched Alice Redfearn's death themselves died, as did their children, and their children's children, and the next three generations that followed.

The tree remained, tall and imposing. Within its core, Alice Redfearn waited patiently, her soul spreading its essence throughout the tree until every leaf, every twig, every branch and piece of bark became one with her.

But it did not stop there, for as Alice Redfearn's roots grew deeper into the Earth, she became aware of other spirits like herself, witches put to death years, decades, even centuries before her; they, too, were imprisoned in the trees, some so close that their thoughts roared into her, others so far away their thoughts were mere whispers.

She heard them all, and they, in turn, listened to her.

The Earth spun. The moon waxed and waned. Villages were replaced by townships. Engineers and architects covered the land with roads and bridges and train tracks.

Alice Redfearn gave some part of herself and her knowledge to each of the countless witch-spirits whose thoughts sang to her an organic song of redemption to come if only one had patience, and the other witch-spirits each gave unto Alice Redfearn some part of themselves and their knowledge.

The Earth spun. Seasons changed. Telegraph wires were replaced by telephone poles.

One night, a ripple of excitement entered Alice Redfearn's roots.

They are coming for me, whispered a distant witch-spirit to all of the others. *At long last, my freedom is at hand!*

Who? asked Alice. *Who is coming for you?*

You shall learn for yourself, soon enough, answered the distant witch-spirit. *But do not weep for me, dearest Alice, for I shall pass on what I have learned from you.*

As shall we all, whispered the others.

And I shall always remember what you have taught me, sang Alice: *The knowledge of the witch is the knowledge of power.*

The Earth spun. Townships were sacrificed in favor of cities, Community was traded for Commerce, cobblestone for asphalt and concrete, horsedrawn wagons for automobiles and airplanes. Telephones gave way to cellular communications.

And the question that had insinuated itself into the minds of the village women the night Alice Redfearn was executed did not die with the witch who had asked it.

People moved on. Families grew larger. Cities sprang up, demanding the death of trees to make room for them.

One of the trees was that in which the soul of Alice Redfearn was imprisoned.

They came for her shortly after dawn.

She waited in her majestic tree as the bulldozers and other heavy equipment came toward her. She listened as they broke through the heavy woods and overpowered the shales beneath the hillsides. Readying herself as they neared her spot, she heard the grinding of their gears, the snarl of their gas-powered saws. She stood tall and proud so she could see them clearly as they arrived. The stench of their smoke and diesel fuel reached her before they did.

Two workmen walked up to her, craning their necks to see all of her glory.

"Damn shame this has to come down," said the first one.

"Don't matter what we think," replied the second. "We got our orders."

The first one picked up his axe. "Trees're supposed to feel things just like a person does, y'know? My grandma told me that. Let's try to make it quick and clean, huh?"

"I've heard enough of that shit from you," said the second workman, powering up his chain saw. "Bad enough we got to cut down all these trees without you bellyachin' over every one of 'em."

"Least they'll be put to good use. That's something, anyway."

They set to work.

Within half an hour, she came crashing down.

This was not death; it was the first stage of Alice Redfearn's rebirth.

And this time, she did scream.

In ecstasy.

It was glorious.

She savored the sensations of every moment as she was cut into dozens of large, heavy sections and loaded onto gigantic flatbed trailers; she admired the world her old body had not lived to see as her pieces were driven to a mill where they were cut into logs; she drank in the cool goodness as the logs were treated in a flow of water made steady and constant by grindstones; she tingled with wild, unbound excitement as the logs were turned into wood chips, then treated under pressure with a solution of sulphurous acid and acid calcium sulfite, then caustic soda, carbon, and sodium sulphide; she centered her consciousness and began to focus her thoughts as the lignin contained in the chips decomposed, allowing a certain amount of dextrose to form as her cellulose was purified; she briefly flashed on the smug expression Witchfinder Bouget had worn the moment he blinded her with his bodkin, but it disappeared from her mind and was replaced by exhilaration as the wood chips were pulped, then immersed in water; the water molded the pulp into fibers; the fibers were felted together as the water was purposefully agitated; then, at last, after centuries of patient waiting, the felted fibers became sheets as they were lifted from the water by a wire screen.

The Witch Alice Redfearn lived again, both in her own right and through the others like her to whom the axe had fallen before.

⚛

The mammoth rolls of virgin paper were loaded onto trailers and hauled away.

Some of the Witch Alice Redfearn became pages in a book used to teach a young girl named Marja Sklodowska to read.

Some of her was made into the contact paper used by a journalist for the production of photographs.

Some of her became pages in a volume of inspirational verse that was given to another young girl named Agnes Gonxha Bojaxhiv as a gift on her eleventh birthday.

Some of her was manufactured into sheets in a notebook purchased by a young Southern girl with money saved from returning empty pop bottles for the deposit; on the first sheet of this notebook she wrote the words, "In the town there were two mutes, and they were always together."

The Witch Alice Redfearn's essence remained strong.

Her ungodly influence spread with every page or sheet of parchment manufactured from her.

None of her was wasted.

Marja Sklodowska went on to discover that the mineral pitchblende contained polonium and radium. For this, she won the 1903 Nobel Prize in physics, an honor she shared with her husband. In 1911 she won a second Nobel, this one for Chemistry in recognition of her isolation of pure radium. The world came to know her as Marie Curie.

The journalist who used the contact paper for her photographs was Margaret Bourke-White, whose pictures of World War II battlefields and American troops in Korea are considered by many to be the finest war photographs ever taken.

Agnes Gonxa Bojaxhiv traveled to India in 1948. There she served and comforted the destitute and dying in Calcutta and later formed the Order of the Missionaries of Charity. In 1979 she was awarded the Nobel Prize for Peace. The world called her Mother Teresa.

The young girl who wrote in her notebook about two mutes later turned that sentence into a novel entitled *The Heart is a Lonely Hunter*. Her name was Carson McCullers.

Two sheets of parchment paper made from the Witch Alice Redfearn were used by Victoria Woodhull to write a speech that she read to the Judiciary Committee of the House of Representatives on January 11, 1871. She was the first woman ever to argue in favor of women's voting rights on the basis of the Fourteenth and Fifteenth Constitutional Amendments.

At night, when the countless women who are the pupils of Alice Redfearn dream, they always come upon a majestic tree growing from a pit of ashes. They approach it respectfully, for something in its stance speaks to them of a deep grace achieved through great and terrible suffering.

The tree bends from its middle and tenderly wraps its branches around them.

They feel, in these dreams, an overwhelming sense of sisterhood with the tree.

Then they awaken and reach for a favorite book left lying near them the night before, and take comfort in the words written on its pages.

The knowledge of power is the knowledge of the witch.

Kanji, CLIVE BARKER

We Find Things Old

Bentley Little

We Find Things Old.

It is the name of our company and a fair description of what we do. We are paid scavengers, tracking down toys from childhood, finding particular decorating items to complete a thematic motif, scouring junk yards and thrift stores and garage sales for the castoff item of one person's life that is the missing jigsaw piece to another's happiness. It's a good job, an interesting job, a challenging job. A fun job.

Or at least, it started out that way.

Our clientele has always been rather exclusive due to the triviality of our profession, running primarily to hip members of the idle rich, and to the major movie studios. It's from the studios that we get most of our business, obtaining period pieces for set designers and prop departments, locating the idiosyncratic items that directors feel necessary to fulfill their visual vision, and it was with a movie studio that the trouble started.

We were under deadline, scouting for freestanding '50s lamps and art studio equipment to fill out one scene of a serious multi-decade love story set in the trendy and ever-changing world of New York bohemianism. Everything else had been found by Tim Hendricks, the film's art director, but the director of the movie, a bad-tempered Brit with an oversized ego, vowed that there would be no fudging with the reality of even the most minor detail on this picture, and instead of allowing the prop department to dummy up some retro lamps and easels, he called us in.

We were given a deadline of a week by the director, but the executive producer told us with a nudge-nudge wink-wink that our stock would not go down with the studio if we failed to find the items at all. I think he wanted to teach the director a lesson and use us as the instrument, but it's always been a matter of personal pride with us to provide the goods as contracted, and though the deadline was more than a little unreasonable, we were determined to meet it.

We had a meeting to discuss strategy, and Tony said he remembered seeing a slew of kitsch items in a Bargain Land in the desert outside Lancaster a few months back, so on the day after we were given the assignment, he and I drove out to the Mojave, leaving Carole and Sims to hold down the fort and make scouting calls to our usual L.A. sources.

The Bargain Land was an empty furniture store in an undeveloped section outside of town, and we found it with no problem, letting a series of paint-peeled billboards and their arrows guide us. We found a lamp all right, and an easel, but the store's stock of artist studio equipment was pitiful, to say the least. The owner, a bearded desert rat who looked like Gabby Hayes and cultivated that resemblance by dressing the part, told us that there was an empty house a few miles down the road that used to be home to a commune. "There was lots of artists there," he said, "but when the leader got busted for pot, the rest of 'em all went their separate ways. They left most everything. The house itself's been pretty much looted, but there's a lot of stuff still rotting in the sand outside, shit that no one else wanted. I think most of the art stuff's still there."

We got directions, thanked him by slipping him an extra five, and walked back out to the van.

"We going to check it out?" Tony asked.

"Sounds like late sixties, early seventies," I said.

"Yeah, but they were poor hippies. If they did have art supplies they were probably secondhand. I bet we could salvage something."

I nodded. "Let's do it."

At the time of its last paint job, obviously several decades back, the small brick house had been coated in shocking pink, with a bright yellow, smiling wavy-ray sun painted on the garage door. The color had faded and chipped in the face of the desert heat and wind, giving it an almost hip, almost current look, but the inside of the building could make no such claims. The multicolored walls were filled with punched holes and flaked peeling plaster, the few items left in the rooms smashed and broken and thrown into piles. Everything was covered with a surprisingly thick layer of sand.

I looked at Tony, sighed. "Why don't you go through the rooms, see what you can find. I'll check outside, in the back."

He nodded and headed immediately toward a pile of what appeared to be bedsprings and blocks of wood in the corner of the room. I walked through the beer-can-littered kitchen and out the back door. Before me, the skeleton of a motorcycle was sticking out of a small hill of sand next to an empty picture frame and a barrel stove. I walked over and pulled the frame out of the sand, but one of the sides was broken and it was too damaged to be of any use. I scanned the area, saw old oil drums, a barbecue, and the cross-post of a downed clothesline. Where were the art supplies?

My eye was caught by a flash of light, a reflection of sun near a patch of brown weeds, and I made my way through the detritus toward it. The reflection was probably coming from a broken mirror or glass shard, but it couldn't hurt to look. Maybe it was part of a sheet metal sculpture or something.

I reached the weeds and stopped.

An object was lying half-buried in the sand before me.

A humanoid figure the size of a small dog.

I stared at the – thing – in front of me, feeling suddenly chilled. I was not quite sure what it was, but I did not like it and there were goose-bumps on my arms as I gazed upon its form. The object looked almost like a doll, but something about it bespoke organic origins. The face was monkey brown and made of a wrinkled shiny material, although its features did not resemble anything I'd ever seen. The eyes were missing, their empty-holed sockets proportionately too small for the rest of the face. There was no nose, no nostrils of any kind, and the mouth was a strangely curved slit which followed the form of a smile but did not give the appearance of mirth. On top of the head was a floppy red clown's hat, and the rest of the body was covered in a garish mummy wrap made from the same material. Elf shoes with bells covered the foot that was not buried under sand, white gloves were on the hands.

Despite having lain in the desert for who-knew-how-many years, the figure was not rotted or at all decrepit. The colors of its clothes were not even faded. Yet, somehow, the object gave the appearance of great age, and in my mind I saw dinosaurs trampling through a primeval forest – while the figure in its gaudy clothes lay unmoving at the foot of a prehistoric tree, looking exactly as it did right now.

That scared me, somehow.

"Anything there?"

I jumped at the sound of Tony's voice.

I wanted to move away from the figure, to steer him toward a different area of the yard so that he wouldn't see it, but before I could even make a move in that direction he was at my side.

He whistled appreciatively. "That's a find," he said, looking down.

I shook my head. "I don't think it's right for this project."

"Are you kidding? Strip off the clown duds and we got ourselves a clay sculpture."

"It's not clay."

"It'll look like it on film."

He was right. We were under deadline, and this was free and it fit the bill. But I still didn't like it. There was something about the figure that bothered me, though I couldn't quite put my finger on the reason. "Maybe Carole and Sims have found something," I said.

"And maybe not. I say we snag it."

He bent down and reached for it, but I was quicker than he was, and I grabbed one of the figure's arms, yanking it out of the sand. I didn't want Tony to touch it. Even through the material, the form felt uncomfortably alien to my touch, and I had to resist the urge to drop it and step on it.

"We'd better get going," Tony said. "It's at least an hour ride, and we still have some more scouting to do this afternoon."

"Okay," I agreed.

I tried not to let the disgust show on my face as I carried the thing back to the van.

On the freeway on the way back, the bells on the figure's feet jingled as we bounced over the bumps in the road.

It stayed in my mind, that thing we found in the desert, and though we soon moved on to another job, trying to find a mint '56 Wurlitzer pipe organ for a super-agent who was turning the barn on his canyon property into a rec-room replica of the pizza palace owned by his father, the figure still haunted me.

I dreamed of it at night, and in my dreams it had claws.

We were, of course, invited to the movie's premiere nine months later. The stars of the film and their friends in the industry paraded in front of the paparazzi on their way into the theater, and a host of wannabes and has-beens arrived as well, hoping to get their faces on *Entertainment Tonight,* or at least on one of the local L.A. newscasts.

We sat in the back row, and I don't know about Carole, Sims, or Tony, but I paid more attention to the sets and art direction than I did the acting and the plot. That's always true for me. Even with a great movie, it isn't until my second viewing that I can enjoy the totality of a film. This, however, was not, by any stretch of the imagination, a great movie, and it was clear long before the end credits that the studio had a dog on its hands.

The stars and starlets who'd been so happily and prominently on display going into the theater avoided the *Entertainment Tonight* cameras on the way out, not wanting to badmouth their friends who were involved with the picture or go on record endorsing an obvious loser.

I still could not get the figure out of my mind. It had been positioned far in the background of an artist's studio, as a failed sculpture or an aborted attempt at something or other, and had been onscreen for a total of no more than a minute, half of that out of focus, yet it had leaped out at me and had so dominated the scene in which it had been featured that I had not been able to look at or concentrate on anything else.

I wondered if anyone else had had the same reaction, but I was afraid to ask.

The strange thing was that the director had not stripped off the clown hat and clothes. That disconcerted me. After all the effort that had gone into making even the most minor detail absolutely authentic, the director had decided to leave in the artist's garish doll. Stripped, it could have passed for a work-in-progress or a failed experiment, but as it was, it seemed jarringly out of place.

I said nothing to anyone, though. Not to Tony or Carole or Sims. Not even to Val, my wife.

We all went together to the post-premiere party.

The next morning, I read in the *Times* that Susan Bellamy, the female star of the movie, had died of a drug overdose.

Val and I read the article together, me looking over her shoulder. She folded the paper when she was through and sat there for a moment, staring silently out the window of the breakfast nook at the other homes on the hill. "It had to be an accident," she said finally. "Susan was fine last night."

An accident.

Logically, it made sense. The movie had been a dud, but the general consensus had been that Susan's star power remained undiminished, and she alone had emerged from the film unscathed. There was no way she could have been depressed enough over first-night reaction to the movie to do something this drastic. Besides, it was well known that she often celebrated to excess, that she liked to party a little too hard. An accident was likely. Probable, even.

But I did not believe it.

I don't know why. And I don't know why I was so certain. Intuition, I guess. Or maybe it was because I had come into contact with that – thing – myself. But no matter what the paper said, no matter what anyone else thought, I knew what had really happened. In my heart, in my gut, I knew.

She had died because she'd been filmed in a scene with the doll.

It made no sense on any sort of rational level, but with unshakable certainty I knew it to be true, and when I called Tony an hour or so later and learned that Robert Finch had died as well, had committed suicide this morning by slitting his wrists in his Beverly Hills bathtub, I could not say that I was completely surprised.

Finch had played the artist and had been in the scene with Susan. And the doll.

I told Tony that I'd be late today, if I showed up at all. I asked him to go ahead with the indie project we were supposed to be working on, and after giving Val the bare facts of Finch's death, telling her nothing, I headed over to the studio.

The place was in an uproar. Both stars dying on the same morning had put people into a panic; and mourning, damage control, and hype were being conducted simultaneously in the suites of offices that served as the studio's nerve center. I bypassed the hurricane's eye, got myself a pass from Security and, alone and ignored, made my way to the props building. I knew Tim Hendricks would be around somewhere, since he was working on a low-budget horror flick with a scheduled release date four months from now, and after following a trail of grunts and nodded heads, I finally found him dummying up a breakaway staircase on one of the soundstages.

I cleared my throat to get his attention and he looked up from his work. "You heard?" I asked.

He straightened, nodded. "Who hasn't?" He walked toward me.

"I need to ask you a question," I said. I wasn't sure how to bring it up, but I plunged right in. "What did you do with the props from that movie? The sculptures and things in the background of the art studio?"

He frowned. "Why?"

"I want to buy one of the pieces back."

"Which one?"

"It's a figure about a foot high. With a clown suit. Looks like it was made out of –"

"That." His eyes widened in recognition and an involuntary look of revulsion passed over his features. "You don't want that."

"Yes, I do."

"No, you don't. It's . . . " He glanced down. "It's unclean."

I stared at Hendricks. He was probably the most rational, practical, and least superstitious man I'd ever met. Even in an industry crawling with cynics, with men and women who would break all of the Ten Commandments and then some if it would mean a bigger opening weekend, Hendricks stood out. He scoffed at all actors' superstitions, scorned all religious conversations, and matter-of-factly admitted his disbelief in God or anything other than the material world around him.

Yet he was afraid of the doll.

I shivered, remembering the chill I'd felt in the desert that first day.

"I know why you want it," he said.

I looked at him, not challenging him, not explaining, not saying anything.

He met my gaze. "I know what's going through your mind, and maybe you're right. Maybe it did have something to do with Sue and Rob. Then again, maybe it didn't. Either way, I don't think you should be fooling with it."

"I don't want to fool with it," I said.

"You're going to do what, then? Harness it? Try to use it on someone you don't like?"

"I'm going to put it back where I found it."

He was silent after that, staring down at his feet, wiping his hands nervously on his jeans. "I believe you," he said finally. "And I'd give it to you if I could. But it's gone. I looked for it myself this morning. I don't know if it was farmed out by Taylor or. . . ." He left the sentence unfinished, and I had a sudden mental picture of the figure crawling out of the building on its own, that mirthless half-smile frozen on its thin mouth as it made its way through the darkened studio at night.

"What were you going to do with it?" I asked.

"Torch it," he said. "Acetylene."

I nodded. "If you find it," I said, "go ahead. But I want you to let me know."

"Yeah." He turned away, obviously not wanting to talk, and I watched him return to his staircase.

I went out the way I'd come in, troubled.

I told Tony about the figure and my suspicions, since he'd been with me when we found it, but I made him a promise not to say anything to Sims or Carole aside from asking them to keep an eye out for it. He did not believe me, but he humored me, and under the circumstances I knew that was probably the best I could hope for.

I did not talk to Val about it at all.

It was nearly a year before I saw it again, lying amidst a bed full of dolls and stuffed animals in the room of a pampered little rich girl in a heartwarming comedy.

The girl died immediately after the film's premiere, supposedly a victim of an undetected congenital heart defect.

No one at that studio, from the set designer to the props men, could tell me what had happened to the figure.

A month later, three elderly stars from Hollywood's golden age who had banded together to do a TV caper about a gang of over-the-hill bank robbers died in a plane crash.

The movie had been broadcast the day before.

The doll had been in the window of a pawnshop the three thieves had comically robbed in order to obtain handguns.

Outwardly, my life continued on as normal. At least I think it did. I took jobs and performed them. I was a friend to my friends, a husband to my wife, an employer to my employees. But inside, I felt as though I were a murderer. I knew that I had caused the death of six people, six actors.

At least six.

Maybe there were others.

I had never thought of that before, and I went to the library and looked up all of the movie people, all of the actors, directors, writers, or producers who had died within the past year. Some of them, I knew, had had films released shortly before their deaths, and I went to a video store and rented those films.

I was prepared for the worst, but, to my surprise, I did not see the figure in any of the movies.

Thank God.

I began thinking about the doll more and more, trying to figure out what it was, where it had come from. I had surreptitiously kept tabs on most of the major players connected with Susan and Finch's film, but there had been no other deaths, and my theory that those two had died because they'd been *filmed* with the doll was reinforced.

My mind kept returning to that first day in the desert, and more than once I wondered what would have happened had I not seen that flash of reflected sunlight in the patch of weeds, if I had not walked into the backyard of the commune house. Most likely, the thing would still be lying half-buried in the sand. It would probably have lain there for years, perhaps decades, the desert covering it up before it was discovered by anyone.

Tony had a part in this, too, I realized. It was he who had convinced me, against my better judgment, to take the doll home. Part of this was on his head. But, ultimately, the blame rested with me. I was the boss. I could have said no, I could have made the decision not to take the figure with us.

But I had not done so.

We Find Things Old.

The name of our company seemed almost prophetic now.

Life went on. I was no longer as excited or as stimulated by my job as I had been, but I had house payments to make and car payments to make and Val was talking about starting a family, and, truth be told, I could not think of anything else that interested me at all. I kept on keeping on, as the song said, but the shine had definitely gone out of Tinseltown for me, and each time I did a studio job, I kept wondering if the people on this project would stumble across the figure some place, if the stars I met would die.

I ran into Hendricks periodically. I even worked with him on a nostalgic coming-of-age film. But we did not speak of the doll.

I finally saw it again two days ago.

On my birthday.

It was one of my presents.

At least I think it was.

Already the memory is fuzzy, the facts jumbled. Val had taken me to Musso and Frank's, where I was supposed to be surprised by a party. The place was packed with friends, acquaintances, clients, and there was a mountain of presents, both real and joke, piled high on two pushed-together tables. We mingled, drank, danced, drank, ate, and drank some more, and by the time I got around to the presents in the wee hours of the morning, I was not sure which were from whom. Nor did I care. The house photographer was recording this for posterity on 35 millimeter, one of Val's friends was videotaping it, and I was nearly through opening presents when I happened to glance next to me and saw, on top of the boxes and wrapping paper, the doll.

It looked just as I remembered it – same shiny brown face and ancient alien features, same brightly colored clown garb – and I did not realize until that moment how clearly and permanently its appearance had been etched upon my mind.

There was a flash as the photographer took my picture, and I suddenly understood that my image and *its* image were being recorded on film.

And videotape.

I leaped up and over the table, knocking down most of my presents. Everyone must have thought I'd gone crazy. I grabbed the camera from the photographer's hand and smashed it against the tabletop before throwing it onto the floor and stomping on it. I looked around for Val's friend with the camcorder, but she was obviously aware of my intentions and was already beating a hasty retreat toward the women's room. I shoved my friends aside, ran through the crowd, caught the woman just inside the lounge, and yanked the camcorder from her hands, using all of my strength to throw it on the floor. The machine was tough and didn't break, but I bent down, popped out the videocassette, and smashed it beneath the heel of my shoe.

I apologized profusely, but everyone was nervous and unsure of how to react, and several people were already making for the exit. I heard the muttered phrase "too much to drink" and the words "nose candy," but I ignored them and shrugged off Val's and Tony's worried inquires as I made my way back to the table.

The figure was still lying on top of the boxes.

"I have to go," I said. "There's something I have to do." I grabbed the thing's arm, and felt again that repulsive unnaturalness beneath the material.

"Wait," Tony said. "I don't think you're –"

Across the room, I saw Hendricks. He met my gaze and nodded grimly. He understood.

"I have to go!" I said.

Holding tightly to the figure's long thin arm, I ran out of the restaurant and jumped into my car.

I drove.

It was dawn by the time I reached the hippie house, sunrise a pink glow on the flat eastern edge of the desert. I parked, pulled a flashlight out of the glove compartment, and grabbed the doll. I had thrown it in the back seat for the trip, and more than once I had worried that it would begin moving back there, trying to get me, to strangle me from behind, but I had resisted the urge to turn around and look, and it lay now in the same position into which it had been thrown.

I hurried around the side of the house.

Though there'd obviously been wind and rain in the two intervening years, though entire drifts had grown, shrunk, or moved, the small niche in the sand where I had found the figure remained undisturbed by nature. Sand had not filled in the small hole, rain had not eroded the contours of its outline. It lay at the foot of the weed patch, vaguely humanoid in shape, a miniature grave.

Gingerly, I took the figure and, using only my fingers to hold the tip of its clown hat, dropped it into the hole. The small bells on its feet tinkled once as the figure fell perfectly into the opening, and then sand settled around the figure, covering the bottom half and the upper left side until it looked exactly the same as it had the day I found it.

I walked to the car without looking up.

I drove home to L.A.

It has been two days now, and I don't know what is going to happen to me. Susan didn't last two days. Neither did Finch. Neither did the others. I see this as a good sign.

I think the fact that I destroyed both the film and the videotape before they could be seen or shown might have saved my life. I am not sure. But I think so. I hope so.

Val still doesn't understand.

Tony does a little.

I'm not sure why I didn't torch the figure as Hendricks planned to do, or why I didn't destroy it in some other way. I was acting on instinct that night, not thinking clearly, and my instincts told me to return it to the desert, to its home. That is what I did. It felt right then, and it feels right now, and I think that perhaps all is as it should be.

We'll see.

All I can do now is wait.

And pray that no one else in the restaurant had a camera that night.

Hexenhammer

Stephen Dedman

Three years ago, I was standing in a courtroom defending myself against an accusation of child molestation.

I'd first heard about this accusation when a neighbor who'd been called as a witness warned me about it. She had been in a quandary about this, because she hadn't known me for many years, and she herself had been molested as a child. The police had questioned her, but not me or any of my family. I didn't know the details – where, when, who – and neither did she. I knew nothing about my accuser except his name and the fact that he'd tried to shatter my skull with a cricket bat. I had known for less than two months that there was going to be a trial, and had not been appointed a lawyer or advised that I had the right to one.

I see you look puzzled. Was this, perhaps, in China or Iraq? No, it was in Australia. As a horror writer, was I not poor enough to qualify for Legal Aid? No – not because the current government had gutted Legal Aid funding (which it has), but because I had not been arrested. Or charged. I was in the box as a witness – specifically, as the victim of an assault.

Four months earlier, a stranger armed with a cricket bat forced his way into my house after eleven PM, asking if I recognized him, asking my name, and incoherently accusing me of selling a friend of his something. He had previously tried the same thing at the house next door, but they had security screens and we didn't (we've since remedied this). My neighbor tried to phone and warn me, but I was online. I tried to shut the man out, but he'd placed his foot in the doorway (apparently this doesn't legally count as entering the house, something his lawyer was at pains to stress, as property crime is treated much more harshly here than assault). Fortunately, my eldest stepson Vic was staying with us, and as soon as the stranger brought the cricket bat out from behind his back and crowned me with it, Vic grabbed his skateboard and ran to my defense. I picked myself up from the floor and grabbed the other end of the bat, yelling for help, and the assailant retreated as a neighbor ran to help me. He was in time to see the license plate on the assailant's car as it sped away, so that the police were able to intercept him a few hours later. I had a bloody coxcomb, a cracked tooth, and bruised ribs, but nothing more serious; he had left part of his face on the rough surface of Vic's skateboard. Because the police found the bloodstained cricket bat buried in his back yard, his fingerprints all over my front door, and a lot of his DNA on the skateboard, he pleaded guilty. Two months later, he changed his plea and I was told I had to appear in court to testify against him. I asked the police how he could possibly claim innocence under the circumstances, and they merely told me it was his right to fight the case.

Obviously on the theory that the best defence was a good offence, my assailant's lawyer immediately became as offensive as possible, accusing me of molesting his client sixteen years before, then attacking him with the bat when he came to my home to confront me. He asked me why the forensic report contradicted my story; I couldn't explain it, but as I said, I hadn't read the report and couldn't comment on it. When he asked about details of my life sixteen years before, I denied ever having known his client or the suburb where the molestation was said to have occurred. When he asked if I'd ever owned a white Holden (the means by which his client was supposed to have identified me), I denied ever owning a car or holding a driver's license. When he claimed that his client had been unarmed when he came to my home, I denied having owned a cricket bat since leaving school. Having had almost no warning of the charges that would be leveled against me, I could not produce witnesses or evidence to confirm any of this except for the bit about the defendant being unarmed; my neighbors had clearly seen him carrying the cricket bat when he tried to enter the house next door.

Fortunately for me, when he was faced with this revelation, the defendant quickly changed his story. He *had* brought the bat. The fight *hadn't* begun with him grabbing my shirt (I wasn't wearing one, just a bathrobe), but with him swinging the bat. If I hadn't lived in the boarding house, I'd driven there. If I hadn't had a car, I'd had a motorcycle. By the end of my testimony (and I was only the first witness), even his own lawyer was finding it difficult to believe him. The magistrate found him guilty and fined him, with $1,000 to go to me as damages and the rest to pay court costs. The defendant then left the state, and the sheriff decided that there was no point in chasing up the fine, as the defendant was unlikely to ever have as much as $1,000; I could, if I wished, pursue the matter at my own expense, and have him sentenced to community service, or I could lodge a claim for victim's aid (also at great expense, with a chance of a payment one or two years later). I declined to do either, but I said would be fascinated to know why he targeted me, and that I would like an apology.

I was never charged with child molestation. The police could have established within minutes that I have never owned a car nor held a driver's license, and if they had access to old phone books, that I'd never lived anywhere near my accuser. But the prosecution didn't attempt to refute this part of the story. I was never charged, *but I was never cleared, either*.

Whether or not my accuser was molested as a child, I have no way of knowing. He came across as an habitual liar in court, but that one detail might have been true, and if so, I pity him. I hadn't been molested, but several of my friends had been (including two of the witnesses at the trial) and I know how it has traumatized them. But to be publicly accused of something so horrendous, then not be exonerated, feels like being branded. Like rumors of witchcraft or satanism in previous centuries or in the Bible Belt, Communist leanings in the McCarthyite 1950s, a fondness for trenchcoats or heavy metal music post-Columbine, or Islamist or terrorist connections post-9/11, the merest unjustified suspicion of child abuse can strike at an emotional, even a visceral level, shocking people into panic and paranoia, making reason and law seem irrelevant.

If my accuser or his lawyer had known anything about me, or done a little research, they could have strengthened a spurious case with even more circumstantial evidence. I've written about child abuse in some of my best known stories. I have several non-fiction books about witchcraft and satanism in my library, as well as shelves of books about forensic science, serial killers, and famous trials – not to mention hundreds of horror novels, thrillers, and fantasies, including complete works of Shakespeare, Poe, and (gasp) Lewis Carroll, plus a few old AD&D manuals. I don't listen to much Gothic music, but I mentioned it in *Shadows Bite*. I married a wiccan in a pagan ceremony. And, of course, I usually wear black, so I must be a villain, right? None of this would have convinced a magistrate, but it might have swayed jurors enough that someone would forget who was on trial, or that my being a horror writer doesn't give some drunk the right to try to hit my head for a six.

This is not justice. It is scapegoating, which is its antithesis – though, alas, more convenient and requiring much less intellectual effort.

I don't know enough about the West Memphis Three case to comment on the specifics, but I do know that scapegoating should not be allowed to overrule evidence, and that the right to a fair trial is as important now as it ever has been. More so now, if the death penalty is being mooted – what with John Ashcroft baying for more minorities to be executed, George W. Bush using spurious evidence to justify a war, Dick Cheney withholding real evidence to cover his ass, and genetic finger-printing revealing more and more fatal miscarriages of the machinery.

The current administration, it seems, likes Justice to have bloody hands, and her breasts decently covered.

But not in gothic black.

The Gemini, CLIVE BARKER

Pisspot Bay

Elizabeth Massie

No, of course. We don't torture people in America.
And people who make that claim just don't know
anything about our country.
– PRESIDENT GEORGE W. BUSH TO THE
AUSTRALIAN PRESS, OCTOBER 18, 2003

Andy had been caught in the sweep. It happened so fast, he first thought it was a gag, something rigged up by that doofus Stephen whose dad owned the farm, something Stephen would have thought was really funny. But it wasn't so funny when all was said and done.

The party had been going on, people were dancing, cussing, laughing in the paddock and in the hot, dusty barn with the windows and doors thrown open. The beer flowed heavy and fast as river water in spring. There were older girls there too, from the community college up the road. College girls at a high school graduation bash was, well, heaven on earth with their tight jeans and halter tops and coolers filled with exotic beers none of the Lee High School grads had ever heard of before.

Strings of lights hung around the inside of the barn, making Christmas in June. Heavy metal and rap music blared from a battery-powered boom box, competing off and on with the throw-together band in the first stall who were trying to get their amps to heat up, but having a hard time with the irregular current that powered the lights in the barn.

There were thirty-some kids, laughing and drinking and taking off to the field to smoke their pot because, while there might not have been a lot of rules they respected, everybody knew it was fucking pathetic to smoke in a barn. Stephen's dad made a living as a farmer; Stephen's dad had said, "Sure, boys, throw yourselves a party in the barn, you deserve it," so nobody was going to take advantage of that and put Stephen's dad's barn or his livelihood in danger. They were good like that.

But then around three AM came the sweep. Blue and red lights in the distance, rumbling through the darkness up the long, pocked driveway

from the main road, chasing down the barn like hounds after a rac-
coon. At first, some of the kids thought a thunderstorm was coming up,
what with the noise and the flashing lights, but before they even had
time to swallow their latest swigs, the Callington County sheriff cars had
slammed on their brakes beside the paddock, spraying grit and straw
dust and gnats, and the officers were out, guns pointing.

"What the – ?" began Stephen, but an officer shouted, "Everyone,
freeze! Don't move a muscle!" and most everyone outside in the paddock and standing just inside the open barn door froze, except for two
kids who were really drunk and fell off the fence railing they'd been trying to walk. They lay, laughing, in the dirt.

Andy was standing in the doorway between Stephen and a really
cute brown-haired college girl named Erin. They'd been sipping on
Sheepshead Stouts and talking about next year. Stephen explained how
he was going to work with his dad. Andy, feeling little pain with the help
of several bottles of stout, claimed he'd been accepted into the state university, but was thinking it might be better to work a year before taking
on another four years of school. This was a lie. Andy had okay grades,
but hadn't even applied to a college because his father was in the pen
down in Mecklenburg and his mother could barely afford to pay for the
rental house in which they lived. But Andy said it to impress Erin and
Stephen didn't contradict him. Andy was starting to think Erin liked
him – that even though he was only eighteen, that was just two years
younger than her, and what was two years, anyway – when the police
crashed the party.

Andy recognized one of the deputies. His name was Conrad Anthony and he'd graduated from Andy's high school three years earlier.
The rest of them he didn't know.

"What the hell is going on?" Andy asked, and Conrad shouted, "Shut
up, Carter! Freeze means your vocal cords too!"

Andy said nothing more. Beside him, Erin was breathing rapidly
and saying under her breath, "Oh, god, my mom's going to fucking kill
me." Andy knew they were in trouble, all of them except the twenty-one-
year-olds maybe, but then maybe them too, for contributing. Stephen
boldly clutched his beer in plain view, his jaws tight.

This was going to go down bad. They'd all get arrested, they'd get
booked. There'd be bail to pay and then fines all around and some sort
of community service. Andy's mom didn't have the money for bail, and
with his new job delivering beds and sofas for Howe's Furniture, he sure
as hell didn't have time for any goddamned community service.

Within ten minutes, all the partiers were separated from each other, standing like scarecrows in the ass-scratchy field, some swearing angrily, others mute, the lights from the cruisers trained on them like spotlighted off-season deer. Each partier was questioned individually, voices kept low so no one else could hear the conversations. Andy shivered in the hot Virginia breeze. He'd never been questioned by police before. What was he supposed to say, or not say? Would they have to read him his rights to talk to him? Was he supposed to admit to Erin providing booze, or should he lie to keep her out of trouble? And what if she admitted to buying it and he was caught in a lie? His heart pounded crazily; it felt like there were spiders on his neck. A gnat flew up his nose and he sneezed and spat, trying to get it out.

Then it was his turn. Two of the deputies, men he did not know, strolled up to him. Their faces were shadowed, but he knew they weren't smiling.

"Hey," said Andy. "What's up, man? Somebody steal a cow or kill a goat? Kiddin'. What's got you so –"

Without a word, cuffs were slapped roughly onto Andy's wrists and he was thrown into the back of a cruiser. As two officers climbed into the front of the car and closed their doors, the one in the passenger's seat glared back at Andy and through the bulletproof glass said, "You have the right to remain silent, you have the right to have an attorney present during questioning. . . ."

The sheriff's department was a fifteen-mile drive from Stephen's farm and in the center of Greeneville, the biggest town and the county seat. Andy didn't know if he was the only one arrested, or just the first.

He sat in a small side room on the second floor. There were three rusty old chairs, a small table, a couple of fading, curling posters on the wall showing sites around "Beautiful, Bountiful Virginia," a footed radiator, and a single window that faced out to a narrow alley and the brick side of Nation's Bank across the alley. It was morning, a bright and sunny day as far as Andy could tell. He had been in that little room for a couple hours. The two deputies who had arrested him had talked to him off and on, and he knew why he was there.

They said he'd planted a bomb.

Someone had called from Stephen's house during the party, and said they'd heard Andy bragging that he'd planted a bomb in the middle of town, a bomb set to go off at 6:52 PM the following day to commemorate the anniversary of the date and time when Andy's father had been found guilty of murder five years earlier. The caller had said that Andy knew his father was guilty of the killing, but it was self-defense, and that Andy was enraged because his father was treated like shit throughout the trial and then even worse down in Mecklenburg's super max prison. Andy wanted somebody to suffer the way his father was suffering.

The initial questioning had been relaxed, almost friendly. When Andy heard the charges, he laughed incredulously and said he'd never done such a thing and couldn't guess who would want to get him in trouble like that. Inside, his guts twitched like a hooked fish on a lake bank and his mind spun with the booze he'd drunk, but he managed to keep himself calm on the outside.

Who the hell would say something like that about him? he wanted to know. Who hated him that much? Or who was insane enough to play that kind of fucked-up prank? The deputies didn't know, and they smiled along with him.

Andy swore his innocence. The two deputies listened and nodded. They asked him if he wanted a Coke and he said no, though his mouth was dry. Conrad came in for a few minutes and they backed and forthed about ol' Lee High, then Conrad left. It was hot in the room, and Andy asked if they could open the window, but they said no, it wasn't that hot. They said Andy probably was feeling it more since he was still intoxicated. They said if they opened the window, flies would come in, and flies irritated the sheriff almost as much as criminals.

The deputies asked Andy about his home life. Andy didn't want to talk about it, but he did, because he wanted to make them happy, make them like him, make them know he wasn't his father's son, really, he was a nice guy. He told the officers his mother worked at the Dollar General, cashiering, doing inventory, that kind of thing. His younger brother was in middle school, a goofy little kid who liked band better than football. His family had gone bankrupt a couple years back when Andy's father went to prison, but otherwise was doing okay. No, Andy didn't hate anybody and nobody that he knew of hated him. What did Andy think of those bombings he'd seen on TV, over in the Middle East? Andy said they were stupid. What did Andy think of the bombing in Oklahoma City, the planes crashing into the Twin Towers and the Pentagon? Andy said they were stupid too.

Andy thought about asking for a lawyer, but he watched TV and knew how once you asked for a lawyer, they thought you were guilty. He didn't want to get booked and get thrown into a cell. It would all be cleared up real soon, so he would hang tight. Soon, whoever had made the call would confess his prank.

The deputies offered Andy something to eat and he said no. Then they said they would wait to talk to him more after he'd sobered up. Andy guessed that made sense, so he leaned back in the chair and closed his eyes, hoping it wouldn't take long. The world spun and he felt like throwing up, so he opened his eyes again.

Now, for the first time since being brought to the station, he was alone. Well, he didn't really think he was totally alone. There was a two-way mirror on the wall. He knew that someone was always watching from behind that glass. Waiting for him to pick his nose or scratch his ass or try to hang himself with his shoestrings or something.

The sun was up and it was damned hot in the room. The radiator hissed softly as if it had been turned on. Andy wiped sweat from his forehead and wished he'd gone for that Coke. When they came back, he'd ask them for one and then asked when he would get to go home. By now, certainly, the truth had come out. Any minute now, they'd come and say go home. It was a joke, a hideous joke, and if he found out who did it he'd beat the shit out of him. Andy didn't know explosives from a hole in the roof. Well, he blew up some toy trucks and soldiers with leftover Fourth of July fireworks back when he was thirteen. That was fun. But it wasn't a bomb.

There was no clock on the wall and Andy didn't have a watch. He wondered what time it was. His back hurt from the chair. Wasn't he allowed a phone call? His head was clearing, and he knew he was supposed to be able to call somebody. He'd call his mom. What would he tell her?

A janitor came into the room, an old man with a blue jump suit and squinty eyes. He said they needed the chairs in the other room, and told Andy to stand up. Andy did, and the janitor stacked the three chairs and took them out. Andy called after him, "I think that radiator's busted, it's pouring hot air," but the janitor didn't say any more, and he shut the door behind him. Andy stood by the wall, and then sat on the table. He wiped the sweat from his brow and forearms.

Conrad came in about a half hour later with Sheriff Bateman. Bateman crossed his arms and said, "Don't sit on the table, son."

Andy stood up. He thought about sitting on the floor, but guessed that might be a bad idea, as unhappy as the sheriff looked.

Bateman said, "Well, the bomb isn't in our building, and it isn't in the courthouse."

"That's good," said Andy.

"I wonder where it is."

"I'm really tired," said Andy. "It's awful hot in here. I got to go home before my mother thinks somebody killed me or something."

Bateman looked at Conrad, then at Andy. He said, "Where's the bomb? We don't have time to mess with you. We need to know. You tell us, it'll go easier, you know it will."

"What?" Andy asked.

"You don't want to hurt anybody. We don't want anybody to get hurt. Let's work together. We know you're upset about your dad, but come clean and it'll go easier."

"What?"

"Talk now, Andy. We can get the state police in here, or the FBI if we have to, and we will, believe me. You know how much harder they'll be on you? Now, where's the bomb?"

"There isn't a bomb!"

"We think there is."

"Well, then somebody else did it, not me."

"You got motive, Andy. We trust the caller. We believe he told us the truth."

"I didn't plant a bomb. I don't know anything about bombs."

"Where is it, Andy?"

"I didn't plant a bomb!"

"We found bomb-making materials in your shed at home."

"You did not!"

Bateman nodded.

Did the sheriff find bomb-making stuff? What's bomb-making stuff? Andy said, "What did you find?"

"You know very well what we found."

What did they find? Some kind of fertilizer or something? Do we have that at home? Mom raises vegetables in the summer. Is that the fertilizer they found? Are they lying? Police are allowed to lie, I know that. Are they lying?

"I want a lawyer," Andy said. He didn't mean to say it, but it came out anyway. He was no longer holding it together on the outside. His hands were shaking madly and his shoulders jumped with every word.

"Hmm. Okay." The sheriff went quiet for a moment, staring out the window. On his forehead, Andy could see sweat beads gathering then rolling. "We'll do that. You got a name? A lawyer?"

"No," said Andy. "I need one, though. I can't afford one."

"Okay. I'll put in a call to the public defender. Might be a while."

"How long?"

Bateman shrugged. "Just hold tight there, Andy."

"I need to call my mom."

Bateman said, "All our lines are busy right now, but as soon as one opens up we'll put you through. That okay with you? Got any problems with that?"

"Yes," said Andy. "I mean, no."

Then Bateman came right up to him, nose to sweaty nose, and said calmly, "You admire those terrorists, Andy? You like their power, the way they teach the world a lesson, don't you?" Spit flew from the sheriff's mouth onto Andy's face, but Andy didn't flinch. "You want to be just like them, to kill people when you don't like something. Following in your daddy's footsteps, huh, but you're going to take it a lot further than he did, huh?"

"What? No!" said Andy. He knew the sheriff wasn't supposed to ask him anything else since he requested a lawyer. But then the sheriff said, "Just rhetorical, Andy. I'm not asking you anything. I know you can't answer me now, now you begged for a lawyer. Fuckin' redneck terrorist."

Bateman glared at Andy, then turned to Conrad. "Here's your little schoolmate, trying to kill people in town 'cause his murderin' daddy doesn't get cable TV down the prison."

Andy saw that Conrad was unsure of what to do or say. Conrad and Andy were on the basketball team together one year. He wondered if Conrad believed the lie.

"If this bastard's your friend," Bateman told Conrad, "then warn him that the FBI's been called. They're on their way. It won't be pretty, lawyer or not. This isn't some purse-snatching or B&E. This is a whole 'nother ball game. We're livin' in a whole different world from a couple years ago. And we don't have time to pussyfoot around threats like the one he's made."

Bateman stormed out and slammed the door.

Andy said, "Con, I didn't do anything! You know me!"

"Phone call said you did, Andy. Said you were high by the time you got to the party, stoned on something. Said you were all riled about your mom being treated like shit because of your dad being in prison."

"She *is* treated like shit," said Andy. "Me too sometimes, and my little brother. But that doesn't mean I'd –"

"Were you high when you got to the party? Just between you and me, I ain't asking as a deputy, okay?"

"Well," said Andy. He'd smoked pot before going to Stephen's farm, half a joint. When he got to the farm at seven, Stephen and a couple other guys were snorting in one of the stalls and offered Andy some. Andy thought about it; fuck, it was a graduation party and time to celebrate. Did he snort? Maybe he did and didn't remember. No, he remembered not going for it. "No, I wasn't high. Well, maybe a little, but I knew what I was doing."

"Then you started drinking," said Conrad.

"Some."

"You remember everything you did before the officers got there?"

"Sure."

"You didn't pass out early in the night, then get woken up around eleven and rejoin the party?"

Did I? "Fuck, Conrad, it's killer hot in here. Can we talk somewhere else? I been in here hours. I feel sick."

"No."

"I don't remember if I passed out."

"Then you might not remember what you said, Andy. People do all sorts of stuff when they're drunk, then they pass out and forget what they did. Some guys even married girls before when they were drunk, then afterwards swore they never saw the woman in their whole life."

Did I? Did I get drunk and make some fucking threat about bombing a building in town?

"Who called? Who said I made the threat?"

"Can't tell you."

"Why not?"

"It's confidential. What if you found out who told us, got mad, and threatened to kill him, too?"

"I don't kill people!"

A pager on Conrad's hip beeped. He said, "Got to go. Think about it, Andy. It'll go easier if you just own up."

Conrad left the room. Andy paced back and forth. The heat was almost unbearable, and his legs threatened to give way beneath him. Blackness gnawed at the edge of his vision. His stomach cramped viciously. He pounded on the door. "Let me out! I'm sick! I'm going to faint!"

No one responded. He dropped down and tried to breathe cooler air through the space beneath the door. He shouted from the floor, "Help me, I'm sick!"

A moment later, the door was thrown open, whacking Andy in the head and splitting the skin of his scalp. He clutched the door and pulled himself slowly to his feet, warm blood trickling toward his cheek. A deputy he didn't know scowled at him. "I don't feel good," Andy said.

"I'll show you the bathroom," the deputy said.

Already, the cooler air coming in from the hallway started to ease his dizziness. "Is my lawyer here?"

"Not yet."

"And I got a call to make."

"All the phones are still busy."

"No pay phones anywhere?"

"The phones are busy."

The bathroom was in the basement. Andy guessed there were nicer ones for the officers and visitors to the department, but this one was down near the holding cells at the back of the building. There were no windows at all in the stinky room, just a vent near the ceiling. One stall housed a john; two hard water-stained urinals clutched the cinderblock walls. The floor was wet and warped. But it wasn't hot, for which Andy was grateful.

The deputy who'd taken him to the restroom didn't go in with him. Andy thought that odd, but maybe hopeful. Maybe they were really starting to doubt his guilt and so didn't think he needed a babysitter. *How would I escape from here, anyway?* he thought, looking around. *Crawl through the toilet?* He finished taking a whiz, zipped up, then sipped water from the faucet. He felt better, though not good. His stomach still hurt like hell.

The door opened and a large man came in. He was an inmate, one Andy had seen in a holding cell as he'd walked past. The man was dark-skinned but white, with several loose hairs on his head and a nose that looked like it had been broken several times. He smelled like old beer and shit. He leaned back against the door. "Hey, fella," he said.

Andy's heart kicked. "I'm through in here. Let me out and you can have the place to yourself, okay?"

"You sure is nothin'," chuckled the big man. "Big mouth, little man, huh?"

"Just move over and I'll get out of your way."

"Welcome to Pisspot Bay," said the man. "Like it in here?"

Oh shit, what's this?

"You ever watch the news?" asked the man. He scratched his neck, leaving long red lines on the skin with his irregular, chipped nails. "They got suspects down Guantanamo Bay and over in Afghanistan, some of those Arab fucks who threaten America, threaten to bomb us and shit. Know about them?"

"I guess."

"Those terrorists don't want to talk, you don't want to talk."

"Let me out of here."

"But you got to," said the man. "Welcome to Pisspot Bay, our own little detention center, boy. And you are going to talk. We ain't gonna let you get away with hurting other people. We gotta get to the truth. I ain't gonna do nothing they ain't doin' for national security. Call it 'stress and duress.' So suck it up or give it up."

Andy screamed at the top of his lungs, "Get me out of here! Somebody get me out!"

He knew they heard him, beyond that stinking bathroom. But no one came to the door.

⚬

"That's all I wanted," said the big man. "Just that, no big deal, right? Now, say it one more time." He patted Andy on the head.

"I . . . planted a bomb. . . ."

"And where is it?"

"It's in the school . . . Lee High School. . . ."

Andy remembered planting the bomb. Not clearly, but as in a hazy dream. He made it in his shed at home, and hid it in the gymnasium where he used to play basketball on the varsity team. He didn't recall how he made the bomb, or actually taking it to the school, but that wasn't the important thing. He was angry that his father was treated like crap and so was the rest of his family. He wanted to get back at the community so he made a bomb. He had confessed. Things would be better for him now, the big man promised.

The man helped Andy to his feet, but his legs would not lock beneath him. He'd been forced to crouch beside the urinals for hours, with his hands bound behind his back. His legs and feet were asleep. The man had also put wet towels over Andy's face time and time again. "This doesn't really hurt you," the man had explained. "It will just help you remember." Andy couldn't breathe when this happened, and he gagged and thrashed behind the wet cloth. He felt close to passing out several times, and threw up twice. The man only laughed and said, "Just cleanin' out the gunk is all. You'll be fine once you fess up."

Andy held on to the big man as the feeling drained back into his legs. And then he whimpered, then cried. With the return of blood came searing, knife-like pains sawing into the muscles of his thighs and calves.

"Oh, shut up," said the man, almost affectionately. "You'll be fine in a while."

The man opened the bathroom door and led Andy, hobbling, into the basement hallway. The deputy who had brought him down was sitting in a folding chair not five feet from the bathroom door, chatting with a jail guard and chewing gum.

Andy didn't ask why he'd ignored the screams in the bathroom. It didn't really matter now, did it? He was a criminal; he'd done a terrible thing. Now they could take care of the terrible thing and no one would get hurt. The deputy helped Andy down the hall and up the steps as the big man was given some cigarettes and chocolate from the guard and put back inside his cell.

Andy blinked in the bright afternoon light that poured through the glass in the front door. He was told to sit on one of the benches by the front desk, and he did so, gratefully. Did he still get a phone call? Had the lawyer arrived? He would tell them whatever they needed to know. He would not go back to Pisspot Bay.

An hour passed, an hour and a half, and then Conrad Anthony came to see him in the hallway. "Your lawyer's here, Andy. Let's talk." Andy was ushered into the interrogation room where he'd first been brought so many hours ago. The radiator was off. The window was open and fresh air coursed through, smelling of a small-town summer. The chairs were back in the room. Andy dropped into one of them and put his hands in his hair.

Across the table sat a man with bushy gray hair. He said, "Son, my name is George Parker. I'm your attorney."

"I did it," whispered Andy. "Find it and get rid of it. It's in the gym at school."

Parker's face clouded. "You are confessing? We haven't even talked yet."

Andy wiped dried tears from his face, feeling as though new ones were very close behind. "Yeah. Find it. Get it out. I never wanted to hurt anyone, really. Do I get it better, for telling the truth? Please? Please?"

There was no bomb in Lee High School's gymnasium, or anywhere else. The bomb squad and their sniffing dogs searched every inch of the school, as well as the buildings surrounding it. There was nothing.

The boy who had called the sheriff's department admitted early in the afternoon to lying to get Andy in trouble. He said he didn't know it would go that far, but that Andy was a pompous son-of-a-bitch who should know his place, what with a killer father and all. "Andy needed to come down a peg," the boy said. The boy would be fined for a false report, but he could afford it; his father owned the Ford dealership in Greeneville.

Andy's mother came to pick him up at six-fifteen that evening, furious that he hadn't called and relieved that he was all right. At home, there was a letter from his father waiting, a cold Coke, and a Hostess cherry pie his mother had brought Andy from the store.

Action, and the Fear of Going It Alone

Jenn Onofrio

"Do you worship the devil?"

"Yup."

"How'd you get into that?"

"My mom." That was me almost ten years ago. Sarcastic, annoyed, and misunderstood. I never tried to let anyone in on my adolescent confusion – I just confused people even more instead.

When you ask people why they defend Damien, Jason, and Jessie's innocence, you hear stories of compassion. We feel like what happened to the Three could have happened to any of us, given the wrong circumstances. Their story resonates with us. It reassures us that what we were going through or are still going through today isn't so lonely. There are other people like us out there.

When I first heard about the West Memphis Three, I was shocked. It felt personal – I felt like what happened to them was about me, about the person I used to be and the person I am today as a result of all the alienation of being an outcast. Naturally, I wanted to do something. My friend Paul Rhyand and I decided to write a play, *Walking Shadows*, aiming to inform as many people as possible about the injustice that was happening in Arkansas. A few months went by, though, and I felt sick with myself because I didn't feel like our play was doing enough. I wanted more – I wanted to call someone, talk to someone – someone who could do something. I wanted to know that in five years I could look back on these times and know for sure I'd done all that I could do in this obscene struggle. But where do you begin? In school and in life you're taught that we're surrounded by great injustice; no one takes the time to teach you how to go about changing it.

In January of 2004, Paul and I became a letter-writing team with the support of Damien, Jason, and Jessie. I used to think we were just actors and playwrights – people who told stories solely through their art. It wasn't long before I became a juggler of letters and not the writer I was before. I was still using my words to speak to an audience, but now the audience was a southern politician, seemingly set in his ways.

We appealed to the Governor of Arkansas, Mike Huckabee, with the hope of spelling out the evidence of reasonable doubt that to us and so many others seemed painfully clear. We wrote annotated letters weekly, copying them to his policy advisors, the Parole Board, and members of the media. It all grew from a need to do more. After Paul and I wrote, I felt accomplished – good – because I knew that even if Mike Huckabee threw away the weekly letters as they came, the topic of the West Memphis Three undoubtedly preyed on him for at least a minute of his day.

Embarking on this campaign proved to be the ultimate test in patience. It wasn't long before I was brimming with frustration and confusion. Those same feelings I'd developed against authority as a teen crept into the way I felt about most of my peers. Why didn't everyone know who the West Memphis Three were? Why wasn't *everyone* speaking out? *We live in a land blessed with freedom and choice! We have the right to free speech, the right to bear arms, the right to assemble, the right to a fair trial! We're given these things as Americans – they're handed to us when we're children, before we've had to do a single thing to earn them!* These are the things that were pounded into our heads in our youth. Are they wrong? Does everything they tell you from the start turn out to not be true?

"Collective fear stimulates herd instinct, and tends to produce ferocity toward those who are not regarded as members of the herd." Bertrand Russell said this and it makes me shake my head in dismay at its truth. This case is proof of that statement. But if we're all supposed to be afraid, I'm not a member of the herd. Damien Echols, Jason Baldwin, and Jessie Misskelley weren't either – and they're paying the price for being "different." They're paying the price for standing alone in the fear-filled face of adversity.

I know there are so many more of us out there. I know that as I write this, there are other people writing things too. They're also singing songs for justice, making paintings, emailing the Governor of Arkansas. I know there are people who believe that our government is tainted, that our politicians don't represent us. But what truly gives me hope and makes me push on is the knowledge that there are even *more* people who want to speak up and shout out – undoubtedly, enough of us to go off and create our own "herd." The key is, we can't let ourselves be afraid.

I hear the clichés all the time about how we're not alone, and I usually roll my eyes and laugh. But the truth is, someone else *is* feeling exactly the way I am – many people are. No matter how hopeless I sometimes feel in this fight, there are hundreds if not thousands of others out there feeling the same way. So if this other community exists – this community of free-thinking, right-deserving, protesting peoples – isn't it time we come together? We have the choice to exert control over a situation that has gotten out of hand. It could be the idealist in me talking, but I do believe all it really takes is a free voice.

As I prepare to write to the Governor yet again, I'm plagued with the usual burden of doubt in figuring out what I'm doing. Does this man even care what I'm saying? Am I going about this in the wrong way? What gives me the right to stand up on the Three's behalf? I can only come back around to the idea that *none of that matters*. It doesn't matter how I feel about the consequences of what I'm doing – it only matters that I'm doing it.

The reality of the situation is that the Governor is just one man. He's a normal person with a wife and a family and a job, just like most everyone else. There's no reason to fear him as if he has some sort of superiority. He is an elected official, elected to represent his populace. His voice is supposed to speak as the collective voice of a people. Though these days our politicians seem out of reach, it's our privilege and responsibility to let them know what we think. A democracy is not a democracy unless you use it.

"Never doubt that a small group of thoughtful, committed citizens can change the world. Indeed, it is the only thing that ever has." I think Margaret Mead was right when she said that. We just have to believe in ourselves. We have to believe that no person, be it an activist, or the Governor of Arkansas, or an average Joe or Janet, wants to see an innocent person face execution. We have to believe that with time and patience, we can band together to free the West Memphis Three.

And until that happens, Paul and I will be writing letters to the Governor. Over, and over, and over again.

You Have to Know This

Simon Logan

"I have to say this to you. You have to know this."

I whisper to her as she sleeps and she stirs at my words.

She lies upon the sweat-soaked sheets, a fractured sculpture touched by the neon glow of the clubs across the street, which staggers in through the bedroom window. Her head seems permanently sunken into the pillow that supports her and her eyes flutter lazily.

"Where have you been? Your shift finished hours ago. . . ." Blurry. Disoriented.

"I know, I'm sorry. I had some things to clear up."

She moves across the bed, closer to me. "I can't stand it in here any more, Alex. I can't stand being stuck in this fucking bed. Will you take me out later? Just for a while?"

I glance at the old wheelchair lying by the door, its broken seat-belts spilling onto the floor. She hates this thing as much as she hates the bed.

"Maybe later," I say.

Her head drops a little because she knows what this means. "I miss walking with you," she says. "That's all I want. Just to walk with you."

"I know. I miss it too."

An uneasy silence falls and she touches my chin with one finger, turns my head to face her warm, brown eyes. "What's wrong, Alex? You're hiding something from me."

I take another breath because I don't want to be here, I don't want to be doing this. And I have to be here. And I have to be doing this.

"You're tired," I say and begin to stand. "I should leave you to rest. . . ."

"*No*," she says, touches my hand. "I've been *resting* for longer than I can remember. I thought we had no secrets. We promised each other that we wouldn't bury anything. So stay. Tell me."

I take off my body armor, gloves, equipment belt, and shoulder holster, reducing myself to a plain black t-shirt, combat trousers, and steel-toe-capped boots. This is me now, not my job.

"We found a body," I say, and in that moment I realize that this is how all my stories start. Each time I have sat with her and told about my day it has started *we found a body*. "A woman."

I help her adjust her position slightly, keeping her fluids moving, her body functioning. "Do you know who did it?"

"We have seven people in custody," I say. "They were formally charged yesterday."

"Seven?"

I tell her, "The seventh man, the main suspect, is called Mijatovic. Pedrag Mijatovic. He's a hemophiliac."

The coffee has been stewing in the pot for eight hours and it moves like blood on my tongue.

"I don't understand," I tell him.

"It means that he lacks a protein that clots his blood and so he needs regular transfusions. Women carry the disease, but only men are affected by it."

"I meant why are you telling me this?"

We are in his office and he has pulled his blinds shut so that we are hidden from the rest of the squad room, but there is still a gap in one corner. There are two others in here with the Lieutenant and me – Mosby from tactical and the plain-clothed Soutar.

"Sit down, Alex," he says to me. He catches me glancing awkwardly at the two seated behind me. "Relax."

"What's going on?"

"Look, we both have a problem that needs to be solved. We've managed to keep the circumstances of Mia's death quiet so far, but if we're going to put some solid cover in place then we're going to need to move now to do something about it."

He shoves the suspension file across the desk towards me and I reach out for it with my damaged hand. Inside is the usual collection of reports, photographs, and other paperwork that I am all too familiar with.

"Mijatovic is at the center of this . . . this . . . I don't know what the fuck you'd call it. . . ."

"Cult," Soutar chips in.

"Center of this cult," Lieutenant Brusnika finishes. "They're into some weird-ass shit: blood fetish stuff. Swapping blood, bottling it, drinking it too, probably. Cutting each other up, for Christ's sake."

I leaf through the paperwork and feel myself drifting. It is as if the words and images are disturbed as I expose them and they flutter up around my head and eyes. I haven't slept for four days.

Days. Days.

The word doesn't sound right.

"Now listen to me, Alex. We've never actually caught them *doing* anything, but you know how it is, right? People like this, you *know* they must be up to something – it's gut instinct."

"What do you suspect them of?"

The question seems to catch the lieutenant off guard. He takes another sip of the globulous coffee. "*Suspect* them of? We *suspect* them of being fucking freaks, that's what we *suspect* them of. These are the sort of people that corrupt this city, Alex. The sooner they're off the streets the better for good folk like you and me." He adds, "And Mia," and it stings like a rubber bullet slamming into my flak jacket.

"Soutar and Mosby have already worked everything out; we know what needs to be done. We just need your word that you are in on this with us."

My attention is distracted by a group of Mohawk-punks that I can see through the gap in the blinds. Their hands are cuffed behind their backs, their faces bloodied. "With you on what?"

"It would do nobody any good if people knew what happened to Mia. We know how much she must have meant to you, but she was one of us too, remember. She deserved better. This way at least her death will not have been in vain. She wanted this city to be clean and safe as much as any of us in this room."

"I can't . . . this . . . this is going too far."

"It's already gone too far, Alex," Brusnika breathed across the table at me. "It's too late to turn back."

I trace the edge of the metal cuff that runs around my left wrist, that fuses the long-ago fractured bones together.

"What do you want me to do?"

She looks at me in a serious and distant way. Her pill bottles are scattered across the bedside table like bomb fragments.

"I don't understand; why would you agree to that?" she asks me.

"Because I felt that what Brusnika was saying made sense. She *didn't* deserve to die in the way she did."

"Brusnika is a corrupt motherfucker, Alex. Don't you trust a damn word he says."

I squeeze her cold hand in some vague effort at reassurance. "I know. But the victim, she was in the force up until a few years ago. She was a good officer, a good person," I tell her. "But then she got injured and after that she got sick."

"What do you mean, sick?"

"Drugs," I say, and the word is like a rock hitting a riot shield.

"She was a junkie?"

"Don't say it like that," I snap. "She wasn't a *junkie*."

"A drug addict," she corrects herself.

"Everyone has their own way of dealing with the job – some are better than others."

"Sounds to me like she wasn't trying to deal with it at all," she sneers.

"*No*. I tried to help her, especially after she got suspended. I got her shifted up the waiting list and into some programs, but they never worked. She just couldn't handle it. I ended up stealing from the narcotics lock-up because at least that way she was off the streets and getting gear that I knew would be safe. Brusnika knew about it."

"But you were risking your job," she says.

"Yes."

"And you did this for her despite that?"

I nod. "And more."

So I stand in the place where she died and it is the sort of place where nobody's life should even touch, never mind end.

It is one of the many squats that have infected the buildings that once housed the fishermen who worked down by the bay, nothing more than a crumbling shell littered with human debris. Strips of crime scene tape are still attached to the door. An old fireplace has caved in, but the frame remains and I lean upon it, staring out the grubby eight-foot window onto the docks below.

In the water I see the small boats that the radio pirates use to broadcast from.

This is where she overdosed. This is what her life came to.

The scene is so vacant, so empty – but Brusnika has given me everything that I will need to change this.

I have some photocopied pages covered in symbols and messages, candles, red spray paint, and a bag of fleshy scraps from a slaughterhouse floor or a butcher's garbage bin. I have some plastic sheeting that is wrapped around a dark bulk.

I set about my task, faltering at first, unsure of how I will go about making it look convincing. I place the photocopies on the fire surround, set up my flashlight to give me some more light, and spray some of the patterns and symbols on the ground at my feet. The paint is a deliberately dark red.

I daub messages on the walls across the graffiti that is already there and across torn posters advertising pirate radio stations.

I light the candles and place them in alignment with the intersections of the floor markings.

I scatter the pieces of meaty trash amongst the scene and then unwrap the torso from the plastic sheet and dump that too.

"What do you mean, a torso? Whose torso?"

"It's a fake, a model, but it looks realistic enough – at least in crime scene photographs. The Medical Examiner's office uses it to train students. The ME owed Brusnika a favor for helping him out with a botched autopsy a few months back and let us take it no questions asked. I got the impression it wasn't the first time."

She flinches in pain and sits up suddenly and I catch her halfway, one hand in her lap and the other at the back of her neck. She goes rigid for a few moments, then softens again. As she lies back I see that her lips have lost all color, her pupils have dilated. I press two painkillers into her mouth and she swallows them with a sip of stale water.

"I'm okay," she says, then to distract me, "You were faking the crime scene."

"I took the pictures back to Brusnika's office. Mosby was already there. He'd pulled a few strings at the lab and was waiting for the results to come back, though of course we already knew what they'd say – that blood splatters at the scene matched Mijatovic's or the DNA found under the corpse's fingernails matched. I never knew specifically what was going on, just what I was told. I think Brusnika was the only one who knew everything."

When she speaks, her voice is frayed and dry like an old electrical cable. "But you *did* know that Mijatovic and his group were innocent. You knew that they would be punished for something they hadn't done."

And I look at her, right at her, and I feel as if pieces of myself are being picked away as I tell her this. "To be honest, I hadn't really thought about it. At least not until the first time I saw him."

As I walk along the long, narrow corridor that leads to the interview rooms, I realize for the first time the ingenuity of the design. The walls and ceiling draw in so slightly that it isn't even noticeable to the naked eye, but as I walk on I get the distinct feeling that everything is closing in around me. I think it is because this is the first time I have walked the corridor feeling more like the accused than the accuser.

I enter room 23B and Mosby and Soutar are waiting. Seated before them is the man I recognize from the Lieutenant's photographs. His shaven head hangs low and I can tell from his posture that he has been drugged. I notice the red ligature marks on his neck that will be hidden by the collar of a prison shirt when he is issued one.

This is before we'd gotten the lab results back.

There is a document, three pages long, on the desk.

"You're late, officer," Soutar says. He smiles and three of his front teeth shine more than they should – metal replacements. "And you've missed the show. Mijatovic has already confessed."

"Watch him for a few minutes," Mosby tells me as they pick up the document from the desk and put their suit jackets back on. "We're going to run this by Lieutenant Brusnika, then get him into the cells."

They leave and I turn to the mirror on the wall behind me, staring through my own reflection to Brusnika, whom I can sense behind the one-way glass. He lingers in that darkened room like one of the malevolent deities described in the photocopied sheets he gave me a few days before, moving his hands, moving events and reality as if they were components of a great machine.

I sit beside Mijatovic and he lifts his head for the first time so that I can get a better look at him. His features are pale and drawn as if they are collapsing into his skull, and I can see a litter of white keloids on his lower arms.

When he looks at me, his eyes are dark and full of whatever chemicals they have fed him.

"Are you here to cut me?" he asks, his words blurring.

"Cut you?"

"They said they'd cut me if I didn't stick to the confession. Just two or three little cuts, they said – but in the right places. They know what it would do to me. They said they'd let me bleed to death and nobody would ever think anything of it."

"I'm not here to cut you," I tell him.

"Alex, you were sitting next to a man that you were condemning to death."

"I know, I know. I looked at him and I understood that he could die because of what we were doing. I was so *close* to him. I wanted to tell him that I was sorry, that I hadn't meant for this to happen. . . ."

"But you didn't," she says flatly.

"No."

And her next question doesn't even need to be uttered – it is conducted through each fine muscle movement of her pale features.

"Because I wasn't sure if I meant it," I say.

There is a moment of silence between us and I think perhaps I am looking for some reassurance from her – that I was confused or misguided and that it wasn't my fault – but she says nothing.

"He was just a man," I tell her. "A sick man who needed near-constant medical treatment for a disease he was born with through no fault of his own. But instead of becoming a victim to that illness, he took control of it. He turned it from the thing that made him an outsider into the thing that made him the focal point of a group who just wanted to do something that was a little different, a little unusual, that was all. Everyone in his group were willing participants. He never hurt anybody. And I could see this as I looked at him then."

"This isn't *you*, Alex. This isn't what you are about. You have to stop this. You have to tell someone."

The light outside is dying now, the sky blackens and burns.

"I don't know who I would tell – I don't know how far this goes. Brusnika. Mosby and his tactical department. The Medical Examiner and his staff. The labs. And now probably the legal teams will take over where we all left off. This has already gone beyond me. It has nothing to do with Mia's death, never has. They've been waiting to get Mijatovic and his group for months and now they have the perfect frame. They're not going to let me get in the way."

Her breathing has become labored and so I tell her to lie down. I adjust her pillow and pull the blankets up. Her breath mists in the air between us.

"You need to get some rest," I tell her.

"I need to get out of this fucking *bed*," she says, her anger directed inwards. "So what's Brusnika pushing for?" she asks me quickly, moving the conversation away from herself once more.

"He wants life imprisonment for all group members."

"And if that's what he wants, then that's what he will get," she says coldly. "What about Mijatovic?"

My head hangs on my neck like a punctured lung. I want to press it to her chest, to curl up with her beneath the sheets and fall into something darker.

"Brusnika will settle for nothing less than the death penalty," I say.

From the streets outside I hear the trampling of feet as the workers from the nearby assembly plants finish one shift and the sirens signal the start of the next.

"Is this really what you want?" she asks me.

"I don't know," I confess.

She takes my hand and it fills me with emotion.

"And what about me, Alex?" she says. "Do you think I would have wanted all this to be taking place in my name? Would I have wanted this man to die on my behalf?"

"I don't know, Mia, I don't know."

And I've said her name, I've said her name.

"You could stop this now if you really wanted to," Mia says.

I press my eyes together and when I open them again, she is gone.

"Mia?"

To the cold air, to nothing.

I lean across the medicinal litter and try to feel her hand within mine as I squeeze, but it's no use.

"I just want you back," I try to say, but I'm not sure if the words come out.

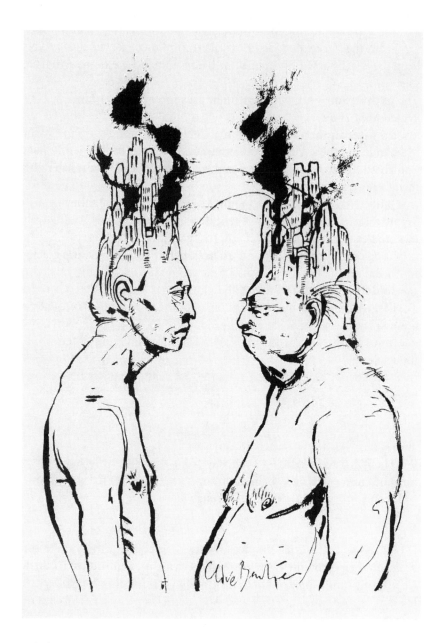

Minds at War, CLIVE BARKER

The Three Strangers

Gerard Houarner

The natives were long gone, but their graves were still around. No one visited them, or even knew exactly where they were. That's why no one saw the three strangers dressed in black climb out of the earth under the pines on a weathered hilltop on a moonless summer night.

They weren't native. Skin as pale as the moon, they might have been mistaken for people of European descent. Except for the glow. They were true children of the moon, rising in the absence of the one they favored as if to take its place in the next generation of night bodies. And like the moon, they had a dark side.

The three strangers turned their backs on the wilderness and headed for the lights of a town in the near valley. Light drawn to light. Darkness repelled the blackness of night, the glitter of stars that shined but did not illuminate.

The owls saw. And the raccoons. Ants abandoned their nests, spiders their webs. Brush withered at their heels, and leaves brightened into their fall colors with a touch of the shoulder. A bobcat slunk away at their approach. The wood rat it had killed came back to life and skittered away.

The three strangers weren't quite right, but thought they were. They headed for town where, some said, things weren't quite right but didn't always look it, and no one cared, anyway.

Having traveled such a long way from the place where they were born but never welcomed, all the strangers in black wanted was to come home. It seemed to them that they finally had.

"Look, as far as I'm concerned, the black man's been getting a free ride ever since we brought him over from Africa and introduced him to Christianity and a pair of pants," said Willard, pounding his empty coffee cup on the table for emphasis. The impact sent ripples through his chins.

Broker laughed and shook his head as he looked up from the paper. He'd finished his breakfast already and really should have been heading to the station, but the radio at his belt was quiet and it was Wednesday morning in Beaumont and things were just about the same as any other morning of the week, so there wasn't much call to hurry in. His deputy, Ty, had the early rounds today, and his sister Eloise was probably just getting into the office. The Beaumont Boys' Club was in full session, and there really was no reason to miss a gathering as comfortable and comforting as an old pair of jeans.

"Wallace had to go ahead and apologize," Giffy said, not noticing Willard had only paused for breath and not actually stopped. Giffy's eyes bulged like they did when his engine was all fired up but the train was derailed. "What the hell was that? Should have shot him in the head and be done with it. At least he would have left us whole, not crippled in the mind like he was. And why did everybody have a fit over old Strom's yard stray? That girl went to the finest negro college money could buy, and he took care of her ma like any man should with what's his."

Willard slipped into Giffy's catch of breath with the practiced hand of a fly fisherman picking a perfect spot between shore and currents and maybe a log or two. "Do you know how much it must have cost to bring over all those folks from Africa?" he continued, sopping up egg with dabs of toast. "Of course they had to work their passage off. What the hell they expect? They got to deal with the cost of a bit of change. Just like we do. And you can't say the change hasn't done their kind some good. Where do you see them now? Mark my words, there'll be a black president, like it or not. You see them sitting on the Supreme Court, in charge of the army, you see them with guns guarding the cities. And look what's coming up: you see kids in all kinds of colors right out in the open with their folks holding hands like there didn't used to be good honest laws against miscegenation. Pretty soon that dream of theirs is going to have them working for us at the top in the White House, and it won't be polishing the silver, either. Don't really know what I think about all of that. I suppose it's all right, as long as they fly right and don't get ideas they're better than us. A man can take only so much change, after all. A little gratitude for saving their black asses from what's become of Africa would go a ways in soothing my aching craw."

"You were born with an aching craw," Broker said, folding his paper and sitting back so the waitress, Cindy, could clear away his plate. He put a shine on his badge with a sleeve and said, "There's nothing no black man will ever do to make that ache go away."

"Yeah," Willard said grudgingly, "but at least they could give it a damn try."

Willard and Broker busted out in laughter while Cindy refilled their cups. Giffy's grin dimmed as he caught a glimpse of a kitchen worker in the back of the coffee shop. "At least they ain't Mexican," he said, with a half-bottle of bourbon edge to his voice.

"Now leave that boy alone," Cindy said, tapping the top of Giffy's head with four fingers. "He's legal, he's got papers, and he's doing a damn fine job."

"No better than I would."

"But you wouldn't do the work he's got to do."

"Damn straight I wouldn't," Giffy said, still staring at the dark-haired stranger as he sipped from his cup. "He just don't have to look that way while he's doing what he's doing."

Cindy's mouth opened and Broker could already hear her answer: how the hell is he supposed to look doing his job? A mild taint of disappointment in the liberalism creeping through town, even through his good old buddy Willard, almost took the sweetness of his last bite of jam and butter right out of his mouth.

The deputy's car rolled up, lights flashing. Broker looked out the window, checked his radio, wondered why he hadn't received a call if something had happened to make Ty turn on his lights.

"Now, Giffy," Willard said, "he can't help the way he looks any more than blacks can help their skin color, except if they marry enough whites and manage to bleach some of it off." He slapped the table again as he laughed.

This time Broker didn't join him. He watched Ty come in, wishing he'd turned the damn lights off. If something had happened that shouldn't go over the radio, those lights were sure to bring attention to it.

Willard and Giffy were still going at it as Ty put his hand on Broker's shoulder, leaned his long, wiry body over the table, and said to the sheriff: "A call just come in, sheriff. There's three boys in black coming down Camden Road."

Willard stopped in mid-sentence and turned to Ty. "Are they our niggers?"

"They're white boys, as far as I know," Ty said, in his slow way, as if he had to test the words to see if they were ripe before picking them off of the tree. "Dressed in black."

Giffy grabbed Ty's forearm. "They got guns? Air support? You see any black choppers, hear any backwash? They can silence the engines, but you can still hear –"

"Who called it in?" Broker said, standing up. Cindy went back behind the counter, called something into the kitchen. The Mexican disappeared.

"Mrs Jefferson. Said they were passing by her house without so much as a look in her direction. She called out to see if they wanted to use her phone if their car was broken down, but they didn't answer. She didn't like the look of them, not that early in the morning. No guns, no uniforms, just three boys, faces and hands pale as fish belly. Shoes, pants, shirts, and jackets all black, even their hair. And she said they had a glow to them, like that fungus that grows on tree trunks deep in the woods."

"How about nail polish?" Giffy asked.

"She didn't say nothing about nail polish," Ty said.

Willard tapped the table in front of Broker. "Could be protestors. Things haven't quieted down all the way since we ran that faggot teacher out of town."

"Still say we didn't get the nest," said Giffy.

"We'll have to see what's going on," Broker said. "Let's take a ride." He led Ty by the arm to the cruiser, and didn't have to look back to know Willard and Giffy were settling the bill so they could follow. Normally he'd advise them to mind their business and let the law handle matters of the peace. But this time around, he had a feeling he'd like to have a set of witnesses he could count on, in case things got out of hand. And if the situation turned ugly, he could always count on them for back up. He was sure the deputizing from the teacher incident was still in effect.

Eloise raised them on the car radio while they were still on their way to Camden Road.

"We're on a call, Eloise," Broker said, hoping to cut off any minor disturbances. "About time you showed up for work."

"You better hear this," she answered. The air crackled for a moment before she continued. "Bobby just found his sister dead when he went over after she wouldn't answer the phone."

Ty pulled over and stopped the car, grabbed the mike from Willard's hand as he was trying to figure out what to say. "I spoke to Mrs Jefferson before you got in and she was fine."

There was a quaver in his voice that surprised Broker. The boy had been in the Gulf. He should've been used to a bit of drama. That's why Broker hired him.

"She's not fine any more."

"Did he see any kids around the house?"

"He didn't say."

"How about on Camden Road?"

"Didn't mention anything. Just about his sister. The boy's in shock, Ty."

"He lives right next to her. She called in a report about three boys in black walking down the road. And he didn't see them?"

"I guess he doesn't look out on empty roads as much as his sister liked to, Ty. I don't know what to tell you except she's dead and you should be getting over there."

Broker took the mike away from Ty and motioned for him to get going. "We're on our way, Eloise. Thanks for picking up the call. Get the Doc over to Mrs Jefferson's place. Tell him forget his black bag, just bring the camera and his recorder so he can make a report on the body."

Ty drove steadily to Camden Road. Willard and Giffy caught up and trailed a hundred yards behind as they headed out of the valley. Broker was glad he'd called for back up, and let his hand rest on the gun at his hip.

There wasn't a cloud in the sky when the cruiser finally came up on the three strangers, but it seemed to Broker that it had gotten darker on Camden Road. Trees loomed overhead, though they were really set a ways back, and the grass and brush seemed to have overtaken the property fencing like the prison road gang hadn't come by in a hundred years. And the strangers, clean, smooth, white-faced, at least, did have a kind of glow to them that stood out in the gloom, though not as bright as that forest fungus Mrs Jefferson mentioned.

Broker stomped down the urge to call Eloise to see if an eclipse was scheduled for today, and told Ty to stop.

The three boys in black kept on coming even as Broker pulled out the shotgun and stepped in front of the car. Ty stayed back by the radio.

"Are you gentlemen in need of roadside assistance?" the sheriff called out. When the strangers didn't answer, he took hold of the shot-gun with both hands and said, "Is there something I can help you with?" They kept on coming, walking in syncopated rhythm with each other, without a word among them. Broker chambered a shell and said, "You're going to have to show some identification, now, or I'm going to have to take you into town and let you straighten this mess out from a cell. Do you understand?"

Still, the strangers said nothing, and now that they were only twenty paces away, he had a cold feeling about them. He thought at first it was something to do with their eyes, which didn't seem to have any whites to them and were all black, or the odd way their arms swung, or the clothes that were such a deep, inky blackness they hardly seemed to show a crease, wrinkle, or fold. But he decided it was their faces that didn't sit right with him, too smooth and even, like they were a bunch of retards that had fallen off an institution bus.

The glow didn't help any, either. He reached for the sunglasses he usually kept in his shirt pocket, remembered he'd left them in the car, then put his hand up in front of his eyes as if the cruiser's search light was aimed at him.

Behind him, someone wept.

Ty?

Willard and Giffy pulled up in their truck. "You need any help, sheriff?" Willard called out while hanging out the open door on the driver's side.

For some reason, Broker remembered Willard as he was when they'd been boys together pulling pranks in school and in church, cutting classes, sneaking into the town movie, watching cousins and uncles and even their fathers planting seed in other men's fields both light and dark, putting on sheets the way some old folks said they did in the old days. Not everything they'd done was harmless. There was that young black boy they'd lynched in the woods for fun, not meaning to kill, only to play at the old ways and put a scare in him. And there was the time they both saw his mother with a black man, though they'd never spoken about what happened next since that day.

Memories of Giffy came back to Broker too, though they were lean and spare, like the man Giffy had become, the most vivid being what Giffy had done to Broker's dog when his older sister proved herself too friendly a girl, this time with Broker.

The sheriff found himself fighting back tears he never knew he had.

By the time he regained his senses, the strangers were past him. They'd gone by Ty, who hadn't even taken his gun out of the holster. He just sat in the front seat bawling like his wife had run off.

The strangers walked past Giffy and Willard, which was a real disappointment, since they'd always been such reliable men. This time neither one of them had anything to say.

Doc Samuels' car raced up the road, but Broker couldn't keep his gaze on what was coming. The backs of the strangers drew him, and he stared into the blackness that was deeper than the color of the clothes he'd seen from the front. It occurred to him that those fronts were nothing more than shells, like cowboy movie towns made of plywood and paint. And just like those movie towns, Broker thought, the strangers' false faces seemed to cover up a vast empty space where no one lived, and might very well set the stage for the kind of fantasies that most people watched once and never thought about or remembered again.

He put his finger on the shotgun trigger, not liking the way that darkness moved, writhed, like a black silk sheet covering a bed full of snakes. He didn't like the kinds of fantasies he felt coming, like a storm, the air tingling with electricity and smelling of too much water. He was an officer of the law. It was his job to quell disturbances of the peace. The shotgun came up against his shoulder. Willard and Ty were in the line of fire. His finger started pulling.

A cry made him turn. It was Bobby, naked, a bloody hunting knife in hand, running down the road at him.

The rage coming off of Bobby was worse than the heat of a forest fire. It dispelled the strangers' darkness, brought the reality of death, the threat of pain, back into focus.

Broker had never figured Bobby for a meth head, but then, he never thought the boy would have spent his life living next door to his widowed sister, either. Judging by the knife, it looked like those days were over.

Broker fired low, hoping to take out Bobby's legs, but didn't do enough damage. He managed to block the downward stroke of Bobby's knife hand with the gun barrel, but they both wound up falling to the road and scrambling.

Willard and Giffy joined in the struggle, though Broker wasn't sure who they were after or what they were trying to do. All four of them wound up with cuts from the blade.

Doc finally pulled up, cried out, and held his hands palms out in supplication like he was pleading for his life, not theirs. Bobby screamed, pulled away, picked up the shotgun which had fallen from Broker's hands in the fighting, and blasted a hole in the black man's belly.

The sound of the shotgun froze them all in place, except for Samuels, who fell back against his car and slid to the ground, leaving a trail of blood across the hood.

"Damn," said Giffy.

"Shit," said Willard.

Their curses snapped the spell of death for Broker, and he pulled his handgun out and emptied the clip in Bobby, Willard, and Giffy. He went to the cruiser, where Ty was holding on to the steering wheel and staring at the Doc's bloodied car. With a fresh clip in the pistol, he put two rounds in Ty's head.

Going back to the bodies, he snatched the shotgun out of Bobby's slack hands. "You need to get home and get into some clothes," he told him. To Willard and Giffy, he said, "Damn lot of use you boys were, today. Same for you, Ty," he said to his deputy. And to Doc Samuels, he said, "Guess that'll teach you to be making house calls."

Broker took a moment to survey the bodies. He breathed deep, and the cordite stung his nostrils and the roof of his mouth. The stuff oozing out of Doc's gut raised a barnyard stink. He gazed down the road at the diminishing shapes of the three strangers and said, "Those boys are on a killing spree."

He went down on one knee and gently patted Willard's leg. "We'll get them."

The three boys in black were sitting at the Beaumont Boys' Club booth by the time Broker finished with the crime scene and got back to town. Cindy served them coffee and danish, though Broker didn't think they'd like that kind of food. She also teased them about their clothes, about the impression they were bound to make in town, and asked if they had any place to stay for the night. She laughed a lot, and stood by the table with the coffee pot in hand when she was done, though the strangers never touched their cups or plates, and didn't even bother answering her.

To Broker's surprise, Giffy appeared by his side as he walked up to the booth.

"She never flirts with me," he said, showing no signs of a gunshot wound, or even resentment.

"Can't say I blame her," Willard answered, bumping into Broker from the other side as he tried and failed to negotiate his bulk between booths and tables to keep up with the sheriff.

"Excuse me, but I've got some business to take care of," Giffy said, and surprised Broker by pulling the sheriff's gun from its holster.

Broker braced himself for the bullet he knew was coming, the bullet he'd been too slow and stupid and confused to prevent from being aimed at him.

But instead of shooting Broker, Giffy went behind the counter, into the kitchen. The Mexican ran out. A shot was fired, and the Mexican fell against the counter, dropped behind it. Giffy came out and put two more in him, looked up, grinned.

There was something that needed to be done. Broker turned to the strangers, walked up to the booth and said, "I need to take you boys in for questioning."

The strangers answered. Their thin, cartoonish lips didn't move, their black eyes didn't look up at him, their faces didn't turn, and their flesh never creased or folded into an expression. But Broker heard their voices, as clear as the town sirens when they warned of fire or flood or tornadoes. He went cold with the sudden realization that the three boys in black weren't quite human, even though, now that he saw them up close, they bore a striking resemblance to people he knew. Cousins and uncles. His Mom and Dad. That boy in the woods. Willard. Giffy.

A strong resemblance, except for the glow.

"Nobody's perfect," one of the strangers said.

"We understand."

Broker shook his head, like that was going to get the fly-buzzing sound of their voices out of his head. "This isn't about being perfect. It's about murder."

Mrs Jefferson walked in, followed by Bobby. Brother and sister showed no signs of violence, and Bobby was fully clothed. Even unusually neat.

Doc Samuels came in next, giving everyone a nod and a smile.

The Mexican stood up from behind the counter, ready to take an order.

"What the hell," Broker said, looking to everyone but the boys in black for an answer.

"You'd like us if you got to know us," a stranger said.

"The hell I would," Giffy said. He still had the gun and he brushed past the Mexican on his way to the table. "You look like three faggots and I ain't queer."

"There's no consequence," a stranger said.

"Nothing to fear."

"We'll fix everything."

"Make everything right."

"Everything isn't right," Broker said. He stared at Giffy standing next to him, aiming his gun at the nearest stranger's head. Giffy, who he'd shot, along with Willard. Everyone dead was back. Alive. As good as new. And, he thought, everything really was right.

"If you give us a chance, everything can stay right the way you like it," a stranger offered.

Broker took the gun from Giffy and shot the stranger sitting by the aisle in the face. In the instant before he pulled the trigger, he saw his father in the pale, stupid expanse of the boy's visage.

The stranger didn't fall, didn't bleed. There wasn't even a hole in place of the nose where Broker had aimed and sent the bullet.

A joke. This was all a practical joke. The gun wasn't loaded, or firing blanks, or just making a loud sound and blowing smoke out of the barrel. He shot Willard and Giffy again to prove his suspicion.

They went down, stayed still. Bled.

Cindy screamed. The Mexican smiled. Doc Samuels laughed and said, "I'd like to give that a try, myself."

Mrs Jefferson turned away and went to the kitchen, grabbing the Mexican by the hand and taking him along. "I'm just going to see if they need any help in the back."

Her brother Bobby took the last empty seat in the booth beside the boys in black and asked Cindy for a cup of coffee. Willard and Giffy got up, the wounds Broker had just given them gone.

"Things sure have changed," Giffy said, brushing his clothes like he didn't quite believe he was still in them. "And then again, maybe they haven't."

"See?" Willard said, slapping Broker on the back. "Change'll do you good. Not everything different has got to be bad."

Broker started to say something back to Willard, but forgot what. Everything was all right, he thought. Changed. But not.

"Can you ask for better?" a stranger asked.

Willard took the gun from Broker's hand. "You've just got to know how to deal with the way things are," he said. He put the muzzle to Broker's temple. Doc Samuels giggled. Cindy stared at the back of a stranger's head and dropped the pot of coffee. "Let me show you how."

Broker closed his eyes.

And when he opened them again, everything really was all right in the glow of the strangers' pale and beautiful faces.

Just like those boys in black said it would be.

An Open Letter to Stephen King, Anne Rice, and Dean Koontz

Mara Leveritt

Little Rock, Arkansas
October 31, 2003

Dear Esteemed Authors:

It's Halloween night. The goblins have gone. My house is quiet but un-settled.

I find my thoughts haunted by you.

Yesterday, the Arkansas Supreme Court rejected the last state appeal of a man who is set to be executed, in part, for reading your books.

No, he was not charged with enjoying the works of Stephen King, Anne Rice, and Dean Koontz. Of course not. Eighteen-year-old Damien Echols was charged, along with two other teenagers, with having com-mitted a triple murder. The three of you entered this story when the case went to trial; when, in lieu of evidence, the prosecutors turned to your books.

This bit of non-fiction is scarier to me than any plot ever devised by you. Unlike your sentences, this court-ordered one really spells death. Yesterday's decision moved Damien Echols considerably closer to the needle that has been ordered for his lethal injection. I sit tonight un-nerved by your silence.

I believe you're aware of the story: West Memphis, Arkansas, 1993. The bodies of three eight-year-olds found in a creek; one dead from stab wounds and loss of blood, the others apparently beaten and drowned. Panic in the community. A month without arrests. Then three teenagers charged with the murders, amid whispers of "the occult."

But there was a problem with the case from the start. The whispers masked a legal embarrassment. Despite the chief investigator's claim that his confidence in the arrests ranked an "eleven" on a scale of ten, the fact was that he and his detectives had not been able to find a trace of physical evidence linking the accused to one of the bloodiest, muddiest, hands-on triple murders in this – or any other state's – history. They had found not a hair, not a fingerprint, not a footprint – not a smidgen of DNA evidence – connecting any of the three teens to the crime.

And what a crime it was. The children's murders were no detached, drive-by shootings, where the killer never came near the victims. Oh, no. These murders were as up-close and personal as murders can get. There was no gun. There was a knife, and a frenzy of stab wounds to one of the boys, as well as a brutal castration. The heads of the other two victims were bashed with a blunt object. Then they were lifted and carried or dragged into the creek, where their bodies, alive or dead, were stuck into the mucky bottom.

The boys were naked by that point; their clothes were buried in the water too. Whoever committed the killings waded through the bloody, waist-deep water gathering clothes, finding sticks, then using the twigs to pin the children's jeans and shirts and underpants to the bottom of the bloody creek. It was ghastly, messy business. Yet, according to the police, the three accused killers accomplished it without leaving a trace of themselves at the scene.

Nor could the police find evidence of a motive. Even as prosecutors prepared to put Echols on trial, they could find no one to testify that he had ever even met the victims, much less that he or his co-defendants harbored a murderous rage against them, or stood to profit from their deaths. Motive and physical evidence were a lot to lack heading into a trial.

What prosecutors did have, though, was a frightened public and rumors that Echols was "weird," "strange," "bizarre," maybe even "Satanic." In this conservative town in a conservative state, it was true: he did stand out. At eighteen, Echols wore black clothing. He'd chosen the name of Damien – perhaps to honor a Catholic priest who'd cared for outcasts like himself, perhaps as a nod to the movie "The Omen," or perhaps as a mixture of both. In any event, he was goth where goth wasn't cool. He liked music by Metallica in a town where heavy metal was damned from pulpits. And he read *your books*, my friends. Even without evidence that he'd committed the murders, prosecutors decided that the combination was enough to present to a jury, with a request that he be sentenced to death.

Their argument was simple. It didn't matter that Echols did not know his victims. He'd killed them as part of an "occult ritual." That ritual was never named, defined, or described at the trial. Rather, the "occult nature" of the crime was established by an occult "expert," a man who admitted on the witness stand that he had "earned" his PhD from a mail-order university, without having attended any classes. Arkansas Circuit Judge David Burnett accepted those credentials and allowed "Dr" Dale Griffis to explain to the jurors how he had detected "the trappings of occultism" in the murders. First, there was the moon. It was full the night the children were killed. There were the three victims. As Griffis explained, "One of the most powerful numbers in the practice of Satanic belief is six-six-six, and some believe the base root of six is three." Then there was blood involved, and the fact that the bodies were found in water – all indications, Griffis said, of the "occult" nature of the crime.

Driving home the point, the prosecutor turned to art. He asked Griffis about the types of art enjoyed by "people involved in occultism." Griffis answered that what he'd seen involved "necromancy, or love of death." He added that Damien's drawings and writings – as well as the books he owned – reflected that interest in "the occult."

Had police found candle wax at the scene? An icon, robe, or graffiti? Anything man-made that suggested a ritual? No, no, and again no. But those absences stood no chance against the potency of the symbols evoked: the blood, the water, the moon, and the mysterious number three.

Lacking any direct connection between Damien and the crime, the prosecutors used triangulation. They linked the crime to the occult through symbol, then they linked Damien to the occult through art. It was a masterful piece of courtroom work, tailor-made for a part of the country where, polls report, nearly two-thirds of all church-goers believe the devil can and does literally possess people.

Echols did not help his own case when he took the witness stand. Asked what types of books he liked to read, he replied, "I will read about anything, but my favorites were Stephen King, Dean Koontz, and Anne Rice." Following that admission, a prosecutor called a police officer to the stand. "In your opinion, is there anything unusual about those being the type of books Mr Echols likes to read?" he asked. The officer replied, "Stephen King seems to be horror movies, horror books. And if you're asking if I felt that was strange, yes, sir, I did."

Your books. Horror. Strange. With that, as the prosecutor told the jury, "the belief system, the state of mind," of Echols was established. Then, in his closing remarks to the jury, Prosecutor John Fogleman tied his case up with a bow. Did Echols' dark and disturbing tastes in clothing, music, and literature necessarily make him a murderer? "No," he answered rhetorically. "Ladies and gentlemen, each item, in and of itself, doesn't mean somebody would be motivated to murder – not in and of itself. But you look at it together, and you get – you begin to see inside Damien Echols. You see inside that person, and you look inside there, and there's not a soul in there." Fogleman concluded: "Scary. That's what he is – scary."

(Mr King, I think of you especially tonight, as you prepare to receive the National Book Award for being so artful, so . . . scary. You wrote. Damien read. And look what was made of that connection.)

In any event, soul-less and scary sufficed for the jurors. They found Echols guilty of the murders – found him to be the ring-leader of the conjured ritual, and sentenced him to death. Two years later, the Arkansas Supreme Court affirmed all three convictions. And yesterday, Halloween's Eve, that court rejected Echols' final state appeal. That is why, on this somber night, my thoughts turn to you – and to your silence.

In the nearly ten years since Judge Burnett sentenced Echols to death, many artists have risen to challenge the abuses of self-expression that were allowed to bear on his trial. Scores of filmmakers, musicians, actors, visual artists, and writers have protested the prosecutors' exploitation of art, as have thousands of your readers. But what has been heard from the three great writers whose works actually figured in his trial?

I hear nothing, and feel a chill.

Your readers have supported you. Now one of them – his fate strangely linked to you – faces a death beyond your conception.

Will none of you spare a word for him in this dark and dangerous hour?

Carnival Knowledge

Scott Nicholson

The sky is hot with popcorn and apple caramel and the diesel exhaust of the big engines. Bright wheels spin, on fire with green and yellow jewels. Screams are tossed from the wheels, brittle on the air like thin shafts of ice. Broad organ notes lurch along to the beat of three. The pounding of the music against your skin reminds you of the thing inside your chest that used to have music of its own.

They cluster beyond the cage, those cruel breathers, those who walk. Mouths and eyes open wide, they give money to the fat man in the long coat. A young one comes close, his mother tugs the back of his jacket, says words that have no meaning. You beg with your eyes for him to put his hand through the bars.

The wheels tilt and whirl, the organ trips faster, a man is laughing. You smell the hard bite of liquor on his breath, though he's at the rear of the crowd. If you could hate, you would wish him in the cage with you. But you can only love.

You look past the crowd, for they will not return your love. Tents with striped roofs lean in different directions, sparks of light and tinkling coins and shouts spilling from the doorways. If you could walk, you would go among them, see for yourself what strange pleasures hide in each. But then you think that the tents may hold only more like you.

The fat man has fat pockets, bulging with money. He turns to you and smiles. You should hate this man, for he is the one who caged you. He rattles the bars with a long stick.

"Give 'em a show, freak."

You know the words, but do not know what they mean. You only know that if you show your love, the man will love you in return. They will all love you, though they eat air and spit air and you are as far from them as the tiny holes in the darkness above.

The crowd shouts and leans forward, their skin electric. The wayward boy comes too close; you reach out to touch and love him. His mother screams and yanks him away. You look at the empty night that surrounds your fingers.

When you die, you should not know these things. You should not see and smell and hear better than when your heart made music. You should not taste.

The fat man beats the bars again and you cannot love any of these people, not the way you should, not with your mouth. You can only love yourself.

You raise your leg, the last remaining one. Flesh hangs in rags around a gleaming knot of bone. The meat is between your teeth and the crowd gasps and sighs and the fat man is smiling.

But they will never love you as you need to be loved.

You feed, you hunger.

You should not know these things.

Beauty, CLIVE BARKER

Fucking Justice

James Morrow

His body was now a sacred place, a sentient temple of Solomonic wisdom, a flesh-and-bone altar at which the innocent would always find relief from persecution and the guilty be evermore called to account. His spinal column had acquired the precise arc of the rainbow with which God had sealed his covenant with Noah. His brain's two hemispheres bulged with the twin tablets of the Mosaic Law. The Code of Hammurabi gave ballast to the vessel of his heart.

Four days earlier, with the full enthusiasm of Andrew Jackson and the qualified endorsement of the Congress, Roger Brooke Taney had been sworn in as Chief Justice of the United States Supreme Court. After the ceremony were a round of dinners, balls, soirées, and, truth be told, visits to the Washington bordellos. Chief Justice Roger Taney had imbibed considerable quantities of wine from crystalline goblets and impressed large amounts of truth on callow journalists, all of them eager to hear what philosophical constructs he would bring to bear in interpreting the U.S. Constitution. An amazing interval – and yet as he stood on the dark chilly banks of the Potomac, the fog enshrouding the trees and the night wind gnawing his innards, he apprehended that the week's most memorable event was still to come.

The stranger had approached Roger at the bar of the Bellefleur Hotel, quite the most grotesque person he'd ever seen, a stumpish crookback whose sallow smile suggested a wooden fence from which every second picket had been removed. He identified himself as Knock the Dwarf. Although Roger's commitment to Aristotelian prudence had obliged him to give the wretch a portion of his time, his sense of propriety had deterred him from granting a full-blown interview. Their conversation was consequently pointed and brief.

"Our republic is young," Knock had said, "and yet already certain ancient and secret societies have established a presence on these shores – though of course such organizations are by definition hidden from view, which is why my employers assume that you are unacquainted with the Brotherhood of the Scales."

"Brotherhood of the Scales?" Roger said. "A musicians' league perhaps? A guild of fishermen?"

"Neither musicians nor fishermen."

Fishermen. Once again the familiar knot formed in Roger's throat, the tumor no surgeon's knife could ever ablate. The late Mrs Taney was certainly no Catholic, and yet she'd insisted that their cook spend every Friday evening frying or baking or broiling some aquatic delicacy. It was surely Satan himself who'd spawned the fatal trout, arranging for one of its vertebrae to lodge in Mrs Taney's gullet.

"Scales as in 'scales of justice,'" Knock explained, handing Roger a sheet of parchment, twice-folded and secured with a dollop of white tallow.

"Your employers are correct," Roger said. "I have not heard of the society in question. And now, if you will leave me to my privacy. . . ."

Knock tipped his ratty felt hat, bowed in a manner that seemed to Roger more insouciant than deferential, and scurried back to whatever moist and gloomy grotto served as this troglodyte's abode.

The message was succinct: a set of directions guiding the recipient to a particular willow tree on the Potomac's eastern shore, followed by three sentences.

> *A choice lies before you, Roger Taney, as momentous as any*
> *you will make whilst heading the highest court in the land.*
> *You can either become the greatest Supreme Court Justice of*
> *this century, or you can add your name to that fat catalogue of*
> *judges orphaned by mediocrity and adopted by obscurity. We*
> *shall expect you at the stroke of midnight.*

The wind rushing off the black river put Roger in mind of his young nephew, Thomas, on whom he had recently lavished a wondrous toy frigate driven by flaxen sails and armed with four miniature brass cannons that, charged with a pinch of gunpowder, hurled glass marbles a distance of twenty feet. On Independence Day, Roger and Thomas had together enacted the Battle of Fort McHenry in a duck pond. As the frigate pounded the little mud-and-wicker garrison, man and boy had given voice to the stirring anthem recently composed by Roger's brother-in-law.

"And the rockets' red glare," they'd sung, "the bombs bursting in air, gave proof through the night that our flag was still there. . . ."

The ship now cruising up the river was nothing at all like Thomas's toy frigate. It was a thirty-foot shallop, the *Caveat* by name, as dismayed and forsaken as anything in "The Rime of the Ancient Mariner," her sails like moldering winding-sheets, her planks like worm-eaten wine casks, her rigging like the curtain-ropes in some unsavory theatre catering to sots and sensualists. The shallop sidled toward the bank. A gangway appeared, bridging the gap between rail and shore. Such a ship, Roger speculated, could only be crewed by pirates, and yet the instant he crossed over – for even a Chief Justice may act against his better judgment – it became obvious that, far from being a privateer, the *Caveat* was a kind of floating academy or waterborne monastery.

Her company, over twenty in number, all wore woolen robes, revealed by the full moon to be of varying hues, each beaky cowl offering Roger only the vaguest glimpse of the face beneath, rather the way his favorite sort of woman's gown provided an occasional flash of bosom. Perhaps these friars were the spiritual descendents of Saint Brendan, the seagoing cleric of Catholic legend. Or maybe their order had gone maritime in homage to *Les Trois Maries* – Mary Magdalene, Mary Salome, Mary Jacob – those pious women who, following the crucifixion, had traversed the Mediterranean and landed in Gaul.

No sooner had Roger stepped onto the weather deck than the tallest monk, swathed in red and radiating an agreeable floral fragrance, clasped his shoulder in a manner he found overly familiar but nevertheless ingratiating.

"You have made a wise decision, Judge Taney," the red monk said.

"How heartening to meet a man who will endure both apprehension and perplexity to increase the quantity of justice in the universe," the white monk said.

"I am indeed perplexed," Roger said, "and truly apprehensive."

"In matters metaphysical," the blue monk said, "confusion and fear walk hand-in-hand with enlightenment and grace."

"The ritual takes but an hour," the yellow monk said. "We shall have you back at the Bellefleur in time for breakfast."

"If you good friars were to lower your hoods," Roger asked, "would I perhaps recognize amongst you a familiar face or two?"

The red monk dipped his head and said, "You would be astonished to learn who belongs to the Brotherhood of the Scales."

The voyage was short and uneventful. For an hour or so the *Caveat* sailed southward from the city, then dropped anchor near a feature that the red monk identified as Janus Island, a gloomy forested mass rising from the bay like the shell of an immense sea turtle. Torches were lit. Lanterns glowed to life. A longboat was lowered, hitting the water with a sound like a beaver's tail slapping a mudbank.

Six monks clustered around Roger. Their sweet aroma and polyphonic humming gratified his senses. They directed him down a swaying rope-ladder to the longboat and positioned him in the stern, all the while chanting a song so beautiful he found himself wondering whether humankind would have done better to remain in the Middle Ages. The monks seized the oars and rowed for Janus Island, the synchronous strokes providing their polyphony with a supplemental rhythm.

Attaining the beach, Roger's sponsors again took him in hand, their skin exuding olfactory choruses of rose and lavender. As the party advanced inland, the terrain became preternaturally dense, the trees packed so tightly together as to make the forest seem a collection of concentric stockades. Chirps and peals and whirrs of every sort poured from the darkness, an insect symphony as pleasing as the monks' sonorous voices.

The moon shone down more brightly still, its shimmering beams spilling through the trees like molten silver from a crucible. Roger shuddered with an amalgam of dread and fascination. His every instinct told him to break free of his sponsors, dive into the bay, and swim to the safety of the Maryland shore, and yet his curiosity kept him on the path, fixed on a destination whose nature he could not divine.

They had marched barely a mile when Roger realized that he and the monks were not alone. A female figure in a flowing gossamer gown darted here and there amongst the trees. She suggested nothing so much as a pagan dryad – though a true dryad, he decided, would enjoy greater freedom than this thrice-hobbled creature, who was freighted not only with a broadsword but also a pair of brass balance-scales and, as if she were about to be executed by a firing squad, a blindfold.

The red monk had evidently noticed the visitor as well, for he now turned to Roger and said, "No, Judge Taney, you are not going mad."

"Nor are you seeing a ghost," the white monk said.

The dryad awakened in Roger's soul a timeless and unfathomable yearning. Her hair was a miracle. The long undulating tresses emitted a light of their own, a golden glow that mingled with the moonbeams to form a halo about her head.

"This island is surely of the Chesapeake Bay variety," he said, "and yet it would seem we've landed in the Cyclades."

"You are most prescient, sir, for the creature in question is in fact the Greek deity Themis," the green monk said.

Even as Roger apprehended the visitor in all her splendor, radiant locks and ample hips and full bosom, she melted into the shadows. Themis? Truly? Themis herself, given flesh and essence through a power that only God and his monks could control?

"The ritual is simple, though burdened with a certain ambiguity," the red monk said. "Before dawn you will perform on Dame Themis an act of raw concupiscence."

"I don't understand," Roger said.

"You will subject the goddess to a vigorous carnal embrace," the orange monk said.

Revulsion coursed through Roger's frame like a wave of nausea. "I am determined to become the paragon of my profession," he said, his tone vibrant with incredulity and outrage, "but I shan't commit the sin of fornication to attain that goal."

"Fear not, novitiate," the white monk said. "Just as Christ is forever married to his Church, so are you now wed to Dame Themis, though for an interval considerably short of eternity."

"Nay, good friar, I am not married to anyone, as my dear Caroline passed away three years ago."

"We know all about it," the orange monk said.

"A bone in the throat," the green monk said.

"Your second wedding occurred last night," the red monk insisted. "The fact that you were nearly asleep at the time does not annul the marriage."

"I find all this most unpersuasive," Roger said, though he had to admit that the thought of conjugal congress with the dryad did not displease him.

"Perhaps you would care to see the relevant document," the green monk said.

From his robe he produced a small leather valise, then flipped it open and retrieved a paper that in the combined light of moon and lantern appeared to indeed consecrate a circumscribed marriage between Roger Taney of Baltimore and Dame Themis of Athens. Their union had commenced twenty-four hours earlier and would terminate at cockcrow. Roger's signature featured his characteristic curlicues. The goddess's handwriting was likewise ornate, a marvel of loops and serifs.

"I am entirely astonished," Roger said.

"In metaphysics all things are possible," the yellow monk said.

"So this is in fact my wedding night?"

The red monk nodded. "Your bride awaits you."

For the remainder of the journey Roger fixed his eyes on that nebulous zone where the glow of the torches and the light of the moon shaded to black. He scrutinized the shadows, studied the breaching roots, fixed on the wisps of fog. Dame Themis was nowhere to be seen. Perhaps she had retired to her private quarters, that she might prepare for the coming consummation.

A shot-tower loomed out of the darkness, a crumbling pile of stone whose calculated verticality had probably not cooled a cannon-ball since the War of Independence. Roger's sponsors led him inside, then guided him up a helical staircase that curled along the inner wall like a viper lying dormant in a hollow tree. A door of oak and iron presented itself. The red monk pushed it open.

Never before had the Chief Justice beheld so sumptuous a bed-chamber, its windows occluded by velvet curtains, its walls hung with tapestries depicting hunting scenes, its floor covered with an Oriental carpet as thick and soft as Irish moss. Dame Themis's sword of justice stood upright in the far corner. The brass balance-scales rested on the window ledge, one carriage holding a daisy-chain, the other a garland of lilies.

Roger's bride was utterly naked, stripped of both her blindfold and her gown. She lay supine on the mattress, her luminous hair flowing across the pillow, her concavity beckoning like a portal to Paradise, whilst east of Eden her firm and noble breasts canted in opposite directions, one north, the other south. Her eyes, unbanded now, were as large and golden as Spanish doubloons.

What most caught Roger's attention was neither his bride's face, nor even her form, but rather the way the monks had presumed to compromise her powers of speech with a silken gag and constrain her limbs through an elaborate network of shackles, chains, and locks held fast to the floor by iron cleats.

The Chief Justice was quick to bring a complaint before his sponsors.

"We can assure you that the chains are essential," the red monk replied.

"In the throes of passion, Dame Themis is known to grasp her lover's windpipe and squeeze," the blue monk elaborated. "Your strangulation would be no less deadly for being unintended."

"And the silken kerchief – likewise necessary?" Roger said.

"Before we added it to the ritual, Dame Themis's ardor would often drive her to bite off her lover's ear," the orange monk said.

"Good friars, I am appalled," Roger said. "How can you imagine I would assent to know my wife in so barbaric a manner?"

"For many centuries the Brotherhood sought a gentler method of instructing its novitiates," the blue monk said. "Alas, they discovered that a certain theatricality is the *sine qua non* of a proper initiation."

"Tonight you will learn exactly how it feels to violate justice," the red monk said, "so that you will never commit such a transgression in the future."

"I would never have a woman against her will," Roger asserted.

"Against her will?" the red monk said in an amused tone. "As you set about acquiring this carnal knowledge, your bride may indeed groan and whimper in apparent distress. Please know that these noises are all for show, the better to impress the event on your psyche."

"For show?" Roger said.

"Dame Themis is a consummate actress," the white monk said.

"My conscience rebels at this arrangement," Roger said.

"And now we leave you to your lesson," the red monk said, resting an affirming hand on Roger's shoulder for the second time that night. "We are confident you will learn it well."

Against all odds and defying his every expectation, the monks were but five minutes gone when Roger found himself in a condition of acute arousal. He fixed his gaze on the object of his desire. His mute bride bucked against the mattress, her chains clanking together with a discordant but oddly affecting music.

He got undressed as quickly as he could, his breeches snagging briefly on his manhood.

The evening unfolded as the monks had foretold, Dame Themis issuing unhappy sounds and muffled protests throughout the ritual. Roger closed his eyes and concentrated on the lesson, and when at last the spasm arrived he understood his seed to be a great gift, a numinous filament from Arachne's loom, perhaps, or a segment of the thread by which Theseus had solved the Labyrinth of Minos. Justice deserved no less.

It was only with the approach of dawn, as the *Caveat* blew back up the Potomac in thrall to a violent tempest, that Roger felt prepared to put his wedding night into words. Sitting with the red monk and the white in their private cabin, imbibing their wine and reveling in their conversation, he attempted to narrate his recent liaison in all its cryptic beauty.

"It truly seemed that my bride did not reciprocate my passion." Roger took a generous swallow from his goblet.

"Dame Themis plays her part with great skill," the red monk said.

"Her bleating still echoes in my ears," he said, recalling her impersonation of agony. "I am hoping this wine might silence it."

"If not the wine, then the passage of time," the white monk said.

The red monk stiffened his index finger and plunged it into the shadowy depths of his cowl, presumably to relieve an itching nose. "What matters is that you have absorbed every sensation that attends the abuse of Dame Themis. In the decades to come, whenever you begin to render a brutish opinion, the erotic fire you experienced last night will start coursing through your flesh."

"Whereupon you will summon all your inner strength and bank those terrible flames," the white monk said.

"With God as my witness, such a conflagration will never again prosper in my loins." Roger inhaled deeply, sucking in the orchid glory of the red monk, the honeysuckle elegance of the white. "I shall resist the enticements of injustice with every fiber of my being."

The white monk filled his third goblet of the evening. "But, ah, such felicitous enticements – yes?"

Roger heaved a sigh. "Felicitous. Yes."

"You can see how easily a jurist might become addicted to iniquity," the white monk said.

"I would never have expected it," said Roger. "I am not so well educated a man as I thought."

"Metaphysics can be as subtle as the serpent," the red monk said. "Welcome to the Brotherhood of the Scales."

In the interval stretching from his first Supreme Court case to the outbreak of the Civil War, Roger Brooke Taney made four separate journeys across the Chesapeake Bay in search of the place where he and Dame Themis had consummated their mayfly marriage. He never found the shot-tower – indeed, he never even found Janus Island. And yet he did not for an instant doubt that the Brotherhood of the Scales existed, or that the friars had sponsored his membership in that arcane organization, or that he had connected with a dryad sometime after midnight on April 23, 1836.

To his infinite satisfaction, not one of the opinions Roger wrote during the first twenty-two years of his career was accompanied by the concupiscent symptoms that the friars had taught him to recognize. Had the despoilment of Dame Themis wrought a cure so complete as to purge pettiness and ignorance from his psyche forever? Or was his congenital sense of justice so acute that he'd never needed the ritual in the first place? In any event, it seemed clear that the name of Taney would be handed down to history as a synonym for integrity, an antonym for malice, and the very definition of fairness.

There were two cases in particular for which he believed he might be revered. The first traced to a suit brought by the Charles River Bridge Company, which charged travelers a small fee to cross its eponymous bridge, against a nascent competitor, who permitted pedestrians, horsemen, and carriages to pass over the same watercourse for free. The plaintiffs contended that their original charter from the Commonwealth of Massachusetts had granted them a monopoly, but the Taney Court took a different view. The charter in question, noted the majority, did not use the word "monopoly." Ergo, the ambiguity would be resolved in favor of the public. Roger Taney: man of the people, guardian of toll-free bridges.

Then there was the controversial and distasteful business of the Negro. Dred Scott was a black African slave whose peripatetic master, an army surgeon named John Emerson, had moved first from Missouri to Illinois, and thence to Fort Snelling in the Wisconsin Territory, and finally back to Missouri. In 1846, Dr Emerson died, whereupon Dred Scott sued Irene Emerson, the doctor's widow, for his freedom. Because Illinois had always been a free state, ran the plaintiff's specious and naïve logic, and because slavery had been banned from the Wisconsin Territory under the Missouri Compromise, he had spent much of his life in a condition other than bondage, and therefore he could no longer be regarded as chattel. For some perverse reason Dred Scott had won his suit in a lower St Louis court, but then the Missouri State Supreme Court had wisely overturned the earlier decision.

In their characteristic arrogance, Scott and his Negro-loving confrères had refused to quit, and eventually they found a way to make a federal case of the matter. For it so happened that the legal administrator of Irene Emerson's property – her brother, J.F.A. Sanford – was a resident of New York, not Missouri, which meant that technically the whole affair lay beyond the jurisdiction of either state. After losing in a U.S. District Court, Scott appealed to the highest court in the land, whose Chief Justice was only too happy to set the plaintiff straight concerning the nature of chattel slavery in America – the plaintiff, the black race, the infernal abolitionists, the troubled republic, and, indeed, the whole world.

In *Scott v. Sanford*, Roger and six other justices ruled that any entity whose ancestors had ever been sold as slaves could never enjoy the rights of a federal citizen, most especially the right to bring a suit in court. Dred Scott and his kind were in fact pieces of property, as befitting the "inferior order" to which they belonged. Negroes, Roger averred, were "altogether unfit to associate with the white race." As for the nefarious practice of chopping up the republic into slave zones and free zones, the Taney Court concluded that Congress had no power to prohibit slavery in the territories. The Missouri Compromise was, in a word, unconstitutional.

If Roger had been forced to make a choice, he would have guessed that future generations would venerate him more for his opinion in *Scott v. Sanford* than for the Charles River Bridge decision. But the issue of the bridge mattered too. It was one thing to earn an honest profit, and quite another to stifle the freedom of a competing corporation.

How strange, this darkness. As usual he'd gone to bed at ten o'clock. Now he was fully awake, ready to hear the arguments in *Torrance v. Ashton* – and yet not a single ray of light pierced his room. Could it be that he'd slept for an entire day? Was his characteristic vigor finally failing? Perhaps he should take his nephew's advice and step down from the bench before the year was out.

He dropped his head back on the pillow and brooded. An insect chorus reached his ears, a noise that made even less sense than the darkness. He had shut all his windows before retiring and, besides, since when had Delaware Avenue become a gathering-place for cicadas and crickets?

His attempt to rise from the mattress perplexed him even more than either the darkness or the insects. Manacles encircled his wrists and ankles, the concomitant chains snaking across his body and disappearing beneath the bed. Whenever he moved, the links of rusted iron gave forth a sound suggesting a bullfrog in pain.

A door swung open. A flickering light filled the bed-chamber. The red monk entered, holding aloft a torch, followed by Knock the Dwarf.

"How long has it been?" the red monk said. "A quarter century? No, longer. Twenty-eight years."

Roger glanced in all directions. Dame Themis's broadsword lay in the corner. Her balance-scales rested on the window ledge, although the daisy-chain and the garland of lilies had long since disintegrated and blown away.

"Good friar, you must set me free," he gasped.

"The Brotherhood has been following your career with great interest," the red monk said. "Alas, I'm afraid we are disappointed with your performance on the bench."

"I've done nothing to deserve these chains," Roger said, straining against the shackles.

"My employers disagree," the dwarf chimed in.

"Did I bring an unconsidered populism to the Charles River Bridge decision?" Roger asked. "Is that it?"

The dwarf snickered. The red monk smirked.

"Perhaps I committed an error or two whilst serving on the bench," Roger continued, "but I always held fast to my principles."

"Dozens of errors," the red monk said. "The first occurred the very week you were sworn in, when you decided that a greater good might come from ravishing Dame Themis."

Anger and indignation boiled up in Roger's blood. "That was your decision, not mine!"

"No, Judge Taney – yours."

"You forced me to ravish her!" Roger cried.

"Shut up!" the dwarf demanded, and then, as if he doubted Roger's ability to carry out the directive, he pulled a silk kerchief from his trousers and used it to render the Chief Justice mute.

Lantern in hand, the white monk strode into the bed-chamber, accompanied by a middle-aged man dressed far too foppishly for his years: blue velvet dressing gown embroidered with golden peacocks, red calfskin slippers, pomaded curls.

The white monk pointed toward Roger and said, "Behold Apollo, avatar of wisdom and probity."

"I was expecting someone younger," the coxcomb said.

"Tonight you will learn exactly how it feels to violate Apollo," the white monk informed the coxcomb, "that you might avoid such a lapse in your coming career."

Roger made every effort to accuse the monks of deception, but the intervening kerchief turned his sentences into absurdities.

"How can a god be so elderly?" the coxcomb asked.

"Metaphysics rarely follows a predictable course." The white monk installed his lantern on the nightstand and headed for the open door. "Cleave to the ritual, and all will be well," he added, vanishing through the jamb.

"Apollo is a *young* man," the coxcomb protested.

"Don't be deceived by appearances," the red monk said. "Your job is not to estimate Apollo's age, but to abuse his flesh as emphatically as possible."

Roger tried to scream, *You have no right!*

The red monk pivoted ninety degrees and marched out of the room, taking his torch with him.

"As emphatically as possible," echoed the coxcomb in a tone of consternation.

Roger wanted to shout, *You must show pity!*

"Might I make a suggestion?" the dwarf inquired.

"Indeed," the coxcomb said.

Knock approached Dame Themis's broadsword and, seizing the handle, brought it before the coxcomb. "What better way to violate Apollo than to excise his virility?"

Have mercy!

"To become a great judge, I shall do whatever is required of me," the coxcomb told the dwarf.

Hear me, sir! I am not a god! I am a citizen of the United States! I am a human being!

The coxcomb went to work, and when he was done the balance-scales of Dame Themis had achieved Platonic equipoise, both loads of equal weight and identical mass, each carriage in perfect harmony with the other.

In 1857, one year after Roger Taney wrote the majority opinion in *Scott v. Sanford*, Irene Emerson of Missouri remarried. Her new husband, Calvin Chaffee, was a devout abolitionist, and so the former Mrs Emerson sold Dred Scott, his wife Harriet, and their two daughters to the sons of the late Peter Blow, Scott's first owner.

The Blow brothers, childhood friends of Scott's who had paid his legal fees over the years, immediately manumitted the African and his family. For nine months, the interval of a human gestation, Dred Scott lived a free man in the city of St Louis, succumbing to tuberculosis at the age of fifty-nine.

Initially Scott's remains were laid to rest in Wesleyan Cemetery, but in 1867 the burial ground was closed and his body placed beneath a blank slab in Section 1, Lot No. 177 of Calvary Cemetery. A commemorative marker was added in 1957, giving the facts in the case, and the grave now bears an inscription: "In memory of a simple man who wanted to be free."

Letter

Margaret Cho

I write a letter, and I offer a plea, a prayer, a hope that He is finished making an example of them, the West Memphis Three. He works in such mysterious ways that I can no longer stand the riddle anymore, and now I desperately want some clues. I outright demand the freedom of these young men, who were only boys when they were caught up in this travesty, this unbelievable miscarriage of justice. I fold it up like a paper airplane, flown straight into the heart of God, buoyed by love and truth and compassion. My correspondence with the Creator is not as satisfying as I would like it to be. I have yet to receive a reply. Perhaps He doesn't understand Himself – why those who would call themselves His servants would act so demonically? Perhaps He wants the same answers I do.

Damien returns my letters. Damien has grown up, no longer a boy, but a brilliant young man. He is incredibly bright, gentle, considerate, sentimental, kind. He isn't seemingly angry, nor is he bitter, as he would have every right to be, having spent the better part of the last dozen years behind bars, vilified and demoralized, imprisoned and readied for lethal injection by an indecently ignorant and hysterical community, so fearful of Satanic cults living in their presence that they commit far more evil in the name of their own blindness and bigotry than Lucifer himself would have the capacity of cruelty for. The suffering that humans will inflict on each other is at times out of the realm of all understanding, and it makes the world sometimes unbearable to be in, yet we, for the most part remain, possibly to comfort those who are in need of it.

In my attempts to comfort, I have made a friend, who I have yet to meet in person, yet I love with a kind of holy impetuousness, for it is neither courtly love, nor is it charitable in nature. I have no choice but to love. He is the victim of a government, a theocracy which has failed us, and for this, he is a messianic figure, yet he will not be martyred, for there are enough of us out there who believe in what is right, and we are warriors and the true protectors of justice, and we have only just begun to fight.

Until he is free, no one is free. Damien Echols is the heavy metal Nelson Mandela.

I write to Damien about Wagner's *Tristan and Isolde*, our mutual fondness for opera, the upcoming presidential elections, which obsess us both, although he will not be able to vote, even when he is a free man, for convicted felons are not allowed this right.

I tell him small details of my travels, which take me everywhere to see everything, from the pilgrims who daily circumambulate the Jokhang Temple in Lhasa, the capital of Tibet, amidst the bustling marketplace, where merchants sell yak meat alongside ornate and expensive silver jewelry to New York City, where everything is happening all the time. It is unfair, for his curiosity about life and the world that lives it fascinates him, yet he can only experience it from messages we all scribble down here and there, when we have the time, when we remember to.

I wish hard, eyes shut and head and heart throbbing, at shooting stars, blowing out birthday candles, every opportunity I have, that Damien and Lorri will make journeys together to the places I have written about, that they will go wherever they like, see everything, visit people who love them, yet have never met them, who have sent letters and cards from far, far away, with invitations to stay for as long as they want, whenever they can, anytime, always, forever welcome.

I ask about his life there in the Arkansas prison in Grady, where his name is a number, and he can only receive paper in the mail. He asks me if they still make cassette tapes, because he has been incarcerated for so long in this terrible place, he has never heard a CD, nor has he ever seen the Internet.

When I write, I use beautifully handmade paper, and I write by hand and by heart, which I have never done with any real knowledge of how to, because I grew up with the luxury of computers and typewriters, and using a pen makes my back hurt, and my neck sore. They are foreign objects to me, but I cannot write him any other way, for in committing the pen to paper, it is a small intimate gesture, a human connection, that I want for him, to ease his loneliness, his boredom, his sadness, even though every interaction we have is surprisingly upbeat, a testament to the enduring optimism of the human spirit in the face of overwhelming injustice and suffering.

I ask what we can do from here to help him survive the daily torpor, the ongoing nightmare of his incomprehensible situation. He loves to read, so I try to send books regularly from his Amazon wish list. His soul is lifted up by the many letters he receives from his supporters, postmarked from all over the world.

Buddhist monks come to pay homage to him, to honor him. He

loves Lorri Davis, and she is his wife, although in our own way, we are all in love with him, for he represents the parts of ourselves we send to the gallows, the freedom we often forfeit, the injustice we commit against the greatest of all enemies, the self.

I send Lorri money for their defense fund, words of solidarity, a pledge of my devotion to their case.

It must be so hard for her. She is also imprisoned, practically the fourth member of the West Memphis Three. We all wait. I do not really understand the court system. It is the crime uncommitted, the time spent waiting to be sentenced for something that didn't bloody your hands, the time in jail, the wait to appeal the crimes that you are innocent of, the wait for the decisions to be made that will decide whether or not they will accept the appeal, the wait for appeals, the wait for the appeal to be denied, the wait to appeal to a higher court, then again another wait for the decision to be re-tried in a higher court for the crime you did not commit, and the wait to wait to wait.

For the West Memphis Three, their families, their friends, their army of supporters, and especially Damien, I wish the minutes, hours, days, years would sprout wings, and fly up and out to the open sky. The cloudlessly blue, unending, borderless, and clear heavens.

Above.

High above.

Free.

Then One Day She Saw Him Again

Peter Straub

Then one day she saw him again. It must have been a year since the first time, because another summer had passed and the weather was now misty gray and the air had turned slightly chilly. She had just realized that, alone of all the people she knew, she was glad to be out of summer. She preferred these days, for summer was a pleasure machine like a strong drink that stroked you and never got you any further than a slow stunned warmth, but on days like this – a slight haze hanging in the air, and the tops of buildings invisible in the fog – she felt a close, lifting sense of anticipation, as if some unforeseen transformation were literally in the air, hovering. Then she saw him walking toward her again and remembered him perfectly, though she had not seen or thought of him in the year that had passed.

He might have been wearing the same clothes – a black sweater and jeans so faded they were almost white. No, the jeans were different, and the long red scarf was new. But it was the same young man. The sense of illumination still clung to him. Neither smiling nor crying now, he was walking along with a comfortable stride. There was nothing special about his face, nor was he as young as she had thought, but a teen-age girl turned to look at him curiously as he passed, and a tall man in a tan raincoat with a heavy, buttoned lining swung his head to watch him go by. It was as if a pale light shone upon him, or within him, a light of which he was absolutely unaware. That was the grace note she had noticed a year ago. He walked past her without pausing. She turned around, hesitated, then began walking after him. She felt faintly silly, even foolish, even a bit ashamed, but her curiosity was too strong for her to let him walk away again. She had a second chance, she saw, and the moment she began to follow him she forgot her plans for the rest of the afternoon in the oddity and interest of her present preoccupation.

She walked down the avenue half a block behind the man. Her life had changed, it came to her, it would never again be what it had been, and with every step she took the change deepened. She had been set free:

this was what had been promised, it was this she had anticipated. An entire year had been wasted in the realm of the ordinary, and now she was slipping away from the ordinary altogether. The air darkened about her, and she followed the man out of everything she had ever known.

From top: Damien Echols, Jason Baldwin, Jessie Misskelley incarcerated, 2002.
PHOTOS BY GROVE PASHLEY

Afterword

M.W. Anderson & Brett Alexander Savory

Isolated societies, dream-bounded within a mythologically
charged horizon, no longer exist except as areas to be
exploited. And within the progressive societies themselves,
every last vestige of the ancient human heritage of ritual,
morality, and art is in full decay.
– JOSEPH CAMPBELL, *The Hero With a Thousand Faces*

What happened in West Memphis, Arkansas – that seemingly unfathomable injustice so many of we social "outsiders" can identify with so deeply – is a gut-wrenching example of how far the American justice system and the basic concepts of Christianity, within Christian communities, have fallen into decay.

Who is to blame for the mess in West Memphis?

Surely there are key figures that could be shouldered with much of the responsibility, but we will likely never know the full story, or who committed such horrible crimes. But in a collective, theoretical sense, two factions, the fundamentalist Christian community of West Memphis, Arkansas, and the American justice system as defined in the state of Arkansas, can reasonably be viewed as sharing responsibility. Religious fanaticism is the environmental foundation that allowed such mindless persecution to become a reality. And the West Memphis Police Department, whatever their true motivations, exploited that environment to their own ends – truth and innocence be damned.

But what does placing blame do for us in this struggle?

Nothing.

Perhaps the West Memphis police department was in some way connected to the crimes, and therefore conducted their investigation accordingly, working to draw attention away from any such connection. But that possibility leads to cold resignation; evidence of such misconduct ever surfacing is indeed unlikely.

And again, unproven speculation gains us nothing.

We, as West Memphis Three supporters, do not claim to know who is to blame for those horrific crimes; our efforts are for those *not* responsible. We work for the release of those who were *wrongly accused and convicted* – for three young men, their lives declared worthless without a shred of hard evidence.

If you've laid down your cash to purchase this book, then you're likely one of us, and you know this struggle is far from over.

All potential recourse for the West Memphis Three now resides at the Federal level of the U.S. legal system, and we must focus our efforts on the fight ahead in that specific venue. But we must also draw attention to this case at every opportunity, raising public awareness through every outlet available, because too many of us – we who practice alternate religions, who live alternate lifestyles, or for whatever reason, have always felt as though we belong somewhere outside of the mainstream human flock – are unaware of this intolerable situation.

It is a terrible temptation for us sometimes to despair for Damien Echols. Like so many others, we've identified with him so closely, and sometimes feel that his situation, as well as our efforts, are hopeless. We think of his Buddhist beliefs and our subconscious minds summon the image of the Vietnamese monk, sitting quite still in the middle of the street, his head and upper torso engulfed in flames.

If the worst were to come to pass, could we bear the equivalent?

But these thoughts must be dismissed (the despair is valid, but premature), because within this young man – who has seen more pain and horror than most horror writers will ever experience first-hand – lies our inspiration to continue fighting for the rights of the West Memphis Three. Despite all that Damien has endured at the hands of religious misconception, he has continued seeking spiritual answers, and has held his own moral ground in the clutches of an oppressive, abusive system intent on its own form of murder.

It is our fervent hope that Damien has found his quiet center – his immovable spot.

> *To take one's stand in the veritable human situation is to*
> *engage oneself in the tasks and pursuits of life in the world*
> *without illusion, taking upon oneself death, suffering, conflict,*
> *fault as bonds and bounds; and at the same time to go forward*
> *as if in the promise of having life abundantly.*
> – H. J. BLACKHAM, *Six Existentialist Thinkers*

As supporters of the West Memphis Three, we must continue our efforts to set these men free, even though we find ourselves weighed down at the seemingly never-ending string of injustices. Hopefully, appeals efforts will have a better chance in the future, but the primary weapons at our disposal – financial support and a greater public awareness – must be diligently pursued until we've reached the end of this harrowing journey.

So let us hope that someday from our outrage and persistent, hopeful efforts, a terrible wrong will be set right.

We hope the stories and essays presented in this volume caused you to stop and think about what happened in West Memphis, Arkansas, and how that unjust travesty continues. Hopefully, when coupled with the knowledge of the facts of the case, these works helped to shine a spotlight on the fundamental *wrongness* of the situation. They were meant to inspire those who already support the West Memphis Three, and to give an opportunity to those who weren't aware of the case to sit up and take notice, to add their number to the growing chorus of voices in dissent.

This cannot stand. It *will not* stand.

Through donations to the Defense Fund, and by getting word out about the case to everyone and anyone who will listen, we can turn this around.

We know this: If at the end of our days we can say that we played even a small part in the effort that set free the West Memphis Three, we will have accomplished something important to the concept of justice.

> *And so every one of us shares the supreme ordeal – carries the*
> *cross of the redeemer – not in the bright moments of his tribe's*
> *great victories, but in the silences of his personal despair.*
> – JOSEPH CAMPBELL, *The Hero With a Thousand Faces*

Birmingham, Alabama, United States of America
& Toronto, Ontario, Canada
May 29, 2004

Notes on Contributors

PEG ALOI is a practicing witch and pagan activist who has written many articles to help raise awareness for the West Memphis Three. She teaches film studies and creative writing at Emerson College in Boston. She helped Joe Berlinger write witchy-sounding chants for *Blair Witch 2: Book of Shadows*.

Artist/writer/editor **M.W. ANDERSON** has had short fiction and poetry published online and in small press venues, and his artwork has appeared as cover art and illustrations in several small press publications. To learn more about his work and upcoming projects, visit his website at *artandfiction.com*.

CLIVE BARKER achieved critical acclaim in the early 1980s with his short story collection *The Books of Blood*. Since then, he has penned more than ten novels – his most recent being the second book of *The Abarat Quartet, Abarat II: Days of Magic, Nights of War*. As much a visualist as a wordsmith, Barker frequently turns to the canvas to fuel his imagination. In addition to the paintings he has created for the *Abarat* quartet, his paintings have been showcased in two books, *Clive Barker, Illustrator: Volumes I and II*, and shown at exhibitions worldwide.

JOE BERLINGER and **BRUCE SINOFSKY** are award-winning filmmakers, best known for their acclaimed 1996 documentary *Paradise Lost*, which first introduced the story of the West Memphis Three to an international audience. Other works include *Revelations: Paradise Lost 2*, *Brother's Keeper*, and *Metallica: Some Kind of Monster*.

GARY A. BRAUNBECK was born in the Year of the Rat and has been apologizing for it ever since. When he's not out and about accosting strangers and begging them to forgive him for his sins, he can usually be found holed up in his office writing stories and novels in a number of genres. Gary was a recent recipient of the Bram Stoker Award for his short story "Duty." His next novel, *Prodigal Blues*, is due out later this year. "From the Books of Alice Redfearn" is from *Things Left Behind* (1997, Cemetery Dance Publications), used by permission of the author.

POPPY Z. BRITE is the author of seven novels, three collections of short stories, and much miscellanea. Early in her career she was known for her horror fiction, but at present she is working on a series of novels and short stories set in the New Orleans restaurant world. Her novel *Liquor* was recently published by Three Rivers Press to general critical acclaim, and her follow-up, *The Big D*, will be released in 2005. She lives in New Orleans with her husband Chris, a chef. "Night Story 1973" is from *Weird & Distant Shores* (2002, Subterranean Press), used by permission of the authors.

MARGARET CHO is a stand-up comedian, a longtime activist, and advocate for freedom. She is also the executive producer, writer, and star of three films: *I'm The One That I Want*, *Notorious C.H.O.*, and the latest, *Revolution*.

STEPHEN DEDMAN is the author of the novels *The Art of Arrow Cutting*, *Foreign Bodies*, and *Shadows Bite*, more than eighty short stories published in an eclectic range of anthologies and magazines, and occasional non-fiction pieces.

ADAM GREENE is twenty-three years old and attends Old Dominion University. He works as a Systems Analyst computer geek. He lives as a music-addicted, free-thinking person who poses questions for the sake of being different. He also enjoys real fruit smoothies.

JAMES HETFIELD is the frontman for Metallica. Since they formed in 1981, the San Francisco Bay Area band have gone from an underground heavy metal group to one of the most successful acts in the world, with an intensely loyal fan base. The documentary film *Metallica: Some Kind of Monster*, nearly four years in the making and directed by acclaimed filmmakers Joe Berlinger and Bruce Sinofsky, premiered at the Sundance Film Festival. "... And Justice For All" is from the album *... And Justice For All* (1988, Elektra Records), used by permission of the author.

Colorado transplantee **BRIAN HODGE** is the author of eight novels, as well as upwards of 100 short stories and novelettes, many of which have been imprisoned without trial in three acclaimed collections. He also tinkers with ungodly noises, composing and recording dark electronic music.

GERARD HOUARNER fell to Earth in the '50s and is a product of the NYC school system and the City College of New York, where he studied writing under Joseph Heller and Joel Oppenheimer and crashed hallucinogenic William Burroughs seminars back in the day. Contrary to popular opinion, he only works for, and does not actually reside in, a psychiatric institution. He shares a home in the Bronx with associated curiosities, including books, music, movies, comics, action figures, and a poet. For the latest, visit *cith.org/gerard*.

PHILIP JENKINS teaches History and Religious Studies at Penn State University. For the past twenty years, he has been writing on issues such as serial murder, cults, and Satanic rings.

CAITLÍN R. KIERNAN (*caitlinrkiernan.com*) has published four novels – *Silk, Threshold, Low Red Moon*, and most recently, *Murder of Angels* – and her short fiction has been collected in *Tales of Pain and Wonder, From Weird and Distant Shores, Wrong Things* (with Poppy Z. Brite), and the forthcoming *To Charles Fort, With Love*. Born in Ireland, she now lives in Atlanta, Georgia.
"Night Story 1973" is from *Weird & Distant Shores* (2002, Subterranean Press), used by permission of the authors.

MARA LEVERITT is an investigative reporter, columnist, and contributing editor to the *Arkansas Times*. Her work focuses on the U.S. legal system, primarily as it has been affected by drug laws. Her two books, *The Boys on the Tracks* and *Devil's Knot*, have won Arkansas' prestigious Booker Worthen Prize.

BENTLEY LITTLE is the author of numerous novels and hundreds of short stories. He has not attended church since 1976 when, while accompanying an Episcopalian friend to a Christmas mass, his hair caught on fire. He assumed that was a sign.

SIMON LOGAN is the author of the industrial short story collection *I-O* and the novellas *The Decadent Return of the Hi-Fi Queen and Her Embryonic Reptile Infection* and *Notes Towards the Design and Production of the Protohuman*. You can contact him and find out all there is to know at his website, *coldandalone.com*.

MICHAEL MARANO is a horror writer and media critic who divides his time between Boston, Massachusetts and Charleston, South Carolina. His fiction has been awarded the Bram Stoker and International Horror Guild Awards. His popular film column, "MedidaDrome," appears regularly in *Cemetery Dance*. He has covered horror movies for the Public Radio Satellite Network program *Magazine International* for fourteen years. His website is at *mindspring.com/~profmike*.

ELIZABETH MASSIE is a two-time Bram Stoker Award-winning writer. Her novels include *Sineater, Welcome Back to the Night, Wire Mesh Mothers*, and more. Her most recent works are *Shadow Dreams* and *The Fear Report*, both collections of her short horror fiction. In the fall of 2004, her novella *Bloodroot* will appear in *The Black Book* by Oblivion Press.

JAMES MORROW is the author of the Godhead Trilogy, a cycle of satiric-philosophical novels about the death of God: *Towing Jehovah, Blameless in Abaddon*, and *The Eternal Footman*. He has twice won each of the World Fantasy Award and the Nebula Award. He lives in State College, Pennsylvania, with his wife Kathy, son Christopher, and two stray dogs, Pooka and Amtrak, the latter rescued from a train station in Orlando, Florida.

SCOTT NICHOLSON is author of *The Manor, The Harvest*, and *The Red Church*, with *The Home* scheduled for a summer 2005 release. He is a journalist in the Blue Ridge Mountains of North Carolina. His website, *hauntedcomputer.com*, contains articles, writing advice, and fiction excerpts.

MIKE OLIVERI writes horror fiction and tech-related non-fiction, and serves as the systems administrator for a small ISP. His novel *Deadliest of the Species* won the Bram Stoker Award for Superior Achievement in a First Novel. More on Mike and his work can be found at his website, *mikeoliveri.com*.

JENN ONOFRIO's work has appeared in *Ink Magazine, The Edward Society*, and *Johnny America*. Her one-act "An American Dream" was a 2004 Festival Selection at the Generic Theater in Norfolk, Virginia. Jenn is the co-author (with Paul Rhyand) of the play *Walking Shadows*. She is the cofounder and executive director of Voices of the Free (*voicesofthefree.org*), an arts and political advocacy organization.

GROVE PASHLEY, cofounder of the Free The West Memphis Three Support Fund, helps maintain the *wm3.org* website and handles many other duties associated with the wM3 Support Fund. He has volunteered his time to this cause since early 1996, and appeared in an HBO documentary about the case called *Revelations: Paradise Lost 2*. He is currently an entertainment photographer in Los Angeles and his work can be seen at *grovepashley.com*.

JOHN PELAN is an author, editor, and publisher. His new novella *The Colour Out of Darkness* is available from Cemetery Dance Publications. A major collection of his ghostly fiction, *Darkness, My Old Friend* is forthcoming in 2005 from Ash-Tree Press. You can find out more by visiting *darksidepress.com*.

ADAM ROBERTS is a writer and academic from London, UK, where he lives with his wife and daughter. His novels include *Salt, On, Stone, Polystom*, and *The Snow*. He considers capital punishment so obviously wrong, he doesn't even know where to start explaining the many reasons why.

BRETT ALEXANDER SAVORY is a Bram Stoker Award-winning editor. His day job is also as an editor, at Harcourt Canada in Toronto. He is editor-in-chief of *The Chiaroscuro/ChiZine*, has had nearly forty stories published in numerous print and online publications, and has written two novels, *In and Down* and *The Distance Travelled* – both of which are currently with his agent. In the works are a third novel and a dark comic book series with artist Homeros Gilani.

PETER STRAUB is the author of sixteen novels, two collections of shorter fiction, and two books of poetry. He has won the British Fantasy Award, two International Horror Guild awards, two World Fantasy Awards, and four Bram Stoker Awards. His amazing website is at *peterstraub.net*. "She Saw a Young Man" and "Then One Day She Saw Him Again" are from *Houses Without Doors* (1990, Penguin Books), used by permission of the author.

PAUL G. TREMBLAY's fiction has appeared in *Razor Magazine, The Book of Final Flesh, and Punktown: Third Eye*. His short story collection *Compositions For the Young and Old* is currently available from Prime Books. For fiction links and other tidbits go to *paulgtremblay.com*.

DAVID NIALL WILSON is the author of over 100 short stories and ten novels. His novel *Deep Blue* is available now – details at *deepblues.net*. He lives and writes in the Historic William R. White House in Hertford, North Carolina, with the love of his life, Patricia Lee Macomber, their kids, animals, and dreams.